Also by Victoria Raschke

Voices of the Dead series:

Who by Water

Our Lady of the Various Sorrows

Like a Pale Moon

Strange as Angels

Voices of the Dead Omnibus

Voices of the Dead Companion: Renegade Tea Cookbook

VICTORIA RASCHKE

Verona Green

A STORY OF ART & MAGIC

For further information, please contact:

1000 Volt Press
info@1000voltpress.com

www.victoriaraschke.com

Cover design and book layout: keifel a. agostini.
Find him at keifelagostini.com.

The book is typeset in Brisio Pro. The font was chosen specifically for the shape of the letters and support of Slovene character sets.

First Edition
ISBN: 978-1-7347422-8-2

ACKNOWLEDGEMENTS

I wouldn't be writing, and you wouldn't be holding this book (or displaying the digital file), were it not for the work, material and emotional support, and love of a great number of people to whom I am incredibly grateful.

Jennifer Goode Stevens continues to be my diligent editor despite my complete inability to ever use further and farther correctly. I am deeply grateful to have her talents in my court. keifel a. agostini, my partner in life and crime, surprises and delights me with covers I never could have imagined and does all the work of layout, book design, and publishing. He also pays the bills so we can still eat while I write, which should not go unremarked upon.

I am lucky to have a cadre of writer friends who encourage and critique. We keep each other sane and writing—no small feat. Thank yous to A.J. Scudiere, D.B. Sieders, Gemma Snow, D.S. Dane, Lulu M Sylvian, Su Fertall, Wednesday Wheeler, Elizabeth Spar, Sally, Yanina, Farriz, and Andrea. Many of them were early readers of parts or all of this book, and it is better for their input. An additional thanks to Eric Ruckart for a vanilla one liner.

Shawn Digney-Peer was kind enough to let me pepper him with weird questions about art conservation and working in museums and helped suggest Verity's not-so-subtle sabotage. Any mistakes regarding painting techniques, working in museums, or art history are mine alone.

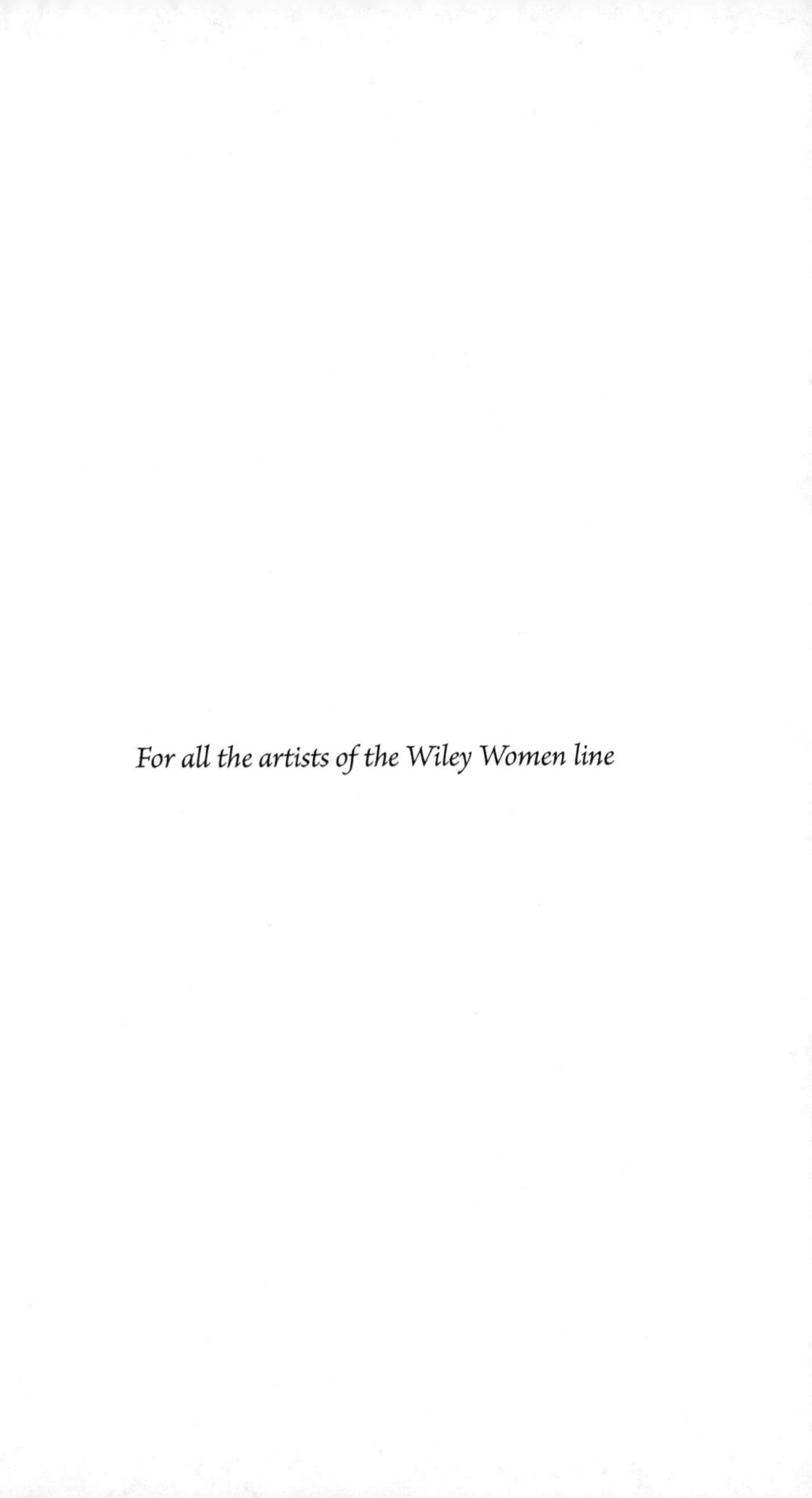

For all the artists of the Wiley Women line

CHAPTER 1

How happy I would be for this commission to be complete, both for the Lady's money and for her absence from my house. Along with her disagreeable nature, she carried the peculiar sweetness of onions gone to rot, making my wife glad to see the back of her and her odor at the end of each sitting.

The departing afternoon light took its warmth with it, and even the fire, recently stoked, couldn't drive out the chill setting in for the night. I pulled my blanket tighter around my shoulders, determined to finish the Verona green underpainting of my patron's hand. She sat, stiff-backed, in the ornate chair she had delivered from her manor across the canal, but she had become bored almost immediately upon sitting, slowing the day's progress with frequent breaks for a warm drink or to relieve herself. One would think a woman bent on surprising her husband with this gift would be more eager to have it completed.

"We are finished," she said as she stood, smoothing the front of her heavy vermilion gown. "The light has gone, and I would return home."

"Of course," I said, setting the palette aside. I moved to drape the portrait with an oilcloth I had fashioned to keep dust and soot from settling on the wet paint between our sessions.

"May I? Before you cover it," the Lady asked as she made to look around the easel.

I quickly settled the cover over. "I would you wait until it is completed."

She gave me a sour look I am certain her own husband often saw and turned to leave without further conversation. After exchanging a few words of departure with my wife, she offered a sharpish instruction to her groomsman in the street outside.

When she had gone, I lifted the cover by half and made an attempt to complete the underpainting of the Lady's thumb before my work and the uncharitable thoughts about my patroness were interrupted.

"Verity. Earth to Verity." My friend George's voice cut through the vision of the painter's studio darkening to the gloom of evening and brought me back into the artificially bright restoration lab of the New Amsterdam Museum of Art.

It was well past dark in New York, and I had to blink a few times to readjust to the present. The aromas of the painter's supper being prepared lingered, making my stomach growl. I looked up into George's face to find her staring at me, concern etched in the line between her eyebrows.

She leaned in close, though we were alone, and stage whispered in my ear, "You were 'gone,' weren't you?"

I mumbled a yes at her, noticing the change to the painting on the easel. Instead of restoring the bits of oil and pigment lost over time, I had completely changed the lay of the frumpy woman's hands, turning the wrist so her fingers grasped the other wrist instead of laying neatly, properly, folded together on the fine, crimson fabric of her dress.

Well, shit.

I hadn't had an episode in public since college—and never at work. Maybe I wasn't sleeping enough, or maybe I needed to do better about keeping my personal wards up. Whatever it was, I needed to get to the bottom of it because this wasn't something that could happen again.

George looked at the portrait more closely, mock horror spreading from the upturned corners of her mouth to her raised eyebrows. With her best fake, down-market London accent, she said, "Well, you've bollocksed that up."

She knew as well as I did that the paints I used were acrylic-based conservator medium, and, though they had already dried, I could remove the overpainting without damaging the original underneath. No one would be the wiser. I figured George, per her usual, was using humor to deflect from the fact that I'd come dangerously close to revealing myself to coworkers or getting myself hauled off to the hospital in a catatonic-looking state. I turned to the cabinet behind me for the necessary swabs for removing the acrylic paint.

"That'll be fun cleaning, but you don't have time to do it now. We have a date." She tapped her wrist where a watch would be.

I had completely forgotten that in George's ongoing quest to find us both some companionship—though I've had my fill of relationships, thank you—she'd set us up yet another double date. She met her prospects on a dating app and then insisted they find a second for a double date if they wanted to meet her. So far, these outings had yielded only lackluster conversation and the occasional free drink.

"What have you got on under that lab coat?" George lifted the lapel to inspect my navy work trousers and russet-colored blouse patterned with stylized bees. "I guess that'll do."

"What?" It wasn't like she was dragging me from the studio at the farm in paint-splattered coveralls.

George rolled her eyes before wandering away to peek at the

other projects in the studio. Everyone had gone for the day while I had been on a time-traveling journey as an obscure seventeenth-century Dutch portraitist with his patroness of the merchant class. I took a cue from D. de Graaf, whoever he had been, and covered the canvas with an odd piece of linen. It wouldn't stick to the varnish or freshly painted area, as the acrylic medium we used dried without tackiness. It made the paints a little more difficult to work with than oil-based mediums, but they floated on top of the varnish, separating the restoration from the original. I put my palette in the drawer, labeled with a piece of peeling masking tape that read V. Green, to the confusion of restoration interns looking for Verona green or terra vert pigment, and I rinsed my brushes at the shop sink.

George stopped me before I got to the door to point out that I still had my lab coat on and to pull an errant paintbrush out of the messy bun on top of my head. I frowned at the evidence of a bad habit and walked back to the sink to rinse the brush before placing it with the others to dry.

Glancing at the obvious covering on my easel, I hoped no one got curious over the weekend and discovered my extracurricular handiwork. It wasn't that big a deal, but the painting made me uneasy now. What about it had made me slip so easily into the painter's past? George and I checked out with the night security desk and launched ourselves into the early December cold.

The New Amsterdam Museum of Art takes up a sprawling footprint on Fifth Avenue, and the streets nearby are dotted with galleries, shops, and eateries. The occasional magical practitioner makes grandiose promises from back doors hidden in the allies. George usually planned to meet our dates at a nearby artsy bar, but tonight we were to meet our evening's companions, Adrien Something French and his friend whose name George had blanked on aside from it being Eastern European, at a pub in the West Village closer to her apartment.

George hailed a cab, having offered to spring for it, and we arrived five fashionable minutes late at an establishment where no one appeared to be waiting outside for us. I had expected some type of hipster bar with industrial lighting and leather-aproned mixologists, but we had been invited to a surprisingly authentic-looking London-style pub—complete with an after-work crowd that packed the bar and booths. I didn't even know this place existed, but, given how little time I spent out in the city, that wasn't too much of a surprise. Inside, shiny plastic garland and twinkling lights had been tacked around the barback, reminding me of the pub we'd haunted at uni that kept their Christmas decorations up until March, sometimes with an errant bat from Halloween festooned with a tiny Santa hat. It was the week after Thanksgiving, but I had to wonder if these twinkly lights were also a permanent fixture.

"Maybe we got here first?" I said, looking around for anyone else who looked to be searching faces. Everyone was deep in either conversation or their phone screens.

George's cell pinged in her hand, and she held it up for me to see the screen. "They're in the snug."

"There's a snug?" I don't think I'd ever seen an American pub that actually had one, or if they did, they definitely didn't call it that.

The barkeep pointed us toward a door that I would have guessed led to the kitchen or a storage closet. The snug was dimly lit and much quieter, with four small tables occupied by a white couple celebrating with champagne, a baby-faced priest drinking a pint alone reading a folded-over tabloid with a bold headline asking "Are Witches Teaching Your Children?", four women with fading summer tans mindlessly stirring neon cocktails as they chatted, and two white guys, a pint each of amber-colored ale half-drained in front of them. I assumed they were our dates.

They stood when we came in. Refreshing, as the last two had had to be pried away from their stock ticker apps to even say hello. The taller one had long dark hair and a full beard, both going gray with sexy gravitas. Guessing, I would have said he was mid- to late forties, and the way he filled out a sweater and jeans spoke more of physical labor than desk jockeying. The shorter one was clean-shaven with jet-black curly hair cut like Gabriel Byrne's in his rakish, younger days. Leaner than his companion, he dressed in tailored clothes that quietly broadcast wealth. Both men looked like they spent a lot of time in the sun, and I had no idea which one was Adrien.

George extended her hand to the shorter man, and I smiled to myself. That meant the taller was the second. Lucky me for once. I hoped against experience that he'd be able to string a few words together.

"Adrien, please meet my friend, Verity Green." George pulled me closer to the table as she said it.

Adrien nodded and shook my hand. "My pleasure. Adrien Travere." Very French name, very New York accent, and zero magic. "And this is my colleague, Matjaž Belak."

"Georgina Burne-Jones, but please call me George." George shook hands with Mr. Belak, whose first name I had missed.

When he offered me his hand, I got the shock of a fellow magic user and a funny kind of warmth flowing up my arm. I could often tell another witch or magician by their presence, but sometimes the magic was discreet enough, or the environment chaotic enough, that it required touch. I doubted that I covered my surprise as Mr. Belak's eyes showed his amusement. He'd spotted me too.

"I'm sorry, I didn't catch your first name," I said, finding it difficult not to stare at him. He had the woo. I had no idea what he could do with it, but now that I was tuned in, he gave off the bass note vibe of very old magic—almost always a complication.

Mr. Belak leaned over and close to my ear said his name again in two distinct syllables. "Mat-jaž. Think 'maht' with an 'ah' sound and stress 'yage' like you say garage." Definitely not a New York accent, but something buttery and cello-like enough to send a tingle down my spine.

Adrien gestured to the empty chairs. "What would you like to drink?"

I pointed at their ales. "Those look good."

"Same," said George while wriggling out of her trench. Adrien dealt with both our coats before disappearing into the main bar.

"So, Matjaž, Adrien said you are from Slovakia?" George asked, giving him her interested but not flirtatious attention. She gave me a wink, making me wonder if she'd picked up on his magic too.

Matjaž chuckled softly. "No. I'm from Slovenia. A bit farther south."

The whole world had reason to know exactly where Slovenia was, magical types especially.

George recovered from our awkward silence at his correction. "Sorry. I'm sure you get that a lot."

I was sure most people immediately asked if he'd been there when The Storm happened, but neither of us did. He nodded and smiled, no harm done, and I would have sworn his eyes even twinkled.

Adrien, bless him, came back quickly, two ales in hand. I don't remember what we talked about after that because I kept sneaking glances at Matjaž, which he caught every time. After all the general chit chat subjects had been covered, Adrien suggested we extend our evening to dinner at a restaurant around the corner. No one objected, and we walked there together, George and I having been graciously helped back into our coats.

Between the shared appetizer and the first course, I left my wine glass to warm. Things were going entirely too well on both sides of the table, and I needed to keep my head screwed on straight. George had given Adrien that smitten smile of hers that I could clock from space, and, by dessert, she and Adrien might as well have been on Mars for all they talked to Matjaž and me.

Between us, we had already established that I worked at NAMA with George and that she and I had met at Central St. Martin's and found our way to New York after grad school. He worked in historic preservation and had moved to New York in the past year. I didn't talk about my family and avoided asking about his, so as to not broach the subject. There was attraction, not that it mattered. I only went on these dates to humor George and, as she and I joked, to keep her from getting kidnapped. I wasn't looking to shack up. I'd had my share of past troubles with men—a man in particular—and I was certainly not looking for whatever trouble Matjaž Belak and his old woo might bring.

"Verity. That's an unusual name for an American?" Matjaž took a sip of wine, the burgundy momentarily staining his lip, as his gaze drilled in like an expert interviewer's.

"My father chose it. He's English. It's more common there, though still unusual." I hoped that was succinct enough to cut off that particular line of questioning. The downside of minimalist modern restaurants—aside from zero sound dampening—is there is no plush booth to sink into and hide long enough to get your bearings.

"It suits you. In Latin it means—" He was interrupted by the return of our server with the check.

Adrien took it without brooking any protests. The server was sent off with what looked like a generous cash tip, and the clinks and humming chatter of the restaurant filled the silence between us momentarily.

"George is coming over to mine for a drink. Any other takers?" Adrien asked out of politeness, and Matjaž and I refused out of the same.

As we all got up to leave, Adrien leaned across the table, put his hand on my shoulder, and said, "You're in good hands." He'd touched me just long enough for me to sense he meant what he said. My watered-down form of empathetic touch, which amounted to being able to sense someone's sincerity and what I would call very intermittent telekinesis, had been The Storm's gifts to me. Some magic folks had gotten juiced up a bit, like George and her astral travel skills, and some of us got brand new abilities—though not always good or especially useful ones.

Adrien's sincerity aside, I wasn't worried about Matjaž being dangerous—even though he was a magic user—or that I couldn't find my own way home, but it was possible my concern about finding my date attractive for once showed.

Outside the restaurant, Adrien and George waved goodbye and got into a waiting car, more proof that Adrien had tailored-clothes-and-a-driver kind of money. Their departure left Matjaž and me standing in the cold hesitating about what to do or say next.

"What were you saying about Latin earlier?" I asked. I wasn't ready to call it a night, even though that was probably the best idea. I was intrigued despite myself.

"Verity in Latin—veritas. Truth." He smiled.

It's surprising how few people brought up my first name. Most preferred to comment on my last being Green and that I'm a painter, as if no one had ever pointed that out to me before. "I doubt that was part of the decision. My father wanted his American children to have very English names. Inescapably so. My brother's name was Percival. Does Matjaž have a Latin secret?" Better turn this line of questioning back around. Trying to explain my family on a first date was not the best way to get a second one. Wait, did I want a second one?

"Not really. It's biblical. In English, I would be Matthew." He smiled. "Definitely not as interesting to English-speakers, I'm sure." He looked down the street and back to me. "Share a taxi?"

"It's a ten-minute walk," I said. I crashed with George at her apartment during the week and took the train up to my place on the weekends.

"I can walk with you." There might have been more on offer in his words, but I was comically bad at being able to tell.

"I . . ." I wasn't going to tell him that I found him attractive and in possession of many of the qualities, physically at least, I would want in someone, if I wanted anyone, but I hesitated in turning down his offer outright.

"I would just like to see you home safe." When he smiled, his eyes crinkled at the corners.

"Sure, but who will see you safely home?" It was impossible not to smile back.

"My place isn't far either," he said and offered me his arm.

I took it, unused to the old-fashioned mannerism but charmed nonetheless. He talked about his work with Adrien restoring a historic brownstone in Brooklyn that was to become a cultural center. His passion for the project was clear, and I found myself asking questions about sourcing conservation-grade materials even though I really wanted to ask him if he'd been in Slovenia during The Storm. I thought he'd picked up on my woo, but I didn't want to confirm it. Mentioning The Storm would either do that, or it could make him think I was one of the "New Great Awakening" religious zealots. The city hadn't drawn many of them, but anyone in New York longer than a day had seen the congregations of "Turn away Satan's minions" and "Cast out the witches among us" sign holders at corners in every borough.

When we got to my stoop, there was another hesitation in our banter. He leaned in to kiss me, and, for once in a very long while, I didn't turn away. His lips brushed my cheek close to my ear as he asked if he could call me the next day. I nodded and dashed up the steps while he waited on the sidewalk to make sure I got in okay. He waved once I was inside and headed back the way we came. A teeny voice in my head chided me for being so closed up. Closed up, yes—and for good reason. Prudish, no. Matjaž had set things stirring that had been quiet for a long time, and I didn't like it. Or at least I tried to convince myself I didn't.

George didn't come home before I went to bed. Good for her, I guess. But her slumber parties didn't always translate into second dates, either, though she often wanted them to.

***

After a night of dreams of Matjaž that would make a sailor blush, interspersed with nightmares of me getting fired for my heavy-handed touch on the restoration (even in my dreams I couldn't just let go and have a good time), I woke up agitated—whether out of worry about the painting or horniness for Matjaž, or both. I envied George the ability to simply see where the wind would take her that day and not sweat the ride. Instead of staying curled up in bed, which I was certain she was doing with last night's date, I got up, made coffee, and set about leaving the city for the rest of the weekend.

There wasn't much to pack, except Hilma. I kept a work wardrobe, seconds of all my toiletries, and a small working altar at George's. It was a two hours and change trip from Penn Station to Wiltwyck and another forty-five minutes by car to get home. Even catching the earliest train on a Saturday, I would lose most of the morning light in the studio there. But going up wouldn't be a complete loss, as I had things to tackle over the weekend besides painting, like beefing up my personal wards again after the slip at work.

Messenger bag and cat carrier secured, I walked to the station gathering wool until my thoughts settled again on the portrait restoration. My assignment was to touch up the missing paint where the canvas had worn through over the centuries and to fill in a larger portion of the back of the subject's hand where an earlier bad repair job of a puncture had caused significant paint loss. Instead I had changed the whole position of the hand and repainted the terre verte underlayer as D. de Graaf must have done before layering red and golden ochres with lead white to create the balance of warm and cool half-tones reflecting the subject's fair skin, an early Renaissance technique called verdaccio. It lead to many paintings of saints looking green enough to vomit when the fugitive red lake they used faded, leaving the light-fast green earth pigment exposed. De Graaf had learned to use a more permanent red.

I'd never even heard of him, but now I knew this woman he had painted was a troublesome client and an impatient sitter. I had been in his body in seventeenth-century Amsterdam and had my own whiff of her rotted root vegetable smell. No wonder he wanted to forgo the demure convention of folded hands for a more aggressive, grasping pose. I still had a few questions about how that part of my magic worked, but there weren't any handbooks on not-quite-time-travel through artwork available. And there definitely wasn't anyone I could ask. My "gift" wasn't common, even among witches. The aspect of it that bothered me most was the thought that de Graaf and the others over the years had also been in my body and what that could mean. It was part of why I'd worked so hard to make sure it didn't happen—and why it bothered me so much that this painting had taken me back for so long.

I would have walked right by the entrance to Penn Station if I hadn't been buffeted back into awareness by a man exiting in enough of a rush to dismiss my solid presence in his path. While getting untangled from each other, I got a noseful of paint thinner off his clothes. He was gone too quickly for even a reflexive apology, and the collision faded from my thoughts before I boarded the train.

CHAPTER 2

Bertha, my beater of a station wagon, was waiting faithfully for me in extended parking at the Wiltwyck station. Pulling up to the newly repainted attendant booth, I waved at Garvey. He smiled broadly, happy to see me, and held up a book behind the plexiglass for me to stop. I would have anyway, even though he'd already raised the black- and yellow-striped gate.

"I thought you might not be coming up this weekend," he said in his Trinidadian-by-way-of-Queens accent, his smile widening to show more of his perfectly straight teeth. It would be easy to mistake him as gruff if you didn't know him, at least until that smile appeared.

"Just a little later than usual. George set me up with another of her dates last night." I punctuated with my usual shrug where her matchmaking was concerned, but my face got warm. I'd given myself away, and Garvey knew me too well to let it slide.

"I think this might not be one of those boring day traders." He had his own crusade where my lack of a love life was concerned, and he narrowed his dark eyes at me like he could see more than the blushing. "You like this one."

"Maybe. Whatever. Whatcha got for me?" I pointed at the book in a transparent move to change the subject.

Garvey pulled it back. "At least tell me this man's name."

"So you and Jon can do one of your all-night love spells? Absolutely not." Garvey and I had recognized the woo on each other at first sight, long before The Storm. We'd been friends and occasionally magical working partners since. His love spells were no joke. "The book?"

"Agatha Christie. *Death Comes as the End*." He handed the novel through his window and mine, but he gave me a look that let me know he wasn't going to give up on getting more out of me about my date.

I propped it against the steering wheel so I could read the back cover. "Is this the Egypt one? I thought it wasn't very good?"

Garvey laughed. "It's better than it gets credit for. She was a racist old white lady, but she could plot the hell out of a mystery." He had started reading her to outline her plots as part of his self-taught degree in fiction writing and had gotten addicted to cozies and country house murders in the process. I nagged him about letting me read one of his Caribbean mysteries almost as much as he nagged me about meeting and getting it on with a nice boy. Or girl. Or anyone.

I dug around in my messenger bag and handed him my trade. "New M.C. Beaton."

"Ooh. Jon was going to buy this one," he said. Garvey had pulled his husband into our book-swapping circle, much to Jon's dismay. He swore that he'd only read horror and the occasional fantasy novel before we ruined him.

"Enjoy," I said as I attempted to grind Bertha back into gear.

"I will. You enjoy that new man. You know you spend too much time alone." He resisted wagging a finger at me, but I think just.

I glanced at Hilma in her crate. "I'm not alone."

He rolled his eyes and waved me on.

My jaw unclenched as soon as I pulled into the driveway of the farm. Calling it a farm was generous. It was more of a cottage tucked into five wooded acres at the foot of the Catskill Mountains in the hamlet of West Kill. My parents hadn't been keen gardeners in the time they'd lived there, but I had planted raised beds full of herbs, vegetables, and flowers—enough that there wasn't a front lawn anymore. The perennials had died back for the winter, but I loved the wild, brittle sculptures of their plant skeletons as much as the leafy green tangles of summer.

As I dug in my bag for my keys, my stomach rumbled, reminding me that there probably wasn't much choice for lunch. I stopped rummaging. Something was off, didn't smell right, didn't feel right. Hilma was silent in her crate. When I grasped the knob to unlock the door, it moved open. I was certain I'd locked up when I'd left on Monday. I was obsessive about checking all the doors before I headed back to the city, and I couldn't decide if I was more angry that someone had broken into my house or that someone had been able to get past the property and house wards.

I set Hilma's carrier down on the square of pavers and swung the door open the rest of the way. No one else's presence registered, but the hair on the back of my neck stood at attention anyway. I inspected the brass lock and strike plate as if I knew what I was looking for exactly. There wasn't any evidence of the door having been forced—no scratches or whatever it was Hercule Poirot looked for after he found a body in the study. I walked inside and closed—but didn't lock—the door behind us.

Hilma bounded out into the entry when I unzipped the carrier, and I relaxed a little. She wouldn't have come out so quickly if there was even the slightest whiff of stranger. While the cat made her way to her litter box in the mudroom at the back of the cottage, I checked every room and closet to see what might be missing. Nothing. It didn't even look like the place had been searched or that anyone else had been there. Maybe I had left the door open.

I went out the back door to check on the studio, and that door was open too. There was no way I had flaked enough to leave the studio unlocked as well. Someone had been there, and they either had lock and ward woo—a real possibility—or keys to the house and the studio—unlikely, but possible. The house had the same locks it had when I was a kid. A few of the blinds were up in the small, airy space. I always closed them when I left. Again, nothing seemed to be missing except my peace of mind, but my burglar had gone through the finished paintings leaning against the wall. Each of them had been turned outward; I kept them facing the wall to avoid light damage. They were lined up, oldest to newest, showing the arc of my painting over the past couple of years—close plant studies to darker blocks of color layered with anthotypes. The sketches on the cork board above my workstation had been taken down and laid in a neatened pile on the glass plate where I mixed pigments into mediums. I had wanted a quiet weekend to paint, experiment with a new pigment idea, and breathe. As much as I loved my restoration work and George, the city exhausted me. Too much noise, too many people. A more perfect life would have been one lived entirely in West Kill, painting, gardening, foraging. Unfortunately, West Kill didn't offer much in the way of lucrative employment, and, though the farm was finally paid for, the state and county still wanted their taxes. And despite its having been transformed into a witch's paradise of herb gardens and greenhouses, no woodland creatures came by to do maintenance on the roof or magically supply electricity.

An unnerved wariness replaced my initial anger as I put the paintings back in their proper places and locked the studio. Most people would have called the police, but anyone with magic avoided law enforcement if at all possible. They were either skeptics who would as soon lock us up as "loonies" or, if they understood magic wasn't a put-on, they would want something. It was never anything good, and no wasn't an acceptable answer.

I had planned to gather the last of the black walnuts from the trees behind the house. The hulls made a fine brown-black ink and wash, and as much of it as I used, I was greedy about collecting all the ground fall. But the thought of roaming around in the woods after finding the doors open wasn't inviting anymore. Maybe it was better to work on another project and go tomorrow afternoon after some time in the studio.

Lunch first. Then make a list.

Back in the house, the yellowed wall phone rang while I was digging in the freezer to find something edible. It startled me enough that I dropped a frozen jar of vegetable stock on the tile floor. There was zero internet or cell service out here, so I had my mobile calls forwarded to the number of the landline my parents had had since my brother was a baby.

It was Matjaž. His voice would have been more soothing under better circumstances. Clearly I was more rattled than I thought.

"I wondered if you were free tomorrow evening and if you liked jazz?" He'd said he would call, and the man kept his word. Check.

"I'm free, but I'm also out of town. Jazz sounds good though." I frowned at Hilma, who had taken the opportunity of my being distracted by sweeping up shards of glass and chunks of frozen stock to jump onto the stovetop. I scooped her up and dumped her out of the kitchen, trying and failing to not completely entangle myself in the spiraling cord that anchored the handset to the kitchen wall.

"I think that's a no?"

"It's a no." My disappointment surprised me.

"Is it a permanent no?"

It should have been a permanent no: I had a job that ate my week, my own work, a house to keep from falling apart, and enough emotional baggage for an all-points world cruise. No would be best. No would be easiest. And yet that little voice in the back of my head pointed out that a drink or two and another human to listen to some music with wasn't going to end the world.

"Verity? Are you still there?"

"Sorry, yes. I mean yes I'm still here, and no, it isn't a permanent no." It wasn't a permanent yes, either, but I wasn't sure how to explain that. "I usually make the rounds at a few galleries on Monday evening. Would you be interested?" It wasn't snuggling up at a table in the dark, but date ideas were George's department.

"I would. Should I meet you somewhere? Pick you up at work?"

And he was a planner. Check.

"Let's meet at the main gallery entrance around five-thirty? George and a couple other folks from work usually come too. Is that okay?"

He assured me it was and rung off. I continued my frozen archeological exploration in the side by side until I unearthed some month-old vegetarian chili and plonked the brick into a pan to thaw. As it began to bubble, I watched the mid-afternoon shadows shift with the wind out the kitchen window. I probably shouldn't be concerned about my unknown intruder lurking in the woods, but an off-ness lingered, tugging at me to look harder. The leaves had fallen, and there wasn't anywhere to hide. Besides, the intruder hadn't done any damage and was unlikely to be hanging around in the cold. They made sure I knew they'd been there, though, and the brazenness of that worried me. Whoever they were, they would find much nastier wards if they tried to get in a second time.

I curled up on the couch with my warmed freezer find just as the phone rang again. I smiled at the thought of unplugging it from the wall and hiding it in a drawer until it was needed.

"So how were 'drinks' at Adrien's?" I took a bite of the chili—slightly freezer burned and in need of some hot sauce—and waited for George to spill her date details. She rarely spared the juicy bits, but this time she hesitated.

"Oh, come on. It couldn't be worse than Steve or Steph or whatever his name was." I leaned my butt against the apron-front sink with the handset tucked between my shoulder and ear.

George snorted on the other end of the line. "Steph. My god, that man is what vanilla thinks of when it wants something vanilla. No. It wasn't worse than that. It just wasn't."

"Just wasn't what?" I didn't like being in the position of asking George to expound on her sexy time details. For one, I couldn't reciprocate and, two, George left zero to the imagination. I was still mildly traumatized by the blow by blow of the last lawyer who'd barged into the bathroom while she was peeing because he'd wanted to watch. No kink shaming from me, but a knock and some consent are minimal requirements.

"It wasn't sex. It was drinks. At his house. Exactly like he said. I just happened to have one too many and slept on his couch."

I couldn't tell if she was surprised or angry.

"He lives on the Upper West Side in a giant flat. Like 'insert fictional billionaire here' money."

Money didn't much impress George, as her family had enough to pave the drive of their Cotswolds pile with monetary paper portraits of the sovereign if they wanted to. For her to mention it at all put Adrien in a completely different tax bracket— probably one that didn't include actually paying taxes.

"So maybe he's a little old-fashioned?" I moved to the dining room table, pulling the plasticized fusilli phone cord to its limit. "It's almost charming."

"It was charming. And he's a collector, and let's just say his tastes run high."

In our world collector meant art. "Like David Hockney high?" I imagined his billionaire pad with gallery white walls and diamond-encrusted skulls on plinths in the living room. But maybe that was more supervillain than billionaire playboy.

"No, like a Rembrandt high."

"That is high. Are you seeing him again?" George claimed to want to couple up with someone, but I had to wonder if her protracted single state didn't have its own tangly roots. Her folks had money, but the Burne-Joneses were in real competition with the Greens for dysfunctional family of the year.

"Tonight. A fundraiser for the cultural center thing he is working on with Matjaž." She sounded excited despite her having said on multiple occasions that any organization who asked for a donation could have it as long as she didn't have to go to another damned dinner.

"Sounds so unlike anything you'd be interested in."

George snorted again. "I'm interested in whether tonight will just be drinks." The wheels were turning in her head loudly enough for me to hear. "So how about your evening?"

"Complete and utter gentleman. He's coming with us Monday night though."

"Well, that's something."

***

I washed the chili bowl and looked out the window again. Something was definitely wrong in the angelica bed. I'd left several of the taller plants to go to seed and overwinter, and they were no longer there. The cottage was in the shadow of the mountain—the downside of living this far north and having a ridge between you and the sunset. I grabbed the solar flashlight off the kitchen windowsill and slid it into my pocket in case I needed to root around for moles.

Out in the garden, the plants had been pulled up by their roots and stacked in a neat pile on the gravel path on the other side of the bed. I might be able to salvage some of the stems, but my plan for self-reseeding was for naught. Whoever or whatever it was had shoveled all the way to the bottom of the bed, ripped through the landscaping cloth, and dug right into the ground underneath. By the looks of it, they had excavated a rectangle the size of a boot box. I'd had herbs in that bed forever, probably since I'd moved back to New York, so whatever my intruder had taken had been there before my parents gave me the house. That it wasn't something I knew about, or would miss, wasn't a comfort. I got my own shovel and a patch for the ground cloth out of the lean-to shed on the studio and filled in the hole as best I could. That left a sunken area the size of the excavation that I'd have to fill in with compost.

While I was out there, I tended the other beds, pulling out some spent plants and gathering a few dried pods, hoping to settle my nerves by sticking my hands in the earth. I took a scoop of the disturbed dirt from the angelica bed to use for resetting the perimeter and all the wards on the house and studio. I also dug up the four jars that marked the corners of the ward protecting the boundary of the property.

After a pantry-foraged dinner and a long soak in my one renovation extravagance—a giant cast iron tub—I pulled on the ivory linen shift I kept only for working. It was too cold outside to be so underdressed, but I had kitted out my old bedroom for spellcraft with an altar and shelves for my supplies when my parents gifted me the house.

I was grateful to have it. The cottage and what remained of the original acreage was the only place in the world that felt like home, and I had been certain my parents were going to sell the whole place off to fund their travels while I was in England finishing grad school. Despite their general disinterest in parenting me after Percy ran away, giving me the house made it seem that at least one of them had finally seen me. I found out later, from one of the piles of self-help books my mother foisted on me when I saw her, that it's common for the parents of missing children to stay in the house their child last lived. Me staying, though, meant they could go. They sold off all but five acres, most of which went straight up the side of the mountain, and deeded it to me, along with what was left on the second mortgage. They promptly took their proceeds to buy their own cottage in Lily Dale so my mother could further her spiritualist work and my father could continue to live off the donations people gave her for putting them in contact with the spirits of their dead. Her mediumship had always been more lucrative than his acting.

I left the door of the working room open because Hilma gets keyed up when I do spell work, and I didn't want to have to let her in or out once I got started. Before my bath, I'd gathered the decorative jars from the corners of the cottage and studio and placed them with the larger canning jars from the perimeter ward on the altar. The jars from outside were cloudy and scratched, but they were sound, so they didn't need replacing. They were going to go right back into the dirt anyway. I didn't really bother with casting a circle anymore, the property had a spiritual ward renewed each astrological Samhain—the midpoint between the autumnal equinox and the winter solstice—which had been about a month ago. I had neglected renewing the physical ward then, which meant the break-in was partly my fault. I wouldn't be slack about it again. I unscrewed all the lids and added a few pinches of fresh salt along with a snip each of mugwort, angelica, and holly, asking these plant allies to protect my home. To the inside jars for the studio and house, I added dirt from outside and a few cactus spines George let me harvest from her collection. To the outside ones, I poured in a splash of my own pee, freshly collected. It would seal the perimeter ward directly to me rather than just relying on the connection to the house.

I also added in some fiery jalapeños I'd grown and pickled and a handful of rusty nails to each. Whoever this asshole was, they would know they were in trouble if they showed up again. I lit a stick of black sealing wax to drip on the lid of each closed jar, then pressed my thumb into the warm puddles, calling upon my ancestors to watch this place.

I still needed to boost my personal wards that had let me slip so casually back to hang out with de Graaf and Lady Onion-Breath. I took off the necklace I wore as a sort of booster for my personal magic—a silver, five-pointed star joined to the silver chain by jump rings through the arms, as it were, of the star. Percy had given it to me for my tenth birthday. The star had rested lower on my chest then, but now it lay in the hollow of my throat when I had it on. I ran the delicate chain through my fingers and coiled it in the small blue dish I kept for offerings on my altar. Maddalena, my teacher, would have given me shit for it, but I lit the candles with matches rather than my own magic. I'd never really been able to pull off that spell; I think maybe I'm too earthy for fire magic. I said the words, and though I was concentrating on empowering the necklace, I couldn't help but think of Percy when I blew out the candles, wondering again what had happened to him.

I gathered the ward jars, and another filled with dried rosemary and yarrow for my patron deity, Minerva, into a basket and went about tucking the house jars back into their places. Then I put on my field coat and Wellies and tramped over to the studio to replace those jars and the ones for the property lines. The moon was high and bright enough to see by as I filled in the holes I'd made earlier and scattered my offering for Minerva at each corner. A doe came to nibble on the kale in a far garden box as I was reburying the final jar. We stared at each other for a long moment before she disappeared across the gravel drive, and I sent a thought after her that she was welcome to what the insects and frost had left of the brassicas.

For the most part, I am a skeptical witch. I know magic is a force in the world and there is more out there that I don't know, but the religious part of my witchcraft tends to be iffy. Then a deer shows up inside the wards I just asked Minerva to strengthen. My personal jury is still out on whether or not the gods of the pagans and witches are real, but I follow Maddalena's philosophy: If the gods are real, isn't it best to have them on your side?

With the jars back in place, I should have been able to relax. The over-fortified boundaries in my personal life are an issue, I know, but I felt justified in making the boundary out here as strong as I was capable of. I would have been happier to stay out longer, soaking up the moonlight. But the cold finding its way up my legs pushed me inside, where I got ready for bed. I did sleep better that night, sensing the ring of protection glowing around the farm, but it wasn't enough to put me totally at ease. Whoever it had been and whatever they had taken were out there beyond the wards, and I couldn't stay here forever.

CHAPTER 3

Getting back to work on Mondays was always a hassle—mostly because I had to get Hilma back to the apartment before I could head to the museum. George had offered on multiple occasions to let me leave Hilma over the weekend, but every time the topic came up Hilma would pee in one of George's shoes. The subject was dropped, and I made arrangements with our director, Dr. Mar, to come in at noon on Mondays with a convincing argument that I was more productive at work having two full days away and that I would be available for the occasional after-hours program.

On my trip from the Village to work, I was preoccupied with thoughts of seeing Matjaž again. Had I bothered to look at my phone on the subway, I would've had warning of the maelstrom I stumbled into. The air in the studios was crackling with anxiety, and every set of eyeballs in the place turned to me with a mix of pity and suspicion when I walked into the studio lab. Immediately I assumed Dr. Mar had seen the overpainting and had made her displeasure public, even though that would be unlike her. I walked by the other workstations and the vacuum table trying not to acknowledge I was being stabbed by my coworkers' stares, but it was impossible not to blanch when I got to my station. My random piece of linen was neatly folded on the cabinet, and the D. de Graaf portrait of *Unknown Dutch Merchant Woman* was gone.

The tap of George's boots announced her. "Did you get my

message? You need to see Dr. Mar."

I probably also needed to clean out my personal belongings and turn in my badge. "Is she in her office?"

"With security." George really needed to work on getting her stage whisper down to an actual whisper.

Things were more serious than I had expected. The painting didn't belong to the museum. It was on loan from a mega donor, mostly so we would handle the extensive restoration work needed to the painting and its frame as part of an upcoming exhibit on Vermeer and his peers. As much trouble as I would be in for a hack job on a museum collection painting, I imagine a donor's painting could be more problematic for Dr. Mar. But my overzealous work wasn't permanent. I had planned to spend the first hour of my day cleaning off Friday's paint. My biggest concern should have been explaining why the retouching and inpainting was taking so long.

Before I could get any more information out of George, Dr. Mar walked through the studio, spreading a hush. Everyone else pretended to be intent on their work as George slunk back to the objects department, or at least as far as the doorway. Dr. Mar, unaccompanied by security, stopped about two feet from my easel.

"Good morning, Verity. Would you join me in my office?" Her brown face was unreadable and drained of the usual slightly mischievous warmth. She didn't wait for my reply before turning and clicking back away from me. It occurred to me that I would never look that good in a suit and heels. I hung up my bag and coat and followed behind her, feeling both scolded and frumpy. Monday was off to a rollicking start.

In her office, Dr. Mar sat on the edge of her desk and stared at me for a long moment as I stood just inside the door, alternately clutching my hands together behind my back and shoving them into my pockets.

"What time did you leave on Friday?" Dr. Mar asked.

"Later than usual. Closer to six-thirty." An instant replay reel of George meeting me in the lab spun in my thoughts.

Dr. Mar didn't seem angry, but an equally strong emotion floated behind the neutral set of her expression.

"That checks with the badge out. And you only saw Georgina?"

"And Tomas, the new night guard. Oh, and Yvette. She was finishing the floor in the main gallery when we walked through." George and I had waved at her while she rocked out on her headphones before we signed out with Tomas.

"Where were you the rest of the evening?" Dr. Mar hadn't blinked in the time we'd been in her office.

"Out with George. Then I spent the night at her apartment and took the train up to Wiltwyck Saturday morning. Pretty much same as always, except I usually take the train up on Friday right after work," I answered.

Dr. Mar uncrossed her ankles and made her way behind the desk. She finally gestured at the leather chair that faced her.

I sat down, still having no clue what to do with my hands.

"The painting you have been working on is missing."

A sigh of relief escaped before I could stop it.

Dr. Mar raised one perfectly shaped eyebrow. "That isn't the reaction I had anticipated."

Before I could dig myself a deeper hole, I decided it was best to explain, or at least sum up, what had been going on. "I thought I was in your office so you could fire me. I was a little overzealous with the paint restoration on the hand and thought there might be a problem." It sounded stupid now that I'd said it out loud. There wouldn't be any issue with removing the conservator paint and redoing the work.

"Why would I fire you? You're by far the best easel painting restorer on staff. It's why I had you working on Mr. Travere's painting." I don't think I'd actually seen Dr. Mar even vaguely confounded before, and the faint smile that followed was incongruous under the circumstances.

"Did you say Travere?" Adrien Travere—George's Adrien Travere—was the mega donor? Shit. I resisted the urge to claw at the slithering sensation under my skin. The tiny voice that liked to alternately berate and cheerlead in my brain was yelling: No way that's a coincidence.

"Yes. Adrien Travere has expressed interest in a sizable donation to the west wing restoration, along with a permanent loan of several key pieces from his personal collection. Why?"

Clearly George had not mentioned that we had been out with Mr. Travere Friday night, or that she had spent the evening on Adrien's couch knocked down on what was surely some quality booze.

"I didn't realize that was who owned the painting." That same little voice, that was usually spot on even when it was being an asshole, confirmed George's omission to be the best course of action. There was a tag on the painting in the inventory. How had I missed that?

"I assume security will also want to speak with you."

"And the police?"

"The board decided to wait until I spoke with you. There was some thought that you might have taken the painting home. We didn't want to involve the police in an internal matter."

I nodded, now not knowing what to do with my whole self, let alone my hands. The de Graaf was the only project I was currently assigned to.

"Jacob is having some trouble with the Rothko. I thought it was a simpler issue but apparently the experimental pigment . . ." her voice trailed off as her gaze moved to the doorway.

I got the sensation of the aura of whoever it was standing behind me without turning to see. Massive, old woo I could feel in my teeth radiated from the doorway.

"Mr. Travere, I didn't expect you to come in."

Adrien had offered no hint of woo on Friday. Woo like that wasn't something you could hide easily, not unless you were into some serious, esoteric magic.

I turned to look at him. The rakish black hair had gone a steely gray but kept its curl, the eyes were piercing, and the suit was expensive but understated. Adrien Travere *Senior* looked very much like Adrien Junior might look in thirty years. If he was lucky.

"Mr. Travere, this is Verity Green, the restorer who was working on the de Graaf." Dr. Mar motioned for me to stand with a glance.

I offered Adrien Senior my hand. "It's a pleasure to meet you, Mr. Travere. I'm sorry it's under these circumstances." I experienced the same frission of magic as I'd had with Matjaž, but any sense beyond that was closed off to me.

There was no doubt he had sized me up as quickly as I had him. He met my gaze with a knowing expression and an almost-pleased hint of a smile. "I'm sure the painting will turn up. It is a pleasure to finally meet you. Your skills are highly spoken of."

His voice, patrician and lightly accented, sent a line of ice down my spinal column.

"Thank you."

"Thank you, Verity. Jacob can brief you on the Rothko, and I'd like to speak with you before you leave for the day." Dr. Mar offered the chair I had vacated to Adrien Senior and closed the door behind me.

I stood in the hallway with my pulse ringing in my ears. Monday was getting better and better. I did still have a job, but someone had presumably taken a painting by a very minor artist of an unnamed woman. From my workstation. In a museum filled with priceless works of art. Someone had been in my house and studio and gone treasure hunting in my garden. And Adrien Travere Senior knew who and maybe what I was. Of those three things, that was the one that gave me the most pause. Aside from George, no one knew what I could do. And I didn't trust anyone with that much woo or cash to burn with intimate knowledge about me, or in general.

Deep in the warren of museum offices, the head of security verified my story before releasing me into the wild. He was disinterested and barely hid his puzzlement of that particular painting being stolen or misplaced. The rest of the day was spent getting up to speed on the pigmentation loss on the Rothko. The damage was extensive, and I was grateful for the distraction. I appreciated the artist's experimentation with mediums and colors. Though I'd built my own work on it, there was no way to know how those experiments would stand up over time. Rothko was hardly the first to lose a novel color or medium to oxidation or light. DaVinci's Last Supper would have disappeared completely without the work of conservators and restorationists—and of whoever sandbagged the wall it was on in World War II. Jacob and I put our heads together and wound up trading research papers and opinions, both scientific and philosophical, about the best approach to take. Whatever we decided, we'd still have to run it by Dr. Mar. Neither of us touched the painting, but it was oddly comforting to have it there on Jacob's easel, even muted by its fugitive colors, while we read and discussed.

Jacob begged off joining us that evening on our gallery crawl to pore over more papers. I shoved two I'd printed off into my messenger bag, knowing I wouldn't take them out until tomorrow, and collected my coat before walking back across the main gallery to Dr. Mar's office.

She'd given no hint of what the second conversation of the day was for—not that she ever shared much. Dr. Mar wasn't standoffish, but she held everything close. One doesn't become the head of one of the world's most prestigious conservation departments as a Black woman without having to be twice as good and twice as professional as everyone surrounding her. She was known to be efficient in dealing with or removing problems, and even those on the receiving end of the solutions had to admit she was always fair. She made her decisions based on what was best for the art, even when the Board didn't necessarily think it was best for the museum. She had an unusual aura. It wasn't one that immediately broadcast "magic user," but I'd learned the hard way to never rule out the possibility.

I knocked on the heavy, paneled door and waited for a muffled reply before letting myself in. She folded down the screen of her silver laptop and motioned for me to sit.

"How did it go with Jacob?" She put the computer into the pencil drawer of the desk and locked it with a small key. Her gaze met mine, and she laced her long fingers together on top of the now empty expanse of wood.

"We're still doing some digging, but my initial assessment is to preserve the current color as best we can and include a discussion of Rothko's process and possibly an earlier photograph in an extended object label if the piece is hung again." Jacob wasn't keen on extended labels but agreed Plum on Red was a special case.

"That. Or the Harvard approach." Dr. Mar tilted her head.

"We discussed that as an option." In the 1970s, Harvard had mothballed several Rothko canvases that had been damaged by light and food splatters from hanging in a dining hall. Now they were displaying them again with projected light filtered to show the original colors matched to an undamaged sister canvas. "We don't have a matching painting to go by, so I'm slightly less inclined."

Dr. Mar nodded. "Tell me more about the inpainting you did on the de Graaf."

I wasn't about to tell her exactly why I had done it, but if the painting was found she would see it. "I would call it overpainting. I had planned to spend this morning removing it and starting over, on the hand at least."

Dr. Mar nodded again. "I'm sure when the painting is recovered, you'll make the necessary corrections."

"Don't you think it's odd that someone took it? If they got in, why bother with that when there was the Rothko and a Klimt, as well as the Picasso sketch, all in the studio? Not to mention everything in the whole museum?" It had to puzzle her as much as it did me.

"Security asked the same question." Dr. Mar didn't elaborate.

"Was that all you needed me for?" I motioned toward the door.

"No. Adrien Travere" (*I had to add Senior in my head*) "would like for you to look at another item in his collection." She fished a thick, cream-colored business card out of a drawer and slid it across her desk to me.

I have a pretty good poker face. Like Dr. Mar, I have to keep a few things close to the vest. But it was pretty unusual to have someone in my position interact with a donor, especially one who was about to shell out enough money to have a wing of the museum named after him. Dr. Mar immediately addressed my surprise.

"I realize it is…" she paused. "Irregular. He asked specifically for you. The date and time are on the back of the card."

I turned it over in my palm to read "Tuesday, 10 AM" in neat, block hand-lettering.

"Tomorrow Tuesday?"

Dr. Mar nodded.

"Is there anything else I should know?" As noted, I'd never gotten woo off Dr. Mar, but it was possible. There were magic users who could keep their status warded enough to be undetectable to most. Those were the ones you needed to be most worried about.

"I'm sure Adrien . . . Mr. Travere, would like to tell you himself, but I would prefer you went in at least somewhat aware." Dr. Mar got up from her desk and walked to the door to lock it before continuing. I shifted in my chair, unsettled.

"Mr. Travere is a Restorationist."

"That's surprising." Though his handwriting had artistic flair, and it wasn't unheard of for a person collecting art to dabble in making it, conservation was a specialized field. Even at a museum with pockets as deep as NAMA's, it wasn't that lucrative. Adrien Travere Senior had definitely not made private collection bank patching up canvases.

"Yes. But probably not how you mean." Dr. Mar leaned against the front of her desk and looked at me for a long, hard moment. "You can do magic. You and Georgina."

Words were nowhere to be found. I may never have gotten a whiff of the woo off Dr. Mar, but there were sensitive mundanes. Since The Solstice Storm, the idea that there were magic users among us had a lot more traction in the mainstream. More people had come out of their broom closets, mostly to do magic for hire, but many of us, inborn or taught, preferred to keep ourselves hidden. There were too many people who still thought witches frolicked in the woods with Satan and ate babies. I worried about them less than I did those who wanted magic users to do their criminal or unethical bidding.

"You needn't be concerned. I doubt anyone else here has figured it out, but for someone who knows what to look for, it's impossible not to see it in your work." Dr. Mar let her personal ward slip, and, for the briefest moment, I got that sense of old magic off her. That kind of magic got passed down, parent to child, building in power with each subsequent generation—

much like the wall of woo I'd gotten off Adrien Senior. Adrien Junior had to be warded like the Crown Jewels.

My tongue remained frozen to the roof of my mouth.

"Mr. Travere is interested in restoring heavily damaged or lost works, especially by artists who are no longer living." She paused again waiting for me to interject with a question.

Restoring heavily damaged work was understandable. Though, after a certain percentage of loss, the artwork became more the work of the restorer than the original artist. But lost works? How exactly did one restore a lost work of art without time travel, or magic?

Oh.

"Why does he think I'd be of any help with that?" I picked a piece of lint off my trousers and rubbed it between my fingers without looking up at her again.

"He does, and that's why he'd like to talk with you," Dr. Mar made a little huff of a chuckle, though I couldn't see what was funny about any of this. "I'll let Adrien tell you the rest." She dropped the "Mr. Travere" pretense without correcting herself. They were at least friendly, if not more.

"Did you tell him about me? About George?" I wasn't going to share George's private dating life. Coincidences do happen because life is chaotic, but in magic circles, it's best to be suspicious of happenstance and therefore best for me to question who sought out whom on George's dating app.

"Not about your magic, no." She shrugged. "Adrien is, as I'm sure you've surmised, a man of means, but I believe him to be fair and as honest as a magician can be."

Damning with faint praise and "magician." It was rare to meet a man who could do magic who chose the title witch. Adrien Travere Senior's use of "magician" added nothing to his plus column for me.

I flipped over the card again. Westchester. That would be a fun commute in the morning.

"His driver will pick you up at eight-thirty. I would advise you not to keep him waiting. And you needn't come in tomorrow."

Dr. Mar stood up and went to the door. I took the cue to follow, and, having been freed, I made my way to the main entrance and found George and Matjaž chatting in the visitor lobby. Matjaž was animatedly explaining something to George but stopped when he saw me walking toward them. He was still far too attractive.

"Oh, good. I thought Dr. Mar wasn't going to pass up a second opportunity to fire you." George threaded her arm under mine, laughing.

"Thanks. Where's everyone else?" It was late enough that I assumed the rest had forged on ahead.

"Just us. Well, just you two." George's smile carried an apology, so she hadn't cooked anything up to force Matjaž and I to head out alone. "Jacob had already begged off, and Harsh and Suzanne said it was too cold."

The temperature had been plummeting all day. I wasn't sure after the Monday I'd had that I was up for being out that much either. "And you?"

"Date with a man who has promised a homemade dinner."

"Three dates in four days? You like this guy or something?" His keenness made me even more suspicious, which felt like a betrayal of George's obvious happiness with said keenness. I wanted to ask her about Adrien Senior but hesitated. She was radiant with that spark of early attraction. I wanted it to be real for her.

George snorted. "I'll leave you two to your evening." She pecked me on the cheek and was out the door before I could change my mind about grilling her.

"It is quite cold out." Matjaž looked around at the emptying lobby; the last patrons were pulling up collars and winding scarves to head out.

George's kitchen was decently kitted out, and I kept it pretty well stocked. If she was going to be out, inviting Matjaž back to the flat suggested the possibility of more than dinner on offer. Still, I didn't want to cancel. He'd come all this way. "It is and, honestly, I've had the weirdest day. I could make a homemade dinner, if you wanted."

"I would like that. Maybe a movie after?"

He'd been a complete gentleman on Friday, and the tiny voice that was so concerned about my cobwebbed vagina noted there were worse things than the possibility of some light snogging with an exceedingly attractive man on a couch.

Matjaž didn't mind the walk and sub ride. I was much less cavalier about paying for cabs or ride shares than George. The mental math that weighed how many plants or how much canvas I could buy with what I'd just spent wasn't worth it to avoid the subway. He also didn't mind Hilma rubbing up against his ankles as soon as he came in. Check. Check. He sat at the counter while I put together my quick version of tom kai gai, with tofu instead of chicken, which he also didn't seem to mind.

We cracked open a bottle of wine and tentatively filled

each other in on our days. I left out some big chunks of mine, for obvious reasons, and asked more questions about the renovation—hoping to keep him replying rather than asking.

"You don't like to talk about yourself, do you?" He poured more wine into our glasses.

"Not really. I'm more interested in other people."

"It's nice that you're interested in plaster and lath work for century-old buildings, but I would like to know more about you." There was that eye twinkle again.

"There's not much to know. I work in easel painting restoration at the museum, and I head up to West Kill on the weekends to paint and dig around in the dirt." The warmth of the soup, along with the wine, was softening my edges. Always iffy territory.

"Why West Kill?"

"I own a house. A cottage, really. I'm only in the city during the week. This is George's flat, and I am a freeloader." The freeloader part was a bit of an exaggeration. I bought all the groceries and split the utilities with George. She wouldn't let me pay rent because the flat belonged to her father, which meant she wasn't paying rent either.

Hilma wove her way between my legs, reminding me that she would like her dinner as well. I got up and started to carry our bowls to the sink.

Matjaž followed and took the bowls away from me. "You cooked. Let me."

Another check in the decent human column. He really needed to start picking his teeth with his fingernails or something.

"Have you decided on a movie?" I poured fresh water into

Hilma's dish and popped her dirty food bowl in the dishwasher next to our dinner dishes. "We could watch something Christmassy if you're into that."

"I'd rather talk." He leaned against the closed dishwasher and crossed his arms, ready to state his case.

"Okay," I said tentatively, bracing for the onslaught of questions.

"Easy question first. What's your favorite color?" He tilted his head at me and guessed. "Green?"

"Seriously?"

"Blue? Orange?"

"The majority of people prefer blue. Orange would be an unusual choice. Brown."

"Brown?" He looked genuinely affronted. "How could an artist pick brown as their favorite color?"

"Because ochres were the first pigments humans used to create art. Because the backgrounds of Rembrandt's paintings aren't black but layered glazes of different browns. Because of the soil. Because most humans have brown eyes. Because—"

"I stand corrected. And I will never malign brown again."

"Good."

"I guess asking who your favorite artist is would be like asking someone to pick a favorite child?"

"It would be. I go through phases." I picked up my wine glass and nodded my head toward the couch. "Currently I'm into Alison Saar's reclining nude pieces and Ana Mendieta's earth/body sculptures."

"I would've thought painters rather than sculptors."

"I hadn't thought of that, though Saar is both. It's more about the idea than the medium. Though if I had to pick who my work is most influenced by, I'd have to say Ithell Colquhoun and Hilma af Klint."

"Hence the cat's name?"

"Hence the cat's name."

There was a brief moment where I calculated how close I wanted to sit, but we ended up bunched on one end of the couch with me tucked into the corner facing him. Matjaž was a big man, maybe seemingly more so in comparison to me. He was six foot two or three compared with my five foot four. We both had what my father—in his less than egalitarian way—called laborer builds. It always made me think of oxen when he said that, but yes, Matjaž and I both looked like we could handle some farm work and wouldn't go down first in a fight. I found his physicality appealing. George tended toward wiry or lean-hard men, but I always wondered if I would break them. Most of the seconds she managed to rustle up were looking for a much younger, willowy trophy wife to match, and dark-haired, dark-eyed, peasant-built, fortysomething me didn't fit their idea of arm candy. I had a good personality, they'd say. "'Tis a pity she's an ox," I'd hear and immediately laugh about it. Don't pine for what doesn't want you.

After several of my attempts to veer the conversation toward politics or religion, Matjaž succeeded in steering it back around to me.

"You were surprised when you met me at the pub." His eyes didn't go full dazzle, but there was amusement there.

I wasn't sure I wanted to step into this water. There were monsters in the deep.

"I was. You . . . have a familiar aura about you." Relatively safe word, aura. Could be the woo, could be New Age nonsense.

"As do you. Do you prefer witch or magician?"

Bold as brass. I guess we were going there.

"Witch. Magicians require a lot more kit." I didn't look away. "And you? Witch or magician?"

"Neither. I tried to put all that behind me, but it managed to bubble to the surface again."

"The Storm," I said. He was from the epicenter. Anyone with any woo at all would have been affected.

"Before that. I wasn't in Ljubljana when it happened."

For people like Matjaž who had wanted no part of magic but had the woo anyway, The Storm was like being plugged into a cosmic battery with no way to unhook the connection. Magic types came out of the woodwork afterward, setting out their shingle to cure, curse, and charm with the mixed results you'd expect. George and I kept our magic on the down low, as we did even before The Storm. It was easy to hide it from mundanes, less so from other magic folk—unless your personal shields were up and fully powered at all times. In a city like New York, where you came into contact with hundreds of people a day, that was exhausting. Low-level shields and an amulet or three kept the most newly minted witches from noticing, but more practiced practitioners were hard to hide from. My work situation, with Dr. Mar knowing what I was without my knowing about her, and Matjaž sitting across from me faintly emanating old magic were excellent cases in point.

He continued. "I have friends who were more directly involved." A shadow passed over him.

"I hope they are well." What could I say? People at the epicenter had gotten eaten by dragon statues come to life with residual magic, and others had disappeared without explanation. Whole buildings had disappeared or been replaced with buildings from the past.

"Most of them, yes."

"I'm sorry." Friends of his were among the missing or dead. It was a strange comfort to have confirmation of what many had always believed: There was an Other, and most likely an After. But that particular window, briefly opened by The Storm, had closed, and we still couldn't physically touch the Other or those on that side of things. I understood why most people wanted to pretend it never happened, but I have to confess I wanted desperately to know how and why and whether it was simply the first glimpse.

He nodded.

"Have you been back?"

"Yes. But there isn't anything there for me now."

"Does that mean you plan to stay in New York?" I hoped it didn't sound like his answer mattered too much to me, but that tiny voice in my head knew better.

"For now." He smiled again, chasing the shadows of the past away.

We both let the pause in conversation hang comfortably. I found myself wanting to know more, ask more. Why was there nothing left for him in the place that had been home? What did he really know about The Storm if he knew people who had been there? Maybe my expression looked expectant or searching. Whatever he saw in my face prompted him to kiss me.

Surprising myself and that damned little voice in my head, I responded. He tasted of Pinot Grigio and galangal and smelled like warm leather and freshly cut grass. He cupped my face with one hand and pulled me in closer to slide his other hand around my waist.

Aside from his polite peck goodnight, it had been a long time since I'd kissed anyone, and it showed. My body responded like it had been starved of oxygen and he was a bubble trapped under the boat. I slid one leg behind him on the couch and ran my fingers up into his hair, pulling it loose from the elastic band. He moaned as I threw my other leg over and sat astride him, pushing our pelvises together. The bulge between us left no doubt he was enjoying himself. That oxygen-starved, wounded animal part of me wanted to feel his skin on mine. I pushed the front of his shirt up and reveled in the soft thatch and the muscle underneath. His fingers were fully tangled in the mess of my hair, and everywhere he touched me felt warm, like red ochre spreading out from the outline of his hand. I wanted to swim in that warmth, soak in it, and forget about work and the break-in and rich magicians who wanted me to come out to their Westchester mansions for gods knew what.

And so much for that.

My brain kicked in and put the brakes on with a screech. Matjaž's eyes opened. He felt the shift. We'd been wrapped in the same space, and I had ripped myself out it. He didn't apologize, which I appreciated because there was nothing to apologize for. We'd gone there together, but there was too much I didn't know about him and his connection to the Adriens Travere.

I didn't move off his lap. Blatant manipulation on my part, I am ashamed to say. "You taste and smell divine, and it has been a very long time since I've let anyone get this close to me." I touched my forehead to his and willed my heart to stop racing.

"I'm flattered."

"You should be."

Amusement replaced the look of concern in those honey-gold eyes.

I smiled and leaned back, shifting my weight from his pelvis to the tops of his thighs. "I'm not saying I don't want to rip your clothes off and have at it, because I think it's pretty clear that I do. But I have concerns."

"That's fair. I will be honest and say I didn't walk in with condoms or expectations."

Check.

"Not those kinds of concerns."

The frown line reappeared between his eyebrows.

"How well do you know Adrien Travere?"

The frown lined deepened, and his left eyebrow arched. "He's a major donor to the cultural center project. I met him on site, and we've had a few beers. Why?" He shifted underneath me, creating more space between us, but he was still effectively pinned to the couch.

"Did you notice anything mag—"

George's keys scraped in the lock, and she was through the door before it even occurred to me to clamber off Mt. Matjaž.

"Oh shit. I am so sorry. I can—" George's horror was an evenly poured mix of walking in on us because that was always seven different kinds of awkward and having interrupted what she quickly surmised might have been the end to a yearslong dry spell.

I slid off Matjaž's lap and landed right beside him on the couch, our thighs still touching. I couldn't actually tell if he was lying, but as long as we were in contact, I could pick up on any mixed signals.

Matjaž stood. "I should be going. We do all have work tomorrow." He looked down at me, frown line still in place. "Call you tomorrow?"

I nodded and stood up to walk him to the door. George waved a mortified goodnight and disappeared into her bedroom.

"What were you going to ask me?" He shrugged into his coat and stood there with that same dis-ease I'd had earlier in the day, having no clue what to do with his hands.

"Some stuff came up at work. It included Travere's name, and I wondered if this," motioning to us, "and that," waving my hand at George's bedroom, "had anything to do with it." The little voice in my head made graphic and distracting suggestions about what Matjaž could do with his hands.

"I don't know that much about Adrien. He asked me to come along because, as he put it, George was being safe and smart and wanted to make it a double. He hadn't mentioned her to me before that, and he didn't say anything about you except you were a friend of hers from work. If it's helpful, I knew you and George were magic users when you walked in, but I've never gotten that impression from Adrien, and he's never said anything to me that would indicate he has any interest." Hilma took the opportunity to rub herself one last time all over Matjaž's denim-clad calf.

The information was helpful, but I had to believe it meant Adrien Junior wanted people to think that, very unlike his father, he had zero magic. It was much more likely that, very much like his father, he had big-time woo and enough power and energy to keep it completely under wraps from us both. Three strikes from me for Adrien the Younger: too much money, too much magic, and much too sneaky.

"I should go. We do all have work in the morning." Matjaž leaned down for a kiss, and I responded. It held a hint of the passion we'd riled up on the couch. "I will call you tomorrow."

I leaned against the closed door after he was gone, still aroused and more curious about who he was to the Traveres and, more importantly, what they wanted from George and me.

George walked back out into the living room and began another round of apologizing.

I put up my hand. "I'd already called it a night. We were just talking."

"Still. Progress."

"Maybe. How was your home-cooked dinner?" George had a glow of happiness about her once the apologetic sheen wore off.

"Tasty and actually made by him, not a personal chef." George plonked herself onto the couch. "And before you ask your next question, it was just dinner. He begged off any after-dinner shenanigans with it being a school night and bundled me into the car with his driver to ferry me home."

I sat down next to her. This reversal of fortunes was amusing and could mean that Adrien Travere was genuinely interested in George for her brilliant, creative mind and not just her Nordic shieldmaiden good looks. Unless he was an insecure git, there was no reason for him to be intimidated by her, which was usually the issue with the men we'd met. Heavens forbid George—a woman—be smart, successful, beautiful, and have her own money.

"Did he mention his father?" I still didn't want to throw water on whatever fire she was kindling, but I had to ask.

"No. Why on earth would he?"

"His father, Adrien Senior, is the donor for the wing renovation. He owns that painting that had me gone at work, and he asked me to come take a look at a few pieces at his house. Tomorrow."

George looked worried for the briefest moment. "It's probably just a coincidence."

"Maybe." I couldn't so easily dismiss the possibility that it wasn't.

"Why'd you slam on the brakes with Mr. Slovenia?" George asked, signaling discussion of Adrien was done.

"Because I like him too much." "Mostly honest" was the best policy with George. She'd sniff it out anyway.

I fully deserved the couch pillow to the head.

CHAPTER 4

Adrien Travere Senior's personal driver pulled up in front of my building in a gleaming black Navigator at 8:29 a.m. Per Dr. Mar's instructions, I did not leave him waiting and had been standing out in the cold in front of our building for a good ten minutes when he arrived.

After confirming my identity, Claus—of course I asked—opened the back door for me and made sure I had my hands and arms inside. Off we went. Even with the blackout tint darkness and the incredibly smooth ride, I was surprised to be awakened by a polite cough in the drive at the senior Travere's Westchester mansion. I'd been too anxious, or too something, the night before to sleep. Claus handed me down onto the sparkling white gravel as I tried to cover my yawn.

The house was French chateau "but make it American" and, judging by the location, had a grand view of the Long Island Sound from whatever elaborate porches were slapped onto the back of it. I expected to be met at the door by a surly French butler. Instead I got Adrien Senior and the wall of woo he projected, despite looking absolutely normal in his knocking about at home outfit of jeans and a dove gray oxford shirt, untucked and open at the collar to reveal a small seal on a whisper of a gold chain.

I followed him to what I assumed was the grand parlor of the house, given the enormous fireplace and walls covered in art from the Western European white dude oeuvre. A small table had been set near the fire that crackled softly in its grate, a coffee pot and a covered plate nestled between two settings of fine china cups and saucers. The whole house seemed to hum with that same bass note of old magic I'd felt in Dr. Mar's office. In different circumstances it might have been comforting. Now it just made me more nervous.

To be polite, I accepted a pour of coffee that I lightened with my choice of whole milk. The covered plate held a selection of small danishes and petite quiche. They looked straight out of a magazine shoot and reminded me of my father's bedtime stories of the perils of partaking of hospitality in the realms of the Fae. The stories had stopped when Percy was too old to want them anymore. I didn't think Adrien was of the Fae, but I stuck to coffee and I didn't sit down. We made small talk about the drive up and how lovely the view indeed was from the porches that he would show me before I left. The longer it took to get to the why of my visit, the more keyed up I got, which made it harder to maintain my personal wards. A jerk move on his part, but clever.

Adrien led me around the room and played at docent, giving me the story of each acquisition. The groupings were largely chronological, aside from a few placements that looked more aesthetic than taxonomic, like placing two portraits of aristocratic-looking women who could be twins but must have lived centuries and oceans apart next to each other. He was enjoying himself, and I maintained an air of being suitably impressed without curling my lip at the fact that most of the work in this glorified hangar should have been available for the public to see and enjoy.

"It's an impressive collection, Mr. Travere, but none of these works appear to be in need of immediate attention by a conservator or restorer."

"Please call me Adrien, and you are correct. They are quite well cared for." He opened a heavy, green baize-backed door that had been camouflaged by the molding on the paneling. "These aren't what I brought you out to look at."

I followed him down a narrow hallway flanked with more dark paneling that smelled of beeswax polish to a room that mirrored the lab and studios at NAMA except for the wall of glass that let in the morning light. Blindingly so. Adrien Senior adjusted a knob on a control panel inside the door, and the glass darkened enough to cut the glare.

We walked over to one of four workstations, and Adrien Senior flipped open an acid-free portfolio on an easel to reveal a yellowed sketch on parchment or vellum.

"Is this real?" I peered closely at the paper. I'd never seen a study of Raphael's *Portrait of a Young Man*. Not only had I never seen it, I was certain it didn't exist. We had covered the painting's theft and disappearance in my seminar on art crime in graduate school, and at no point was there any evidence of a study. The only photographs of the painting that exist are in black and white, and the digitally colorized prints of those could never do justice to the layering of paints and lake glazes we see in Raphael's other paintings.

"Yes. I've spent a great deal of time and money tracking it down." He ran his hand down the side of the portfolio.

"It's remarkable. And it really shouldn't be in private hands." My comment wasn't going to win his friendship—not that I cared—but that this existed was a miracle and was as close as most of us would ever get to seeing *Portrait* in person.

"But it is," he said. "And it may be the key to ensuring that the self-portrait can be seen again."

I turned around to glare at him. Art historians were split on whether the painting had been destroyed by the Nazis or passed around in private sales after the war. The Polish government believed the painting still existed. Personally, I assumed it was destroyed but didn't rule out greed and the mania that could overcome people when it came to art, especially a piece with a price experts believed would easily top 800 million in U.S. dollars if it came to auction. I imagined Adrien Senior as the exact kind of person who would seal away an artwork like Raphael's *Portrait* without a second thought.

"The painting is not in my hands. I can state, with only the slightest hesitation, that it was destroyed." His face stayed neutral, but there was a bit of amusement in his eyes.

I didn't appreciate being toyed with. "The study is in very good condition. You hardly needed to have me out here to tell you that."

"I do need you, and your particular gift, to restore the painting." He opened a large flat drawer in the cabinet next to the workstation. The de Graaf portrait, complete with my terre verte overpainting of the Lady's hand, lay on the drawer's cork lining.

"You stole your own painting from the museum?" I tried to back away, but he'd blocked me in with his body and the open drawer. No wonder security had been so weirdly disinterested in the theft—the owner hadn't been that concerned about it.

"The painting is unimportant aside from its age. I wanted to see your work for myself. I didn't share all our research on the piece with the museum. I told them enough to show we had been thorough, but not enough to reveal that the painting had been overpainted by another artist, changing the lay of the sitter's hands. You corrected the change that had been clumsily made long before the canvas had been damaged. De Graaf had painted the woman with grasping hands, as did you." His looming over me was effective, but it was also infuriating.

"That doesn't mean much." Only George knew about my episodes, and she would never divulge that information to anyone. Yet, Travere knew, or thought he did. "And besides, I can't restore a painting that no longer exists."

He laughed, brushing away my comment. "I have no desire to force you into doing anything for me. I would prefer you let me make it worth your time."

"You'll have to excuse me if I find that hard to believe." There was no way my poker face was good enough to hide the fear pooling in my gut. We were alone. Only George and Dr. Mar knew where I was, and who knew how involved Dr. Mar was in this business.

"You can believe what you want. My intentions are noble." He and Dr. Mar had the same unblinking stare. Despite the fact he seemed to believe what he was saying, collectors could be pathological shitbirds—like that guy who wanted to have Van Gogh's *Portrait of Dr. Gachet* cremated with him and, for all we know, did.

"What do you want from me?" I left off the *and how unethical or illegal is it* part.

"As I told Hannalore, I want to make you a partner."

Hannalore? If Dr. Mar was that involved, had she lied to me about not telling Adrien Senior I had magic?

"Is that why you had your son hit up George? To get to me?"

Adrien Senior looked baffled. "George?"

"Georgina Burne-Jones. My friend, objects restorer at NAMA, who has spent the last few nights with your son. I assumed George was—"

"I had no idea. I've never spoken to Ms. Burne-Jones. Though I am aware of her family." He played confused well.

I couldn't believe that both Traveres would enter my life so close together without there being any connection. He had to be lying, but I didn't have any desire to touch him to get a better idea. There was no telling what he would pick up from me.

"Could we continue this conversation somewhere less claustrophobic?" Anger slowly edged out fear for control of my brain, and mouth. Who did he think he was to drag me out here and obliquely threaten me?

He closed the drawer but didn't offer to move.

He smiled and seemed to take my change in tone as an opportunity to expound on why he'd arranged this viewing. "Hannalore and I, with some associates, work together to restore lost artworks. We call ourselves the Restorationists. Pretentious perhaps, but we were young, and it stuck. We work with a network of dealers, scientists, and others to locate or reacquire stolen and destroyed art."

"Reacquire destroyed art?"

"That is a more contentious part of our work and less easily accomplished. There are very few people in the world who can do what you can do, and none of them has your talent."

"And what exactly is it that you think I can do?" He hadn't

come right out and said it, and I sure as hell wasn't going to.

"Communicate with artists over time through their work, a very specific form of psychometry and channeling combined with nonmaterial time travel." His expression gave no hint of doubt about his correctness in what particular shape my woo took.

He was right, though not completely. I could do more, or discovered I could do more after the magical hit from The Storm, but I'd been channeling or time-traveling or whatever you wanted to call it since I was a kid. Back then, anything could set it off, like holding a postcard. It wasn't always the full episode like with the de Graaf, but there were hints, the smell of linseed oil, the feel of a brush in my hand, the whisper of voices. There were a few episodes when I blacked out completely, scaring the crap out of my mother. Aside from George, I hadn't ever told anyone the full extent of it. I learned pretty fast from the grifters and charlatans my mother's mediumship attracted that it was better to keep anything supernatural to myself. My mother was convinced I was channeling spirits or had what amounted to the party trick of being able to tell you the history of a thing by touching it. Token-object reading was a great favorite of the Spiritualists and parapsychologists, and it was very lucrative with the right clients. My father had been thrilled at the prospect. When it turned out I sucked at "divining" which object belonged to whom in a gathering of my mother's followers, it was all but forgotten, and I'd never shared with either of my parents that I could tell all those things and more from paintings. I thought I had done an excellent job of keeping it secret. Until now. Adrien Senior knew, maybe even better than I did, what I was capable of.

"I've never heard it described so succinctly."

"From my research, I've gathered that money doesn't interest you, though joining us would mean you wouldn't need to work at the museum. Hannalore would be disappointed to lose you of course. But you'd have the security you seek and the time to focus on your own work. And you would be ensuring the preservation and restoration of art thought lost to current and future generations." He smiled, the warmth and sincerity were startling, especially considering he also sounded like a stalker.

"And what's in it for you?" Money couldn't be the only reason, though billionaires did seem to enjoy piling on the zeros. And it couldn't be fame, unless there was a plan to reveal their machinations later.

"The art. That's all." He moved, opening up my path to leave if I wanted. "You don't need to tell me now, but soon."

There wasn't an overt threat in the statement, but his tone didn't soften it much.

"Claus can take you back to the city. I'll have him meet you out front." Adrien Senior walked away and left me standing alone with the Raphael study.

I brushed my fingertips over the worn edge of the parchment, stirring up the scent of gallnut and bister inks and the lightness of a reed pen in the hand. The bustle of a working studio began to materialize around me, and I pulled my hand away before I went any further into the past—or the past went any further into me. The signature in the work, not Raphael's hand, but the signature of his art—its own kind of magic—permeated the drawing. The *Portrait* wasn't his finest work, but it had been important to him. It had been his own, and not the fulfillment of yet another commission. I took a last look at the sketch on the easel, reluctant to leave it, and picked my way back through the enormous house to the front foyer, where Adrien Senior was waiting for me with my coat.

"I hope you will consider my offer, if for no other reason than the protection we can provide." He didn't elaborate, leaving me plenty of room to wonder about who or what I needed protection from. He helped me into my coat but didn't touch me, at least not long enough for either of us to glean much. Or I didn't, anyway.

Between the traffic and the new dread I carried in my stomach, the ride home took twice as long. Claus dropped me at my door, and I watched the hulk of black car disappear into traffic before I turned to go inside. It felt like I had spent all day at Adrien Senior's house, but it wasn't even quite two o'clock. The little voice snarked about not even getting to see the view from those porches. It wasn't the porches I cared about; that brief glimpse of Raphael's talent and his creative drive made me want to see the drawing again—if it weren't in Westchester.

Hilma pounced on me when I got inside and then backed off, sniffing the air and hissing. She detested the smell of other people's magic—except for George's, and that had its limits. Before stripping down for a shower and a change of clothes, I fished my phone out of my messenger bag and called Dr. Mar to let her know I was going to take the rest of the week off. She refrained from asking for any details of my meeting and agreed a few days away to consider my conversation with Adrien would be a good idea. Then I texted George to let her know Hilma and I were vacating to the farm. She replied with a frown-y face emoji and "I'll call you when I get a chance." I'd have time on the drive to figure out how to tell her I thought there was something fishy about the younger Travere's interest.

Hilma was more friendly and cooperative after I washed Adrien Senior's smell off me. She happily snuggled into her carrier because it meant she was going home, and she was always up for that. I was running away, but I had told everyone who needed to know where I would be, and I was literally going to my own house. If that was running away, I was doing it wrong, no matter what the tiny voice in my head had to say about it.

I had planned to read on the train but found myself staring out the window instead. I couldn't concentrate on anything except the replaying loop of every word of my conversation with Adrien Senior. I needed to get to the farm as soon as possible. My heart raced in my chest like it did when I was a kid and got frightened outside in the woods at night. I would sprint for the front door like the threshold of that house could save me from anything that was out there in the dark. There was safety within my wards, but there was a different kind of safety in the city surrounded by people. It was hard to judge which was best when I didn't know what I was afraid of besides Adrien Senior's magic and the mundane power and money that backed it up.

The train arrived in Wiltwyck without problems. It was Garvey's day off, so there was no pause at the gate. I drove a fraction above the speed limit to quench my sense of urgency but not fast enough to get a speeding ticket on my way to the farm. I mentally checked all of the wards when I got there and did a visual sweep of the gardens before I went inside. The front door was still locked, and everything seemed to be in order. Hilma only mewed at me once to let her out and bolted for the litter box as soon as I unleashed her. I unwound the tiniest bit, relieved as the cat was to be home.

There were tasks in the garden that I'd left undone over the weekend. Anything to keep busy. I checked on the last batch of indigo paste from the plants I'd grown in the greenhouse. It made a better dye than it did ink or paint, though it could remain lightfast under the right kind of varnish or when processed into Mayan blue. Learning to grow, harvest, and ferment it had been on my list for years, and I loved working with it on the anthotypes. Tanya, an art school friend in New Mexico, traded me her foraged desert ochres for a couple dried disks of indigo. If you were going to have adult pen pals, having one with the same obsession for natural pigments was the way to go.

The indigo was dry enough for me to package and take to the post office in the morning. I turned my attention to finishing the candied angelica I'd decided to make with the plants that had been so unceremoniously uprooted by my intruder. Making the syrup to poach the stems in gave me time to think about what Dr. Mar had said about knowing the signs someone was a witch. Of course there were clues in my work that gave away my secret. I'd just been too close to see the pattern, like standing too close to a Seurat painting. So much for hiding in plain sight.

I tucked the last of the hollow, sugar-encrusted stems into mason jars from my hoard of glassware, leaving out one long piece I was going to test as a cocktail straw. I'd found an article about it being nice for gin drinks when I was looking for recipes. If any day deserved a drink, it was this one.

No word from Matjaž despite his promise. Why was I disappointed? I'd seen him all of two times. George finally called just as I sat down with my thrown-together cocktail of Hendrick's, frozen lemonade, and leftover angelica syrup. It wasn't going to be much of a dinner. I needed to hit the grocery on the way back from the post office in the morning.

"Was it that bad?" George was outside on the street. I could hear traffic in the background, and the wind that whipped between the canyons of buildings took her next question with it.

"I can't hear you. Where are you?" Hilma jumped up on the counter and headbutted the handset against my ear. "Ouch." I scooped her up and put her back on the floor.

"On my way to meet Adrien. Are you okay?"

That morning there had still been the slightest possibility that her crossing paths with Adrien Junior just as Adrien Senior maneuvered his way into my life was a coincidence. Chaos did still contribute in this world, and, if it was truly happenstance, I hadn't wanted to ruin anything for her. Now my opinion had shifted toward the negative, despite Adrien Senior's reassurance that he hadn't arranged for George and me to meet up with Adrien Junior. The timing was too odd, but I had zero evidence something was wrong, other than my gut—which was enough for me. But I didn't want to lay it out for George over the phone.

"I'll fill you in when we can both hear. You should come up to the farm this weekend."

She said goodbye, but I caught her before she hung up. "Be careful."

I could hear the smile in her voice. "Now look who's worried about my heart. I'll be fine."

Having a witch's intuition sucked balls sometimes, and this was definitely one of those times. There had to be more to this whole thing, but my intuition ran more toward the sketch of a hint than a mural of explanation.

The sun had set before five o'clock, one of the joys of early winter in northern climes, but I still needed a preoccupation to keep the hamster wheel of my thoughts at bay. It was too dark in the studio and too cold to do much outside. The best I had was the book Garvey had given me and a drawerful of old DVDs. The book turned out to be one I had read but had forgotten the ending, not that it mattered. I fell asleep with it open on my stomach, Hilma snuggled on top of it.

A piercing pain in my chest woke me, and I knocked both book and cat to the floor as I tried to turn over to stand up. A heart attack was the first thing I thought of. The second was that someone had crossed the wards I'd set on the gardens around the house. The curtains were open, as I rarely bothered to close them. Instinct said turn off the lamp so whoever it was couldn't see into the house.

But they would know I was awake if the light went out.

Better that they can't see you.

I pulled the chain under the shade and rolled off the sofa into a crouch. Hilma hunched down next to me, and I held my breath and listened. Nothing. I sent my senses out to each jar in the ward at the edges of the property. No one was there that I could feel. A witch or magician could try to cloak themselves, but it would be almost impossible to do so inside the wards—especially since I'd beefed them up. I pushed my senses past the bright line of protection I pictured in my mind, to the edge of the woods and the road. The sound of an engine turning over and pulling out onto the gravel was just at the edge of my hearing. Whoever my intruder was now knew I had gotten their message about being there, and I hoped they remembered the sting of trying to cross my wards again.

I slid down and sat on the floor in front of the couch, stroking Hilma's fur. It was too dark to see the kitchen clock face, and I'd left my phone in my bag. I stood up and closed the curtains before walking into the kitchen to turn on the light over the stove. Ten o'clock. Hardly the witching hour, but long past dark enough to prowl about, especially here where there were no streetlights and no security lights. I abhorred that weird orange glow, and I wanted to be able to see the stars if I was outside at night. The first time she'd been here George had suggested putting up motion sensor lights. They might help keep the raccoons out of my trash, but they would wake me up every time a deer farted in the yard.

My wards had held, and there was nothing more to do about any of it that night except try to get some sleep and let my brain marinate on how all these threads might come together. I put my cocktail glass in the sink, wishing I'd had the wherewithal to eat some dinner or, come to think of it, lunch. Coffee with Adrien Senior had been a long time ago.

Too much had happened too quickly for me to process it all. Feeling uncomfortably and unusually alone, I padded off to the bedroom, the one that had been my parents' when we had all lived there together, before Percy had run away, and before my parents had lost interest in being parents. George's mother had always told her that benign neglect of children made for better witches. Given my childhood, I'm fuzzy on where the border lies between emotional unavailability and benign neglect, but I don't think it makes for better adults. I had the house, though, and I was protected in it by my own magic. For tonight, that would have to do.

CHAPTER 5

With dawn comes clarity, usually. I was less emotional about the pool of concern and memories my unwelcome visitor had stirred, but I was no closer to understanding or knowing what to do about the Travere père et fils suddenly taking an interest in me and my dearest friend—and why the two had to be connected despite Adrien Senior's confusion, feigned or real. There hadn't been enough hours of twisting and turning, and definitely not of sleeping, to figure it out. I needed more information, and I was in a spot where any internet sleuth-stalking of the Treveres was impossible. There was also no food or coffee in the house, and that would absolutely not do.

I fed Hilma and dressed for the unseasonable cold. Some mornings I wished Bertha were newer, with heated seats and a remote start. But it would be warm enough at the Creekside, and whatever the vegetarian breakfast special was would be worth the chill to get there. The heater fully kicked in about the time I pulled into the last empty parking spot at the cafe. They had a cup of coffee on the counter for me before I could even get my coat off.

"Usual?" Darryl held the paper order pad in his hand, pen poised.

"Um, no. Could I get the four-grain flapjacks instead?" Darryl's granola was excellent, but I wanted something hot sitting in my belly. "And a side of the veggie sausages?"

Darryl nodded and smiled, highlighting the deep laugh lines

in his face. "Good thing I didn't have your breakfast already made to go with the coffee." He headed to the back to give his wife, Bunny, my order.

Small town life has benefits. Massive choice in eateries isn't one of them, but getting friendly with the proprietors of the only place with good coffee—and better breakfasts—definitely is.

Fueled and warmed, I headed to the post office to send Tanya the fermented disks of indigo. Then I dipped into the tiny local market for a few pantry items and a week's worth of produce before steering Bertha back to the farm. Wednesday was starting out with fewer surprises than Monday or Tuesday had offered, but, given their riches in the what-the-hell-now department, I shouldn't have gotten so cocky.

The house phone was ringing when I opened the door, burdened with an armful of canvas bag. I had expected an update from George or even a check-in from Matjaž, who had said he was going to call on Tuesday and hadn't—earning him another check in the Maybe Not column, along with the one for being far too attractive for me to keep my wits about me.

Adrien Senior's faintly accented voice greeted me, if you could call it a greeting.

"I'm sending my driver to collect you."

"I'm not a painting, Mr. Travere."

"But you are valuable, and you will be safer here." That didn't ring with any less objectification than his first statement had.

"The farm is heavily warded." He didn't need to know I'd run someone off the night before, but I knew it and mentally dusted off my shoulder at him.

Adrien Senior laughed.

Objectified and insulted. Definitely a people person, this Adrien.

"I appreciate that you are quite skilled, but I meant what I said yesterday about offering you protection, and it has become necessary sooner than I anticipated."

The little voice in my head took that moment to chime in with a comment about not being obstinate when I was in danger. "I can't just leave. I have Hilma with me, and I just bought a week's worth of groceries."

"Hilma is?"

"My cat." My cat who loathes magicians.

"Please bring her and your perishables. Claus is already on his way."

"You can't just snap your fingers and expect me to comply."

"I'm not snapping my fingers. Have you spoken to Ms. Burne-Jones?" His words were clipped. I didn't care if he was annoyed. So was I.

"Yesterday. She was going to see your son. Why?"

"They are both missing." He hung up.

That couldn't be. Why would they be missing? I called George's phone from the landline, but it went to messages immediately. But why did I need to go to him, of all people? How the hell had my life managed to get so complicated in a span of days? Clearly "no" wasn't a word Adrien Senior was familiar with, and maybe now wasn't the time to school him on it.

There wasn't a landline at the flat, so I called the concierge desk—yes, it's that kind of building. Martin, the day-shift doorman, answered.

"Have you seen Georgina?"

"No, Miss. She hasn't left for work this morning." I heard him flipping through the guest book on the desk.

"Has anyone been in to see her?" No. "Martin, I hate to ask, but can you go check to see if she's there? I've had some worrying news, and I need to find her."

Martin adored George, and though he couldn't leave the desk he sent the super up to check with my permission to go in if she didn't answer. No George.

"Let me know if you find her, Miss. You've got me worried now too." Martin rang off. It occurred to me that he might call George's family's secretary in New York, but I didn't have time to worry about involving them.

Harsh hadn't seen George that morning either, and Dr. Mar had been by to ask her about the vase she was working on. I even called the coffee house George haunted when she stepped out of work to read papers and do research. They hadn't seen her. This left me with the sinking feeling that Adrien Senior was telling me the truth.

If nothing else, I had to go to find out what he knew about George. I called him back.

"Have you confirmed that no one has seen Ms. Burne-Jones today?" He almost sounded bored with my predictability, but why wouldn't I try to track her down?

"Yes. But I'd rather go check myself."

"I understand that, but the city is a big place, and I have reason to believe you are also in danger."

"Why?"

"I won't discuss it on the phone. Claus should be there in fifteen minutes. I'll share what I know when you get here." He hung up again.

I stared at the receiver in my hand and then at Hilma, flicking her tail to and fro. "Okay, Hil. I guess we're doing this." She looked at me with all the indifference a cat could muster and walked away.

I spent the next fifteen minutes alternately thinking up ways to tell Adrien Senior to back the hell off and assembling a bag of clothes and sundries and dealing with the groceries as best I could. It felt weird to be taking my produce, but I didn't want to come home—whenever that would be—to a science project in the fridge. Hilma was uncooperative about getting into her carrier, but by the time Claus arrived in the black Navigator, I was both resigned and packed.

Claus met me at the door and walked me to the car after insisting I leave my cell phone on the table next to the entryway. Despite my many protestations, he won by threatening to throw my phone into the woods and manhandle me into the SUV at Mr. Travere's request. That didn't sit well, but Claus looked like he really wasn't going to have any compunction about following those orders. He handed me up into the backseat of the SUV and closed the door with a heavy metal thud. He slid Hilma's carrier in next to me from the driver's side before he got in and closed his own door. The ward came together like plate mail around the car. Being transported in a magically armored vehicle did nothing to make me feel better about agreeing to this. Claus made a U-turn around Bertha, and we were back on Highway 42 headed toward Wiltwyck before I could gather enough thoughts to tell him this was a mistake on my part. I had the whole of the drive to imagine several scenarios in which

I was putting myself in the care of the murderer in one of the country house mysteries I read for escape.

Upon arrival at Chez Travere, I was escorted to the front door by Claus and handed off to the much younger and more attractive than I had imagined French butler. He took my suitcase and Hilma and led me up the grand staircase to a room suitably decorated to receive royalty, or at least a president. A litter box, a few cat toys, and bowls of food and water had been set up for Hilma in the adjoining study. Someone must have made a run to the nearest pet supply in the time it took Claus to get me to Westchester. I let the cat out to sniff around, which she did with her usual suspicion for the novel.

The butler, Fontaine, did an admirable job of ignoring Hilma's hissing and set my bag down beside the armoire.

"Mr. Travere and the others are waiting for you downstairs."

Images of scarlet hooded figures surrounding the empty slab of a stone altar slipped through my thoughts. I wasn't virginal enough to make a very good human sacrifice, though I had probably been celibate long enough to be in the running. George would have laughed at the thought.

Fontaine led me to a room that would best be called a dining room—if your average house had a dining room with a crystal chandelier, a giant tropical wood table, and chairs that had to cost more than my house. I had to calm the urge to touch the walls to see if the wallpaper was actually silk.

Adrien Senior stood when Fontaine announced me and motioned to the empty chair to the left of him at the table. Dr. Mar sat on his right, and two other people, a white man and a woman, I'd never seen before occupied other spots at the table.

"We are waiting for one more." Adrien Senior looked at the door in anticipation.

I sank into the deeply upholstered chair with a sense of trepidation and mentally kicked myself for agreeing to this nonsense. It was for George. I could find out what Travere knew and leave. The tiny voice in my head pointed out that I had been invited for my safety. The tiny voice in my head could go pound sand. I am allowed a bit of anxiety when the situation calls for it.

Dr. Mar nodded at me in greeting, as did the other two extras at the party. Adrien Senior looked again to the door. It was probably thirty seconds, but felt more like thirty minutes, before Fontaine reappeared with Matjaž Belak in tow. That red flag had not announced itself, or I was an idiot who completely missed it. If there was something suspect about Adrien Junior's interest, of course Matjaž could be involved, and he'd been brought along as the second if only to entice me. The surprise on his face when he saw me said he had expected the ruse to last longer. His lie at the apartment about not knowing anything had been impeccable. My chest flushed, and I berated myself for being taken in by twinkly eyes and some hot snogging. Matjaž took the empty seat next to Dr. Mar. The subtle inlay work on the dining room table was fascinating, and I refused to look at him again.

Adrien Senior finally spoke, but only to ask Fontaine to bring in the coffee and tea. Fontaine stepped away and returned pushing a cart. As he wordlessly served us, Adrien Senior began the introductions.

"Verity, you know Dr. Mar." He continued introducing the other two people who were already there when I arrived. I couldn't have told you their names if my life depended on it.

Niceties were hardly important at this juncture. "And this, as you know, is Matjaž Belak. I'm sure he has as many questions as you do."

I finally looked Matjaž in the eye.

"I do have questions," I said, buoyed by the warm cup of coffee. "Mostly I'd like to know why I'm here. You could have told me what you know over the phone."

"When did you last speak to Ms. Burne-Jones?" Adrien Senior's gaze was intense to the point of discomfort.

"I told you, yesterday afternoon. She called on her way to meet with Adrien." Everyone at the table maintained neutral expressions except Matjaž, who looked more puzzled.

Adrien Senior pulled out his phone and laid it on the table before tapping it a few times. A choppy, digitally manipulated voice let Adrien Senior know that they had Junior and if he wanted to see his son again, he should be prepared to meet a list of demands. The cartoonish menace dripping from the caller's mechanical intonation made the whole thing sound like a scene out of a bad thriller, but the somber faces around that table made it clear the kidnapping was very real. The message ended without any mention of George.

"And what does this have to do with George?" I addressed my question to the table rather than risk another of Adrien Senior's high-wattage stares.

"Georgina appears to be missing as well," Dr. Mar responded.

"If they were together… I mean, you don't think she's involved?" I looked at Matjaž because I didn't know where else to look, and at least his face was nice.

Adrien ignored my question. "Given the demands, it seemed

wise to collect you and Matjaž until we could get to the bottom of this." Adrien nodded at Fontaine again. I hadn't even realized the butler was still there. He laid a piece of white printer paper on the table in front of Adrien, who pushed it to me.

It was the printout of an email, but there was no greeting or intro, just a short bulleted list of things Adrien Travere Senior would be required to fork over to retrieve his son. The first was an eye-popping sum to be transferred to a bank account with an incredibly long number. I don't know jack about high finance beyond what George's seconds droned on about, but my immediate thought was that it had to be off shore. The second item was a Titian painting I thought belonged to a national gallery in Europe. The third item was the Raphael study. That was weird enough, as I had to believe there were a very limited number of people who even knew it existed. The last item was the kicker though. It was me.

Two trains of thought left the station at the same time. How many people knew about me and what I could do? And, where the hell did this kidnapper get the idea that Adrien Travere Senior was in a position to trade me for anything? Both trains derailed on the first turn, and I sat on the edge of my seat wondering how fast and how far I needed to run. Adrien Senior slid the sheet over to Matjaž so he could read it. Matjaž blanched before pushing it back, locking eyes with me.

"I don't understand what this has to do with me." Matjaž's confusion was now tinged with anger.

Adrien Senior handed the paper back to Fontaine, who disappeared again. "You've been working closely with Adrien, and you have been seeing Ms. Green. Of course you seem likely to be involved."

Matjaž blinked. "I can assure you I am not. I explained to Verity that I hardly know Adrien outside of work. I was surprised he asked me to dinner with her and Georgina."

"Based on what I've learned about you, that's most likely true. But." Adrien looked at Matjaž, as if waiting for the younger man to say more.

A question formed behind Matjaž's eyes and then faded. Adrien Senior's bullshit spiel was apparently enough for him. Matjaž tried to catch my eye again, but I avoided his.

Dr. Mar spoke. "I want you to know that I didn't fully understand what you can do and that I am certain Adrien has not shared his knowledge beyond this table."

Matjaž looked even more confused when I chanced a quick glance at him.

I sat back in my chair and took in the bizarre assembly of people, not in the least comforted by Dr. Mar's words. "So how did you find out?" I met Adrien Senior's laser-like gaze head on.

"A friend in the Carabinieri Art Squad in Venice shared a story a suspect told him that he'd found hilarious, a story about a painter who could copy any Old Master's technique by talking to their ghost. I've learned there's always a kernel of truth in such things, though it took time for me to trace the rumor to you. I set a test."

"Without informing me, I might add." Dr. Mar was salty about it. Good.

I hadn't been in Italy in years, not since coming back to New York. I'd never shared what I could do with anyone when I was there. The only tenuous connection I'd ever had to the Art Squad was dead, and, besides, I'd never told him anything about what I could do.

"Does Georgina know about you?" the other woman asked.

"Yes, but George would not be involved in something like this." George was a lot of things that rubbed people the wrong way, but she wouldn't be involved in kidnapping, and she wouldn't have told anyone what I could do. I knew what she was capable of, and her ability was far more likely to get her into trouble with the kind of people who hired kidnappers.

"I know she's your friend—" Adrien Senior said.

"No. You don't know. George isn't 'my friend.' She's family. She doesn't give a shit about money, mostly because she has more than she knows what to do with. And she would never, under any circumstances, tell anyone anything about me." Another warm blush rose up from my chest, but this time it was anger.

Matjaž had finally had enough. "Could one of you please explain what the hell is going on?"

I opened my mouth, but Adrien Senior cut me off. "This person and whoever they are working with has set things in motion to gain access to a great deal of money, a painting, a sketch that only a few people know is in my possession, and control over someone who has the potential to be the greatest art forger in the world."

Matjaž looked even more confused as Dr. Mar hastened to add, "But isn't."

He closed his eyes for a long blink that looked as if it pained him. "You can talk to ghosts?" I couldn't decide if he was incredulous or disappointed.

The others looked at me expectantly.

Adrien Senior set me up to fill in the remaining information gaps, but I was too busy watching Matjaž's face and hating myself for wanting to keep looking at it despite his being part of this whether he was truly involved or not.

"Verity is a remarkable artist, but she also has the ability to connect with other great artists." Dr. Mar filled in the silence I left.

Matjaž raised an eyebrow at me.

"It's complicated. I can," I had to go with Adrien Senior's description here, "perform nonmaterial time travel and channel at the same time, but only through works of art." My other talents hadn't been hinted at, and I intended to keep them to myself. This was already too much like being stripped naked.

"What does 'nonmaterial time travel' mean?" Matjaž asked.

I explained what happened with the de Graaf painting, getting a little more into the story than I had intended. It had been vivid and the first time it had happened in a long while. They were all staring at me when I finished the telling with me blinking into the light of the lab at George's face.

"And you have always been able to do this?" the other man asked. I think his name was Kaspar, Dr. Kaspar something. His white eyebrows disappeared into his whiter hair, giving him the air of a startled yarn mop.

"Yes and no. It was more random when I was child, and other things set it off. Coloring books. Photographs of artwork. I couldn't control it at all. Now it is mostly paintings and drawings, but until recently I've been able to rein it in before I'm too far gone." I still didn't know why an artwork like the de Graaf could drag me back even when I was being careful, unless Travere had done something magically to the painting to make it more likely for me not to realize I was slipping back.

Dr. Mar said, "You neglected to add that because of your work in restoration and conservation, you also have expert knowledge in historical pigments, mediums, and varnishing techniques."

It had never occurred to me until that moment that I could package my woo, talent, and academic knowledge for such nefarious purposes as forgery. I'd always been too worried about being put on display like a sideshow act to my father's advantage. Good for me that my brain didn't work like that, I guess, but bad that someone else had figured it out first.

"I can see why you would be a valuable asset." The other Dr. Art Historian—Jennifer, maybe?—chimed in.

"She isn't an asset. She's a person, and her friend is missing." Nice of Matjaž to stand up for me, but it didn't elicit any more information from our host.

"Matjaž and Verity will be staying here. I have some calls to make." Adrien Senior got up to leave. "Fontaine will see to your needs."

Dr. Jennifer stopped him with a question. "You must have some idea who is behind this?"

The list of people who knew he had the Titian had to be short, and the one about the Raphael study even shorter. And as far as I knew, the list of people who knew about me had been two, including me, before yesterday.

"You know what I know." I didn't even need to look at him to know that was a lie. He left before any of us could call him on it.

I took the opportunity to leave with minimal politeness, hoping to be able to navigate my way back to my room and plan what to do next. Matjaž caught up with me on the first landing and would not be brushed off.

"Look. I don't want to talk here. I'm going back to my room, if I can find it. Feel free to join me." I took the next flight of stairs and realized halfway up that my room was on the second floor. Matjaž followed me back down without a word.

With only one more switchback as I walked right past my suite, we arrived at my luxury accommodations. I had no intention of staying there long enough to enjoy them. I didn't have a great chance of finding George on my own, but I had no desire to make myself of service to any of the people at the table downstairs—or to the criminal enterprise that had taken Adrien Junior and George if the Restorationists voted to send me off like a door prize. I had enough magic to take care of myself despite Adrien Senior's earlier derision. I couldn't go back to the farm or to George's apartment. Thankfully, I didn't have to. One upside of having been a mostly feral child who also has trust issues—see previous bad relationship with an artist named Theo—I always have a backup plan.

Matjaž closed the door to the room, and Hilma came barreling out from under the bed to wend her way between his calves and rub her gray tabby face against him. While we'd all been downstairs, my clothes had been tidied away into the armoire. I perched on the edge of the bed and took a long look at Matjaž as he scooped up Hilma and cradled her against his chest. She tucked her face under his beard and purred loudly enough to be heard across the room.

"Just because Hilma likes you doesn't mean you're off the hook. You're here, so it seems you're involved in this whether you say you are or not." It was hard, though, to maintain suspicion of a person my cat melted into.

Matjaž crossed the room and sat next to me on the bed, thighs touching. He didn't know that meant it was easier for me to sense if he was being honest, and I didn't tell him, though I knew it was shitty not to. A girl has to have some secrets, especially when people are clearly not being straight with her.

"Did you get the 'I'll have a car there in fifteen' call?" I scratched Hilma between her traitorous little ears.

"I got a call from Fontaine to set up a restoration estimate for two nineteenth-century greenhouses on the estate. He did say I should pack an overnight bag—which was odd—but I've worked with people like Travere enough that nothing much surprises me anymore." Hilma had her fill of Matjaž and scampered off to stalk one of the felt mice in the study.

"You didn't know I was here?"

"No. Since I missed you yesterday, I tried to call this morning, but it went straight to messages," he said.

"I was out running errands." This morning seemed like three days ago. Matjaž shifted back on the bed and planted his hand behind my butt to support himself. I stood up, breaking contact. "Now that you know what my woo is, I think it's only fair you share yours."

"Woo? I used to have a friend that called it that. Nothing as impressive as yours. A little intermittent clairvoyance, heightened senses, and some spellcraft." He flopped back onto the bed. My bed. Or at least my bed for now. "But I don't work at it or use it. Like I said, I wanted to wash my hands of it."

Heightened sensitivity—especially to other magic users—had popped up or increased for most of us after The Storm. Despite the Veil being open long enough to supercharge every magical person on the planet, my episodes hadn't changed much, as I had spent twenty years honing that ability to have what I thought was absolute control. Popping off into the past every time I brushed up against a sketch wasn't very practical. The Storm had amped up my senses and spellcraft, but it also revealed I had empathic touch, which I hadn't refined yet, and telekinesis. I hadn't even told George about the telekinesis. It was too intermittent and unpredictable, and I needed to practice more to make it useful. I'd had to tell her about the empathic touch because we lived together, and it could be considered manipulative not to.

"Are you self-taught?" I asked. It was a cheeky question and one that could result in shunning in polite magic circles. Witches get weird about their bona fides.

"No. My mother and my sister were both witches, and my father was . . . complicated." He sat back up and reached out for me. "You?"

He referred to his whole family in past tense. I took his hand, and he pulled me to him, close enough that I was standing between his knees. The scents of leather and freshly mown grass blurred out all the old furniture and house smells.

"Mostly self-taught. My mother is a medium—a good one—but she wasn't keen on my explorations of witchcraft. Communing with the lesser spirits, she calls it. I didn't find a teacher until I was at uni in England."

He nodded but didn't probe further on that subject. "I promise you, there was no angle in my joining Adrien for his date with your friend. He asked me, which surprised me enough to take him up on it. I figured I would get a free beer out of him and be done." He took my hands. "And now I'm tangled up in mystery, kidnapping, and intrigue with . . ."

Damn his crinkling eye smile.

"I believe you." I let go and walked to the armoire to start repacking. "But Adrien had to know you had magic. His father is far too powerful for him not to have any. Since neither of us picked up on it, I'd say he has a lot of magic himself." How had someone managed to kidnap him then, with George?

"What are you doing?"

"Getting out of here. I don't trust the elder Travere or his cronies, including my boss. And I'm not sure where that leaves me."

Fontaine had hung up all of my clothes, but the bag with an extra bra and my underwear was on the shelf above the drawers in the armoire. I found my suitcase in the bottom drawer and unzipped a side pouch to pull out Hilma's harness and leash. Sneaking out with a cat carrier wouldn't do. I slipped the pouch of underwear, the harness and leash, and a long-sleeved shirt into my messenger bag.

"How? There have got to be cameras everywhere. Where will you go?"

"Don't you think it's better if I don't tell you that?" I pulled my coat off the hanger and laid it over the desk chair covering the bag.

"I'm coming with you," he said.

"No. You are not. I can't get us both out of here." I'd had enough of people telling me where I was going to go and what they were going to do for the day. I wasn't even sure I could get myself out of there. I should have worked harder on the telekinesis. I was going to be relying on my wonky ability to mess with the cameras, and I didn't need the distraction of worrying about anyone else.

"If you're going to look for George, I can help, and some things are easier with two people." He didn't press his case beyond that, and he didn't approach me. He sat on the edge of the bed and gave me time to think about it. Check.

The little voice in my head nudged me to take him up on the offer and see where things went. The word "things" had a definite lusty vibe to it. Not the time, little voice. Not the time.

"Fine. We'll need to wait until dark and probably after dinner to give us a lead before we're missed." It would be nice to have help with Hilma. She hated the harness and could be an ass about it, flopping over on her side like having it on had taken her will to live.

"Sounds like you've done this before," he said.

I flinched. He had probably meant to tease, but it hit a little too close to home. There had been a lot of time—and more self-help books because it's not like there are listings for magically inclined therapists, yet—between bad college boyfriend and standing in that over-decorated boudoir with Matjaž, but thinking too long about the night I finally got away from Theo still left me in a cold sweat, and I didn't have time for that.

Matjaž got up and walked over. He kissed me on the cheek in that European greeting kind of way and said, "We probably shouldn't look to be plotting. I'll see you at dinner."

I stood there for a long time after he left, reminding myself it was better to rely on only me. I needed to regroup before I went looking for George. Matjaž with his good smells and twinkly eyes had me all mixed up. That voice counterpointed that there were good people in the world. There probably were good people in the world, but I was reluctant to bet everything on any of them being in that house, Matjaž being the possible exception.

CHAPTER 6

Dinner at Chez Travere was much less pretentious that I had expected. There was no dinner gong, and no lady's maid showed up at my door with a borrowed frock and a mouthful of hairpins like in a Christie novel. The food was good. The conversation less so. Two of us did an admirable job of pretending we were friends at a dinner party. One of us—that one being me—made a point of being sullen and almost bitchy. It was much easier to pout and let Adrien Senior think I was sour about my predicament rather than mentally plotting my way down the trellises.

Halfway through dessert, I stifled an enormous fake yawn and begged off, a little bit sad to leave the other half of a perfect crème caramel uneaten. Fontaine followed me to the staircase.

"Do you need anything else this evening?" he asked.

It was probably best not to ask him for fifty feet of sturdy rope and an accidental blackout around midnight.

"I'm fine, thank you." I waved goodnight and tromped the rest of the way up the stairs to the landing and hesitated again. Second floor. Fourth door on the left.

Hilma was sound asleep at the foot of the bed. A nap might not be a bad idea. I curled up on top of the blankets and tried to shut my brain down enough to drift off. I would have set an alarm on my phone if I'd still had it.

A light knock against the doorframe woke me. Matjaž stood in the door to the study and gave an awkward wave.

"I didn't want to wake you, but I also didn't want to stand here creepily while you slept," he said.

"Thanks." I stifled a yawn and scritched Hilma, still curled in sleep, between the ears.

Matjaž had dressed in darker clothes than he'd had on at dinner and only had his coat and a cross-body messenger bag with him.

My city wardrobe stuck to a darker palette of navy, brown, and black, but my farm clothes tended to be a little more lived-in and faded. A quick rifle through the options yielded a dark pair of jeans and a charcoal sweater.

"I need to change, if you don't mind." I pointed to the unlit study.

Having buttoned up the jeans, I walked to the door between the rooms. His presence was a bright, warm spot in my senses. The furniture creaked, and his footsteps fell muffled on the rug. That bright spot shifted until he was close enough to touch. I wanted to reach out but didn't. He hadn't mentioned empathic touch in his catalogue of woo, but he had mentioned heightened senses and there was no need to risk him getting a hit of the inappropriately timed physical need he stirred in me. Imagining a cold shower would have to do.

Hilma fought the harness, but Matjaž was able to persuade her with a few nibbles of salmon jerky from the basket of food and supplies on the desk in the study. He stuffed the rest of the bag of treats into his coat pocket and scooped her up. I envisioned a future of buying expensive cat treats for Hilma.

"Where to, Captain?" he asked.

The front door was out of the question. I would've given

anything to have George plotting this escape with me. She would have already explored the whole house without anyone noticing. All I had were my wrong turns, which had yielded only one other obvious exit, a large window in the main hall where Adrien Senior's collection hung. The sashes would be alarmed, and the room would be full of cameras and sensors—making it worse than the front door. I relayed these facts to Matjaž.

"I took a stroll around the estate after we spoke. I had those greenhouses to look at." He smiled at me with a conspiratorial glint in his eye. "There's a service entrance at the side under the wraparound porch with a stand of trees about ten meters away. Would that work?"

I nodded. "If we can figure out how to get there from inside."

Matjaž led the way with Hilma zipped into his coat. We missed the service door the first time we walked by, but Matjaž looped back. He had to have a better sense of how these manses were laid out. Drop me in the middle of the woods and I'd be fine, but in here I was the mouse that would never make it to the cheese. With the navigation left to him, I felt out for cameras, surprised to find only one—which we could easily avoid. I was genuinely relieved that I wouldn't have to try to disable the CCTV with my questionable telekinesis.

"Shhh." Matjaž reached out and flattened me to the paneling with his arm.

Claus walked across the end of the hall with an unlit cigarette hanging out of his mouth. He was headed the same way we were, and he would turn off the alarm on the door to go outside to smoke, saving me the trouble of having to magic that and possibly set it off anyway. Convenient, except for the part where he would be standing outside the door smoking. We gave him a minute head start and crept to the service entrance. He'd left it wedged open with an upended pot that had been emptied for the winter. The lit end of his cigarette glowed in the air about five feet from the door. Beyond the shadow of the porches, the dark lawn led down to the Sound, and the waxing moon hung too low in the sky to brighten the night.

Matjaž searched his pockets.

"What are you looking for?" I mouthed the words more than I said them.

"Something to throw."

"Let me." I focused down the lawn opposite the way we planned to run.

The dark shape of a planting or a group of bushes hulked halfway between the house and the water. I closed my eyes and sought out a finger-sized branch, pushing my senses to the limit imagining the branches growing up from the ground. It was much more difficult when I couldn't see where I was aiming. I said a little prayer to Minerva and an image of a twig snagged in my mind. I mentally snapped it in two. It was louder than I had expected, and I could smell burnt wood as the center of the brush caught. Whoops. Claus's energy immediately sharpened, and he moved cautiously down the lawn toward the mass of bushes and the glow of a small fire.

I grabbed Matjaž's hand and took off at a sprint toward the small stand of evergreens. The feathery needles of the white pines brushed my face and pulled us into the woods. It was much darker in the stand without even a hint of the moon, and I kept Matjaž's hand clutched in mine, pulling him through the groupings of trees muttering a cloaking spell under my breath. I expected to hit a fence, but there was nothing to prevent us from following the tree line up to the main road. Neither of us had a cell phone, as Matjaž's had been taken when he arrived. We walked toward the orange glow of a business district, stopping along the way to put on gloves and reposition hats and scarves. The wind off the Sound was sharp and wanted to get as close to my skin as possible.

I don't put much stock in cloaking spells. Making humans invisible, making anything invisible, is incredibly strong magic. The best I could hope for was that people's gazes slid by us, especially anyone who might be looking for us since I'd made a bit a scene to get past Claus. We walked on through suburbia, avoiding streetlights where possible and keeping our heads down.

Bless the soulless business strips of America. There was a no-brand motel next door to the International House of Pancakes and an all-night convenient store next to the motel. We made a pit stop to let Hilma have a pee in the dirt of the median and get some gas station coffee and a few things that passed as food, just in case, before checking into the motel. The night desk clerk was uninterested in the fact that we wanted to pay cash and that we didn't have a car to give him the plate number for the honor of parking in one of their spaces. Hilma stayed silent and still in Matjaž's coat so we didn't have to ask about the pet policy.

We were a little too close to Chez Travere for my comfort, but it was cold enough to worry about hypothermia and we wouldn't be able to get far without any gear. I needed to make a phone call. I had exactly one contingency plan, and I hoped he wouldn't mind a late-night request.

When we got to the motel room, Matjaž sprung Hilma from his coat. I fashioned bowls for her food and some water out of our rinsed and folded over paper coffee cups and closed her up in the bathroom. She wailed her complaint, but it would be easier to clean up messes on the tile in there than it would off the carpet. I was going to owe her after this. Salmon treats for days.

Matjaž sat on the edge of the bed and popped open a small bag of cheese popcorn. "You left firestarter out of your 'woo' list."

"Everyone has secrets." I smiled. "But seriously that's a new one. I've had shaky telekinesis abilities since The Storm, but pyrokinesis was not part of the package as far as I knew." It was going to make practicing a lot more dangerous.

Matjaž was weighing the truth of my words. "Thank you. For explaining and telling me about the rest of your abilities." He doubted me less, though the smallest trace of distrust lingered in his tone.

He was right to wonder. I still hadn't told him everything. Empathic touch—even as minor as my ability was—could be used in the worst of manipulative ways, and I had already used it on him without his knowledge or consent. The thought of him being angry with me left a knot in my stomach, but we were in a situation that required trust. He was going to have to trust me, and I him, or there was no point in us continuing on together.

"There's more." The knot tightened, and I almost faltered under the shame that washed over me. My reaction to the thought of him being angry surprised me. I hardly knew him. Yet I'd trusted him this far, and there was more. A feeling, a knowing almost, growing inexplicably.

"It can't be that bad." He smiled, but his eyes didn't crinkle at the corners this time.

"Empathic touch. I get a sense of emotions when I am in contact with people. It isn't exact at all, but I can generally gauge if what someone is saying vibes with the energy they are giving off." I looked past him to the bathroom door where Hilma was poking her paws underneath.

"Have you used it on me?" He said it so quietly.

"Yes. When I started to ask you about Adrien on the couch at George's. And back there when we were talking about you coming with me." I had believed him on his own merit then, or convinced myself that I did. I finally looked at him, and there was hurt there but something else.

"What did you sense?" He didn't look away.

"It isn't like a lie detector, and it isn't really clear. It's more sensation. Like when people are lying, I get mixed feelings from them. On the couch, I mostly got heat because we had steamed each other pretty good. At Travere's, nothing. So I didn't think you were hiding anything," I said.

He would have been justified in getting up and walking out. My magic is supposed to stop where his skin starts by common courtesy; manipulating other magic users is not "done." Instead, he stood and walked the few steps to me, pushed up his sleeve, and held his arm out. Part of a dark, curved tattoo showed on his muscled forearm, but not enough of it for me to tell what it was. "Tell me what I'm feeling now."

I shook my head no and looked away again.

"If you are willing to do it when I don't know, the least you could do is do it when I ask." He wasn't angry, but there was steel in his words.

I didn't want to drag this out any further. I wrapped my hand around his proffered arm like I was going to pull him up onto a ledge. There was a trace of something that felt like anger, which could have also been projection. But the overwhelming sensation was a warmth beyond body temperature. I couldn't name it, but my throat tightened around the feeling and my eyes burned.

"What do you sense?" His voice was soft; its low, cello-like quality had returned.

"Anger? Disappointment?" It was only heat now, and it spread from him up my arm and across my chest. I let go and backed away.

"What was that?" My voice was still tight, and I didn't want to look him in the face yet.

"What was what?" He asked.

"You didn't feel that?" The warmth faded slowly back down my arm.

"Feel what?" He pulled me into him and turned my face up with his hand cupping my chin. He brushed his thumb over my lip then kissed me, softly.

The same warmth there. I pulled away enough to speak. "I'm sorry."

"I believe you. I don't know why you're so distrustful, but I'm sure you have your reasons."

He kissed me again, and the warmth spread through me down into the earth beneath us, creating tendriled roots as it burrowed. He pulled away and looked at me for a long moment. "I have my own reasons to be wary of manipulative magic. I'm not going to say, 'you can trust me,' because if I have to say it, it doesn't mean anything."

I nodded, wondering if he had more magic then he'd let on. Maybe he had some kind of calming magic that radiated like heat? Though I can't say that it was calming every part of me.

He stepped back and gave me some space. "So what now?"

"Now I call Garvey." I was going to owe Garvey more than Hilma, but I didn't have any other outs. Adrien Senior had done too much homework for me to call my parents, and they wouldn't have been my go-to anyway. It did occur to me that my life of solitude had left me with exactly three genuine friends and two parents who were only semi-reliable on a good day. The little voice in my head had a good I-told-you-so laugh, but I pushed the thought away and dug out my notebook with Garvey's and George's numbers written on the inside back cover. Never assume your phone will work when you need it or that you'll remember a number you never have to punch in.

The call went to voicemail because no one in the twenty-first century bothers to answer an unknown number—especially if a call wakes them up. Garvey's voice asked me to leave a brief message and assured me he would get back to me at his earliest convenience.

"It's Verity. Please call me back at this number." That was safe enough. As far as I knew, only George knew Garvey and I were friends. He hadn't met my parents, and he'd never visited me at work.

Matjaž and I both sat on the bed, and I pulled open the other single-serve bag of popcorn to wait.

"Who's Garvey?" Matjaž asked. He crumpled up his empty bag and walked to the bathroom to throw it away. Hilma dressed him down loudly enough that I could hear her over the water when Matjaž washed his hands.

I waited for him to reemerge from the bathroom. "He's a friend."

"I assumed that much. Why is he part of your plan?"

"He has a cabin in the Catskills—an old one his husband's family has had for generations. It's off grid and nearly off road. I figure it's a good place to figure out what to do next and far enough away that no one will look for me there." I had dragged George up to the cabin the night of The Storm. The dread that that tear between the worlds roiled up had made me certain it was an apocalypse, and I'd had to get out of the city as fast as humanly possible. I'd been sure that once those clouds crossed the Atlantic everything would collapse into panic. It hadn't ended the world, but it had changed things in ways that were apparently still being revealed. "More importantly, I trust him."

"Travere knew we'd been out together. You don't think he'll have eyes on all your contacts?" Matjaž sat back down next to me, both of us facing the hideous curtains covering the picture window and its view of the parking lot in front of the motel.

"Garvey and I don't know each other from work, and he doesn't know my family." Hell, George barely knew my family aside from what I'd told her. I had managed not only to have just a handful of people in my life but to keep them mostly separate. Maybe it was time to seek out that magic-informed therapist.

"Do you have a backup if you can't reach him, or he doesn't call back?" Matjaž moved his arm around my back and planted his hand in the squish of the mattress as he leaned. I could feel the warmth of him through my sweater. I did not need to get distracted, but I did want it and there was really no denying it at this point.

"Maybe. But I'd rather not." The phone rang, and I dusted the cheese residue off my hands before picking up.

"Verity?" Garvey's baritone sent a flood of relief through my system. "What have you gotten yourself into?" Apparently Jon had had one of his gut feelings as soon as Garvey's phone rang and pestered him into waking up and checking his messages.

"It's a story best told in person. Is there any way you could collect me and a friend in Larchmont?" I gave him the address of the motel and the International House of Pancakes landmark and hung up the phone.

"He said they can be here in an hour and half. Maybe an hour if Jon drives like he usually does." I got up and paced the floor between the bed and the window. "I don't have any outdoor gear, but there is stuff at the cabin." The cabin was old but had been retrofitted with off-the-grid modern conveniences and filled with supplies. I wouldn't call Jon and Garvey preppers in a tinfoil hat sense, but I would say they made an effort to be prepared for the worst. The wards on the cabin made my piss and rusty nails look like amateur hour.

Matjaž reached out a hand for me. "Sit down. You'll wear a rut in the carpet. Though that might be an improvement." The carpet was a particularly heinous motel pattern of harvest gold and burnt orange designed to hide all manner of stains. It was doing a poor job.

I sat next to him, thighs touching. He put his arm around me and pulled me to him so my head rested against his shoulder. "Do you always have a plan?" he asked.

"Usually. Aside from George and Garvey and Jon, I'm pretty much on my own." It had never occurred to me that could sound sad to anyone else. It did then.

Matjaž straightened and turned so I had to sit up too. He looked at me for a long moment before leaning in to kiss me again. The rough of his beard and the faint taste of processed cheese soon gave way to not thinking about anything but the smell of him and his hand clutched in the mess of my hair. If the little voice in my head hadn't chimed in to gloat, I probably would have let things progress. I did "see," as the voice had chided, and that was the problem. It wasn't that I thought men or relationships or kissing until you lost yourself were awful things, it was that they often lied, rarely lasted, and made it too easy to let your guard down. I pulled away. Reluctantly.

Matjaž's pupils were wide in the dim light and hooded with the unmistakable look of desire. I didn't need any kind of woo to sense where he wanted that kiss to go.

He didn't push. Check. He reached out and tucked a lock of my hat-matted hair behind my ear. "There are other people you could count on."

"You don't even know me." We were in a strange situation that required trust and intimacy, but that wasn't the same as knowing me. And I couldn't afford to let my lust for him sub in for knowing him.

A smile played at the corner of his mouth. "Not well, no. But enough to know I want to."

Honesty is the best policy. I didn't need the little voice to tell me that. "I am attracted to you. Hilma clearly loves you. It isn't that you aren't exactly what any well-adjusted, mostly straight woman would want. I'm not well-adjusted though." I stopped myself there because the reasons I was maladjusted for relationships were more than I wanted to explain.

"We all have baggage." Said like a man who might have his own vintage world traveler set stashed away in a closet.

"I don't think any of us make it to adulthood unscathed. That's not what I meant. It's not just the woo, you pretty much know all that now. There's shitty family stuff and bad—really bad—relationship stuff. Whenever I think I've dealt with it all, something climbs up out of the dark to remind me all I've done is rearrange the furniture," I said. There wasn't a good reason for me opening up that much to him, but there I was, spilling about as much as I was willing to spill with anyone aside from George.

"Some scars heal better than others." He wasn't saying it just to say it. He spoke like he'd had to contend with his own darkness, which did make me trust him more. There wasn't much he could say that would make me trust myself though.

A faint knock prevented me from having to say anything else. Matjaž went to the door and peered through the peephole before turning back to me. "Not sure why I felt the need to look. You know them."

I had to stand on my toes to see, thanks to whoever thought that only the statuesque would stay at this motel. Jon and Garvey stood side by side, looking around suspiciously.

I took off the chain and invited them in.

"Grab your stuff and let's go. Jon has one of his feelings," Garvey said.

Matjaž gathered up Hilma, and I corralled what few belongings we had with us. We locked the door and slid the key under. While we were inside, Jon had gotten back in the car and had the engine running. Matjaž and I piled in the back of his kicky little SUV and slunk down in the seats for good measure. Hilma, in her harness, insisted on being between us.

Garvey didn't look back to speak to us but asked, "Care to make introductions?"

"Garvey Deverteuil, meet Matjaž Belak. Jon Telford, Matjaž," I said while trying to keep Hilma from rubbing her butt on my face.

"Now that the niceties are taken care of, what's going on?" Garvey flipped down his visor so he could see me in the mirror. As with George, there was no lying to him.

"Someone's taken George and the guy she's been seeing for all of five days. They want money, of course, and a painting, and a sketch his father owns. And they want me," I said the last bit more quietly still marveling how my secret had managed to so thoroughly escape into the wild.

"Rich people problems, except for you," Garvey said. "What do they want from you?"

"Magic." I didn't explain further. I hadn't told Garvey and Jon what I could do, but since everyone else seemed to know, maybe it was time. "I can do something like channel dead artists and let them paint."

Garvey and Jon gave each other a knowing look, and Jon let out a little "whew, girl."

"We knew you had some big badass power, but not that." Garvey readjusted the mirror so he could see me better. "How did they know?"

"That's what I'd like to know."

"Ummhm." Garvey nodded. "Did George know?"

"Yes. Only her. And before you say anything else, she wouldn't have told anyone." I had to hold on to that. George sharing that secret would be too much of a betrayal to contemplate.

"Even if she were in trouble or needed money?"

Garvey liked George okay, but he was even more suspicious of the obscenely wealthy than I was. I only got a pass because my father was all snobbery and embarrassed former gentry without any actual money or land to back it up.

Jon coughed either to curtail Garvey's further poking or to get us back on track with Garvey's original question. "Is that why you were hanging out at a questionable motel in the middle of the night?" I watched his eyebrow raise in the rearview mirror but couldn't see the teasing smirk I knew was on his mouth.

"Something like that." We were on the highway where the streetlights were more spread out. I straightened up in my seat to keep my back from hating me later. "Would you take us to the cabin?"

Garvey put his hand on Jon's shoulder and nodded. "Jon already knew that's what you needed."

Matjaž had been quiet other than to acknowledge the introductions. Garvey was not going to let him stay that way long.

"And you, sir? How are you involved in all this?" Garvey tilted his head and looked at me rather than Matjaž in the visor mirror. I could hear Garvey thinking that I'd finally met a decent human and gone out of my way to sabotage it.

"Other than working with Adrien Travere, I have no idea." He stroked Hilma's fur as he replied.

Garvey raised an eyebrow again. "Did Verity drag you into this or vice versa?"

"I attached myself to the expedition as cat wrangler." Matjaž pulled Hilma closer to his thigh then searched out my hand to squeeze it. I didn't bother trying to take it back—a move I'm certain did not go unnoticed by Garvey or Jon.

"I'm surprised she let you. Good surprised," Garvey said. His smile beamed in the mirror. He was dropping the three of us together in the woods, and he radiated with a self-satisfied glee.

Matjaž and I fell asleep, waking to find ourselves bouncing along a rutted track barely recognizable as a road. After half an hour of Jon's careful but still teeth-rattling maneuvering through the darkened woods, the SUV pulled into a leaf-covered clearing. The cabin was tucked back under the trees, and if everyone in the car didn't have some magic in them, we wouldn't have noticed it. Jon's family had built the cabin generations ago, and decades upon decades of careful warding had all but hidden it from mundane eyes.

I snapped the leash back onto Hilma's harness to keep her from scampering off into what was left of the night and scooped her up before sliding out of my seat onto the crunching carpet of leaves. One deep breath of the cold air—free of all the irritants of the city—reassured me I'd made the right call. The others clambered out of the SUV, and our few possessions were gathered and carried in. Hilma refused to walk in the harness, so she got carried in as well.

The interior of the cabin had that flat musty scent from being empty and cold, but that could be quickly chased away with a fire and some breakfast cooking.

Garvey ran his hand over his mouth, cupping his chin. "I'm afraid you're going to have to share." He walked over to the smaller second bedroom I had planned on laying claim to and opened the door. Since my last visit, the bed had been disassembled and laid against the far wall where the mattress leaned. The room was filled with boxes and crates.

"After The Storm, Jon ran amok on the survivalist sites and well…" Garvey swept his arm over the gathered supplies like a showroom model. "We haven't had time to get everything properly stored."

"I don't mind if you don't mind," Matjaž said.

Garvey was excellent at hiding his thoughts, but it didn't take a psychic to see the smile playing at the corner of his lips.

CHAPTER 7

Matjaž took it upon himself to make everyone breakfast. Garvey had thrown together a bag of perishables from their house to supplement the dry goods stored at the cabin, knowing I wouldn't be dipping into their homemade jerky supply. Matjaž made some kind of boiled Slovenian coffee that required grinding the beans to dust in a mortar and pestle. He could cook and make decent coffee. The number of checks accumulating in the Pro column continued, to my dismay.

Garvey and Jon left, but not before they each wink-winked, nudge-nudged me to an embarrassing degree. With them gone, the cabin was very quiet except for Hilma zooming back and forth like she'd drunk her own pot of coffee. I quickly noted the downside of hiding out was not having much to do aside from the dishes, or talk.

"I'm fascinated with this idea of your 'nonmaterial' time traveling. How does it work? Can you interact with the past when you're there?" Matjaž clearly had no intention of making chitchat.

"I'm not a hundred percent sure how it works. A painting or artwork triggers it. With the de Graaf painting, I was working on the inpainting—"

Matjaž interrupted. "Sorry, what's 'inpainting'?"

"Touchups where paint is missing or where the canvas has worn through the paint layer."

He nodded and motioned for me to continue.

"Usually when artwork triggers things, there's a sense that I'm slipping back, I hear things, smell the boiled walnut oil used to mix the paints, feel the brush in my hand or just that spark the artist felt during creation. That gives me the opportunity to pull back, but that didn't happen with the de Graaf. I disappeared into seventeenth-century Amsterdam without any warning that I remember. I was just gone until George came in."

"So it's like possessing the artist?" he asked.

"No. I've described it that way to George before, but it isn't accurate. I am the artist. I'm seeing and feeling and painting as them. But the memory of it stays with me, just like any other memory I have, so somehow I am still me as well."

"So where does the artist go?"

Matjaž seriously missed his calling as an interrogator. "I don't like to think about it much, but given what happened with the de Graaf, it's definitely a two-way street. They inhabit me in the present—the future to them—but I don't know if they are more themselves than me. I think de Graaf must have seen the damage to his painting, and what I now know was a significant change to the composition, and attempted to correct it. Or maybe I was just repeating what he painted in the past without him really taking my place. I don't know if they can remember it when we switch places again and they go back to the past, their present. I hope they don't. Twenty-first century New York would be nightmare fuel for them."

"But if they can work through you, that means they are possessing you, to some extent. They must know something has happened."

"Yes." He had a point, not one I liked. My mother had always made it clear in her mediumship that she didn't just let any spirit possess her and took precautions to make sure only those entities she wanted to communicate with could come through. There were costs to every exchange, and you had to be willing to pay the price. "But, I am in the past. It isn't like a channel medium who calls upon the dead and brings them into the current realm of the living. Part of my consciousness goes back. I can smell things, taste them. It isn't just visual."

He looked at me thoughtfully for a moment before responding. "And it really never occurred to you before that you could repaint lost Van Goghs?"

I saw a clear flash that he had his own running checklist of "The Pros and Cons of Verity" in his head, and I had to wonder what column "clueless master forger" belonged in.

Our conversation had veered into troubling territory. I got up to put the dishes back in the cabinet. The plates were still wet, so I grabbed a towel from one of the two kitchen drawers and studiously wiped them before stacking them in the cupboard, avoiding answering Matjaž's question for as long as possible.

He crossed the small space and took the last plate from me. "You really never thought to use your powers for gain?"

"I do use them for gain. Knowing the artist's intent makes me a better restorer. I have to back up my decisions with research, but I have an edge no one else that I know of does."

"That isn't what I meant."

"I live off what I make at NAMA, but my own art is my priority." My voice rose. "The thought of repainting another artist's work or allowing some dead white guy to use me to crank out new work or fix his old work? I have zero interest in that."

"I didn't mean to rile you."

"I didn't mean to get riled. It's a sore spot." And had been for as long as I could remember. Percy had accused me of just copying things like a baby. I idolized him, so it hurt more, and I was still mad at him about it when he took off. I doubted at age eleven that I would ever be the artist I imagined him to be at his advanced age of seventeen. It worried me that he had never surfaced in the art world. He was too good. And, after all this time, it was impossible to imagine that he was still alive and not painting.

The shadowy place my thoughts went must have registered on my face. Matjaž took the towel away from me. That warmth grew again where he brushed my hand, and I let it, without trying to think my way through what it was.

"Are there any games or anything in this place?" he asked.

"Yes. Garvey insisted. I think there's a Sorry board in here somewhere," I said over my shoulder as I headed for the cluttered former bedroom.

The trunk where odds and ends were kept yielded the Sorry board and a deck of Uno cards. I regretted teaching Matjaž all my Sorry tricks after he beat me three times in a row. We switched to Uno, where my luck improved. After we'd both had too much sitting and too much avoiding the fact that we were alone together in the woods with nothing but time, I suggested we bring in some wood and do a perimeter sweep before it got dark, one of the things Jon insisted be done nightly when anyone was staying at the cabin.

The temperature, already cold, had dropped to frigid, and the sky had turned that strange luminous gray that promises snow. I pulled Jon's borrowed puffer coat tighter around me as Matjaž and I made a clockwise turn of the ward perimeter. Garvey and Jon had strengthened it over the years, layering their workings over those of Jon's ancestors and living older relatives. Walking just inside it, I could sense the shift from inside the boundary to outside the boundary with my arm outstretched, like a curtain of dense air had been hung at the property line. Matjaž walked across it and stepped back.

"That's powerful." He stepped back over the line, straddling.

"I wouldn't do that for too long unless you want to summon Jon back up here." He had tuned the ward to himself in a more binding way than I had with a few drops of his blood— as his ancestors had done. Matjaž had missed Jon's mouthed incantation when we had come up the driveway, letting the cabin and land know that Matjaž was welcome. Jon had held my hand and recited the words out loud when I had been invited the first time. The strength and nature of the wards wasn't information he shared with everyone.

Matjaž pulled his leg back, and we gathered wood from under the protective lean-to on what had been the original outhouse. I was grateful for the newer septic system and indoor plumbing, which meant no freezing dashes to the toilet in the middle of the night. With the wood stacked neatly in the cast iron log rack next to the fireplace, Matjaž set about checking all the cupboards for ingredients for dinner while Hilma wound through his legs hoping she was going to get fed as well.

"I've only ever cooked for one other vegetarian," he said with his nose in a cupboard full of neatly ordered jars and cans.

"Ex girlfriend?" After pouring out some kibble in a bowl for

Hilma, I sat backwards on one of the kitchen chairs and propped my chin on the top of the curved back.

"Funnily enough, yes." He pulled down a storage jar of twist-shaped pasta and a can of black beans. "She hated vegetables, though, which never made any sense to me."

"There are a surprising number of anti-veg vegetarians."

"And you? Why are you vegetarian?" He rooted around in the fresh stuff Garvey and Jon had brought with them and placed a small onion and a bag of spinach with his other finds. "There should be some oil somewhere, shouldn't there?"

"Check that other cupboard. There's usually some ghee and stuff in there." I pointed to the last cupboard over the modest prep area. "My parents were full-on hippies at some point, and my mother hated the smell of meat cooking. So, post-hippie lifestyle, they stayed vegetarian. I never bothered learning to cook meat, and the few times I've tried chicken or beef, the texture was off-putting. I will occasionally eat fish, but usually only what Jon and Garvey catch on their trips."

He nodded, seemingly satisfied with my explanation, and set about putting together a black bean spinach pasta I would have happily ordered at any restaurant. With the dishes done and dried, we were back to the same problem of time on our hands. The sun had fully set soon after we'd come inside from our wood gathering, and the cabin assumed the intimacy of darkness. The fridge gave up two beers left over from a previous stay, and Matjaž and I wound up on the couch watching the fire, beers in hand.

"You said that your mother and your sister had been witches and your father had been complicated. That's a lot of 'hads,'" I said. It might not have been my turn to probe, but his earlier statement rested heavily on me.

"My father died in a car accident when I was at university. My mother was badly injured and used a wheelchair after that. My sister was murdered, and then my mother died, both before The Storm."

"I'm sorry." What else could one say?

"Thank you. My sister's death still troubles me, but I've long come to peace with my father's death and, more recently, with my mother's." He stared into the fire, but his eyes were seeing another place or time.

"Did your mother not offer to train you? As well as your sister?" Nosy question. Magical families could be weird about how things were handed down.

"She did, but I didn't want any part of it. My parents were complicated."

"You mentioned." I unlaced my boots and pulled them off so I could tuck my feet up underneath me on the couch. I wasn't going to prod if he didn't want to explain, but I left him space to if he wanted.

"My parents did some unethical things to be together, and my mother used her magic to control and hurt people." A shadow passed over his face. "I thought my sister had gone down the same path after I learned what she'd been involved with before her murder, but I was wrong."

I moved closer to him on the couch. "We aren't our families." I'd had to say those words to myself enough times that there was real conviction behind them.

"We aren't, but we do sometimes have to answer for their actions." He found my hand and squeezed it. I squeezed back. "I think I'm ready for bed." He covered a yawn with his free hand. "I can sleep out here, if you don't want to share."

"You won't be able to walk tomorrow if you sleep on this couch. I really don't mind sharing." I wouldn't mind the extra body heat, and maybe I did trust him, if not myself.

"If you want to do whatever you need to do before bed, I'll bank the fire."

I popped up from the couch and grabbed my boots to put by the bed. A rummage through my bag produced a small toiletries zip pouch of basic needs—toothbrush, toothpaste tabs, floss, deodorant, and a slim tube of moisturizer. You could probably call me a prepper as much as Jon or Garvey, but in a much smaller way. If I had my bag with me, I'd make it. Brushed and slicked and dressed in borrowed PJs, I climbed into bed, cold despite the down comforter. Matjaž came in and stripped down to his T-shirt and boxers, revealing a body more attractive than I had imagined.

I could see most of the tattoo that I had glimpsed at the hotel. The part I had seen was the tip of a feather on a black-winged person, their head hidden under the sleeve of his tee. It was too large and too dark to not have significance.

"You played me so you could get pre-warmed sheets."

He smiled and scratched his arm above the tattoo in that sleepy, sexy way that would usually melt down any underwear made of manmade fibers, before sliding under the duvet next to me. Should I look at the ceiling? Turn my back to him? Turn my face to him?

He turned on his side to face me. "Are you cold?"

I nodded, concerned about the words that might tumble out

of my mouth if I opened it.

Unconcerned with the fact that I was no longer breathing, he reached his arm out and pulled me into him. How could he be that close to naked and that warm?

"We can just sleep." His voice at my ear made it even more difficult to remember what my lungs were supposed to be doing. "Take a breath."

Sleep seemed impossible, but I took the breath and pulled my hand up out of the blankets to touch his face.

"Why do I feel like I know you when I know hardly anything about you?" That wasn't an answer to his half-asked question, but as much as I wanted him to kiss me, to touch me, to absolutely fuck my brains out, I couldn't say it. I had barely admitted it to myself.

"I don't know, and I don't know that it matters." He pulled me in closer and covered my mouth with his, taking the breath I had just found.

Kissing him was like falling through warm summer air. I was completely enveloped in the scent of him, the warmth of his body, and that flooding of liquid heat that spread wherever our skin met. Our breath meshed as the kiss deepened, and the tip of his tongue gently teased against mine. I pulled his lower lip into my mouth for a tiny nip.

"I need both hands on you." In one fluid movement, he rolled us together so I was on top, straddling his hips. His T-shirt rode up, and there was another tattoo visible down his sternum. It was too dim in the light of the oil lamp to make out the details. I ran my fingers up the image, pushing his shirt up. He tilted me back before taking his T-shirt off entirely. I ran my fingers down the tattoo again before he pulled me back down to him, kissing me hard, his hands thrust into the mess of my hair.

His skin was so warm, I wanted to feel it against my own and leaned back to undo the plastic buttons on my borrowed PJs. Matjaž stopped me. "Let me."

He sat up and turned so he was sitting on the edge of the bed, my legs wrapped around him. He nuzzled his face against my ear and gently bit the lobe. "Stand up."

With his help, I extricated myself and stood in front of him, suddenly shy. It had been a long time since I'd been naked in front of anyone, except Hilma, or George on occasion.

Matjaž picked up on the change in my demeanor and put his hands on the tops of his own thighs. "We can stop." He smiled and raised his hand to tuck my hair behind my ear. Check.

I shook my head and took a breath. "I don't want to stop. It's been a really long time, and I have a scar."

He shook his head and started to undo the first button. "May I?"

I nodded.

He undid the button and pulled me in closer and brushed his lips against the newly uncovered skin, the hollow between my breasts, and lower to the visible top of my scar, silvered and faded. He reached for the next button. "May I?"

"Yes." My voice was breathy and shaking.

His breath against my skin sent a wave of electricity across my nerve endings. I knew there was more scar to reveal, and I wasn't sure how he would process that or how much I could tell him.

"May I?" He undid the last button I had done, and he could see that the scar went farther.

"What happened to you?" He wrapped both arms around me and buried his face in the crook of my neck.

"Trauma surgery. A ruptured spleen."

"Were you in an accident?" His voice was muffled, and I appreciated that I didn't have to look him in the eye because I wasn't ready to tell the whole story of the night I finally left Theo.

"Something like that."

He took my face in both hands and looked at me for a long time. "I'm sorry that happened to you. You don't have to be shy with me about your body. I want to see all of it. Touch all of it. Worship all of it." He kissed me hard before I could respond.

I slid my pajama pants down before he had the chance. I had made peace with my body, it was only the story that scar held that was hard to share. It could wait for another time.

***

Afterward, I got up to pee and looked at myself in the porthole mirror over the sink, smiling at my reflection. Maybe it had been foolish to let him get so close, to leave myself open. For that brief moment, I didn't care.

Matjaž was asleep when I got back to the bedroom. I will never understand how men seem to be wired to pass out after sex, and I will always be envious. I put my pajamas back on to ward off the cold and curled into his warm back, my mind spinning out too many tales of what happened from here.

The adrenaline spikes and crashes of the past twenty-four hours eventually got the better of my hamster brain. Despite the exhaustion, I woke with a start sometime after midnight. I'd been dreaming and heard George call my name, but not in the dream. Matjaž was spooned around me with his hand draped across my stomach. I hesitated to move, but I was too jarred to go back to sleep. He didn't wake when I lifted his hand. I sat up and reached instinctively for my phone to see what time it was. The nightstand was bare except for a lantern and a box of safety matches.

"Verity." The voice came out of the darkness in the corner of the room. "Verity, please don't scream." I had not imagined George's voice.

"I'm not going to scream," I whispered. "Who's there?"

"It's me, George. Are you daft?" It was hard to believe anyone else could fake that posh but trying really hard not to be British accent.

"Am I still dreaming?" I pinched the top of my thigh hard enough to wince. Nope.

"Sorry about that, but it's the first time I've been alone enough to look for you."

George had some serious explaining to do. "You weren't at the flat or at your place. I thought you might be at Matjaž's, but I didn't know where he lived and didn't have enough of a link to find him. Then I heard them talking about tracking you." The voice came closer to the bed. It was too dark to see, and I didn't want to strike a match or light the lantern. It was better if Matjaž stayed asleep. My witchy gift wasn't a secret anymore, but George's was, and it needed to stay that way.

"Tracking me? How?" The cabin wards would have dispelled any magical tracking as soon as I crossed the boundary.

"Something in your bag. It doesn't matter. They know where you are. You have to leave." George breathed in audibly. "I think he's coming back. I have to go. But you can't stay here, you have to leave."

"How? Where are y—"

"Leave." With that, her presence was gone.

I knew George was able to remote view, but I had no clue she could bi-locate. Clearly we both had been keeping our own little secrets since The Storm. I lit the lantern to look for my bag, which I had put on a chair next to the nightstand with my clothes. Jon always insisted that you had to be ready to dress, with shoes, without having to run all over the cabin. I said a little thank you prayer to him for his useful paranoia.

I turned my bag out onto the quilt, finding nothing that I couldn't identify until I unsnapped the wide pocket on the outside and a small, shiny disk the size of a shirt-collar button dropped out into the pile. Whoever it was hadn't tracked me with magic but had used good, old-fashioned technology. It was probably too late to do much, but I put the bug on the floor and whacked it with the heel of my boot until it cracked. Matjaž grumbled in his sleep but didn't wake. I wasn't sure which column being able to sleep through a witching hour visitation and bug smashing went into.

The more pressing issue was what to do about George's warning. There wasn't anywhere for us to go or any way for us to get there except on foot. I hadn't filled George in on how powerful Jon's wards were as he'd whispered her invitation to the land as well. No one was going to barrel in quietly. Famous last words those.

CHAPTER 8

Engine sounds and the crunch of tires on frozen ground were finally enough to wake Matjaž.

"Did Garvey—" Matjaž's question was cut off by loud swearing from outside. Hilma made a beeline for the bed and shimmied under the covers.

"It isn't Garvey and Jon." I wanted to peek outside but didn't dare move the curtain to see who was coming. They'd gotten through the ward, but how could they even find their way up here with a signal from a tiny piece of metal and silicon? This place wasn't even on current surveyor maps.

The cabin itself had another layer of wards, but if our uninvited guests had gotten through the blooded land ones I didn't have much hope for the cabin protections. I started pulling on my boots. If I was going to run for it, I wasn't going to do it barefoot. "Get dressed."

Matjaž nodded and searched around for his boxers. There were guns in the cabin, and I knew where the locker key was, but I had zero training and wasn't about to endanger myself or Matjaž trying to shoot our way out of there. I did whisper a petition to my ancestors and Minerva and whoever else might be listening to get all three of us out of this situation alive.

Another loud swear came from the cabin porch—another breach. They were at the door and the last ward.

"You aren't welcome here, and you should leave." I didn't

scream but said it at the top my voice and pulled in every scrap of magic I could find in the wards and myself.

Three pounds against the door answered.

Matjaž started to walk toward the bedroom door, but I stopped him.

"They don't want you. They may not even know you're here."

"I'm not going to just let them take you." His face held all the markers of someone in fight mode. My gut said fight mode would get us killed, get him killed. And it was too late for flight.

"We don't know if they have guns. We do know they have serious magic. Very few people could have gotten through Jon's wards." They had to have an artifact older or more powerful than Jon's ancestral magic. Matjaž was listening, but I hadn't convinced him to stand down.

"If they take us both, no one will know what's happened." George would know, but she wasn't in any position to help spread the word.

That made him stop. "Let them take me."

I looked down at the lump of Hilma under the quilt. I was terrified that whoever those goons out there were, they would shoot Matjaž rather than leave a witness. "They aren't here for you."

That sunk in. He nodded almost imperceptibly. "What do you want me to do?"

"Take Hilma and get in the closet. When we're gone, get on the ham radio, it's in the closet in the other bedroom, and contact Jon—he'll already know the wards have been crossed. All the information you'll need is with the radio." I pulled on the puffer coat and grabbed my bag. They probably wouldn't let me keep it, so I stuffed my emergency magic kit and a few other items into the inside pockets of the coat.

"I can't believe I am letting you do this." Matjaž stared at me for a long moment, looking like something inside him might break. He pulled me into him and kissed me, hard and angry.

The warmth was there again, but more like flames licking at us than the sun-warmed skin feel of earlier. He pulled away. "Please be safe. Please come back." He started to say more but stopped himself.

All I could do was nod. I dug Hilma out from under the quilt and thrust her at him.

Three more pounds against the door.

"Closet. Now."

He Tetrised himself in with Hilma wrapped in his arms. I pushed the door to without letting it latch and walked to the main room to face my kidnappers. The look on Matjaž's face as the door closed would probably haunt me forever.

I opened the front door as the very large man who had been pounding on it raised his fist to do it again. His surprise would have made me laugh in different circumstances.

"I had to get my boots on. You didn't expect me to wander out into the night barefoot, did you?" My words were shaky, but I was going to keep as much control in this situation as I could. I stepped out onto the porch and closed the door behind me. Looking up into the face of my kidnapper, I noticed one eye was swollen and his cheek looked like it had been raked by a claw. I didn't really want to know what crossing Jon's wards uninvited would do, but I had a better idea now. His ancestral spirits or the land spirits totally played dirty. Good.

I walked past him and another man with his own wounds, down the steps toward the waiting SUV. A few inches of snow had fallen after dark, and the headlights illuminated the heavy flakes still coming down.

"Do you want me to sit in the back or the front?" I smiled politely, as if we were taking a Sunday drive. My knees were about to go out from under me. Every self-defense class I'd ever had drilled into my brain: don't let them take you to a secondary location. I wasn't worried for my life, because whoever these people were, their boss wanted me to paint. But there are a lot of things that can be done to a body that don't impair the physical ability to hold a brush. That's why my knees were Jell-O.

The men bounded down the stairs, their heavy boots thumping against the wood. The taller one opened the back passenger-side door and motioned for me to climb in. "Move across."

As he pulled up to slide in next to me, he gave me the perfect opportunity to run for it. I could have slipped out the other unprotected, unlocked door and into the darkness of the woods. It was snowing hard, and I didn't doubt they were packing more than magic in their tactical black ensembles. But whoever they were working for had George, and I wanted to believe that together she and I could free ourselves and her new boyfriend. So I sat, hating that I might regret not taking the chance for the rest of my life—however long that was going to be.

The other man climbed in behind the wheel and drove us slowly back down the rutted track. Any marks the SUV's tires made coming in had already been covered with fresh snow. I hugged my bag to my chest and stared at my face in the window, its contours dimly lit by the glowing panels in the dashboard.

The window was too darkly tinted to look out. No one spoke until we got to the first turn onto what most people would consider a road.

"That was pretty ballsy, what you did back there," said the dark bulk next to me in the back.

I shrugged but didn't answer.

"Those were some serious wards you had set up." He was impressed and maybe a little afraid of me, given his tone. Let him think it was me who'd used the power of generations of magic users to nearly put his eye out.

More snark bubbled to the surface, but words were power and energy, and I needed to conserve what I had. Matjaž had probably already gotten through to Jon. He and Garvey would have been waiting to hear from us unless Jon had pushed Garvey into the car as soon as the wards were broken. Given that whoever crossed my wards at the farm had made me think I was having a heart attack, I didn't want to think too much on what Jon experienced at the breach of his protections. If I ever got the chance, I would ask him if he had a way to mitigate the pain of the connection.

The SUV turned onto the highway, and I tried to figure out which way we were headed. The snow was nearing whiteout conditions, and we would have to stop if it got any worse. The best I could tell, we were headed south and back toward the city, but that could mean anything. The little voice in my head had been quiet but took the opportunity to kick me when I was down and pointed out I would have been fine if I'd stayed at Adrien Senior's. Better the devil you know and all that. But I didn't really know that devil either. Adrien Senior, Dr. Mar, and their compatriots were in a gray area of business, if not actively dealing with outright stolen or forged art, whatever they called it. A shiver went up my spine. If the Restorationists were already the villains, the person these two henchmen worked for could hardly be an improvement. I hated to give the little voice a win but conceded I might have acted in haste.

The snow worsened, and the driver took the next exit. The muted glow of an all-night gas station beckoned not far from the turnoff, and Driverman Dan pulled the SUV under the canopy of the pumps. Several other motorists had made the same decision, turning the station into an impromptu parking lot. This would have been another opportunity to give my new friends the slip, but nobody was going to be going anywhere fast in these road conditions.

"Can I go pee?" I asked.

The driver and the bulk next to me exchanged a few glances. Driverman Dan said, "Go with her and stay close."

I reached for my door, but my seat mate indicated I should follow him out the passenger side. "Leave the bag here."

I tossed my bag back onto the seat and walked ahead of him into the gas station. There was a line for the ladies, of course, and he had to stand with me trying and failing to look nonchalant. More than one person gave the two of us the once over. We definitely made for an odd couple, me in my winter boots and borrowed, oversized PJs and him dressed in black tactical gear, gaiter up, looking like he'd been mauled by a bear. At least one of them had to have blood-stopping magic, or that cut above his eye would have been a waterfall of crimson. The toilet was single occupancy when I finally got to use it. I took the opportunity to actually pee—because never pass that up—and pulled my emergency magic kit out of my coat. I'd like to say it was the first time I'd ever used the back of a public toilet as an altar, but it wasn't. I didn't want to take the risk of setting off any smoke alarms, so I skipped lighting the stump of a black birthday candle and poured some salt and moon-blessed water from a small glass vial into the tiny dollhouse punch bowl. A few words asking for a window to deliverance for George and Adrien and me and the focus to see it when it presented itself as well as safety for the three of us. I dipped my finger in the water and dotted my forehead before pouring the rest into the toilet and flushing. Not the best way to dispose of spell remnants, but witches make do.

My new friend was waiting for me, as expected, with the rest of the impatient line.

"Do you want anything?" he asked.

"A coffee maybe." I shrugged, and for you and your friend to get me to George in one unmolested piece.

The coffee machine was broken, and the cashier offered me a bottled coffee drink for half price to make up for it. Cold coffee wasn't my first choice, but I took it for the caffeine. My companion had to pay because he'd made me leave my bag in the SUV. He patted himself down, trying to find which of the many pockets he'd put his wallet in. While he was fumbling around, I was watching the other people in the gas station. Two women were standing next to the pyramid of Coke and Diet Sprite cases strung with blinking Christmas lights by the door, whispering to each other and looking my way.

The automatic doors swished open, letting in a rush of swirling snow and two police officers. They both scanned the scene, focusing on me and the group of people crowded around the checkout. The cashier gave me a look she assumed I would get the meaning of and then jutted her chin toward the door where the officers stood. I looked at them and then the two women who had moved closer to them and realized what had been going on while I was having a pee and petitioning Minerva. They thought I was being trafficked and had alerted the cashier. I mean, I was being trafficked, but this wasn't really going to help the situation.

The officers approached, and I thought one more prayer to the goddess. I doubted my kidnapper would give up his prize easily. There was still the question of how much magic or metal he was carrying, and I needed to get to George. How much charm could I summon, sleepy and cold and genuinely afraid, to convince these two I was just fine, thank you?

Tactical Jack stiffened and gave me an unparsable look. I nodded at the officers and followed them with my guts churning. I didn't know where George was, but she was alive if not exactly safe. I had no idea what these two henchmen would do if they thought they were going to lose their quarry, and there were a whole lot of innocent people who were only there because of the snowstorm. Was it better to let these officers take me away or stay with the henchmen and get to George? I was only one item on their boss's list of demands, and there was no guarantee I or George or Adrien Junior would be safe with a partial fulfillment of their request. There were too many questions, and I had zero answers for any of them. Best to stick to the plan.

"Ma'am, are you with the person inside of your own volition?" the first officer asked. His patches marked him as a Greene County Sheriff's deputy. Dark hair, dark eyes to his partner's blond and blue.

The words of his question tumbled over each other in my

brain until they didn't make any sense as words. I pulled my coat closer and looked for the SUV in the parking lot. The driver got out but stayed near the car, watching.

My seat mate walked outside, bottled coffee in hand. "Is there a problem here?" He'd pulled down his gaiter to reveal a nearly pleasant, clean-shaven face marred with animal-like scratches around his eyes. He'd nearly lost his right eye, and the edge of the bruise spreading across his cheekbone had already purpled.

"We have the situation under control. Please return to your vehicle."

Tactical Jack stiffened and looked to the SUV for his compatriot who, I imagined, stood ready to intervene.

"Officers, yes, I'm with them. We got a later start than we'd intended and hadn't counted on the storm." I dug my hands into my coat pockets. It wasn't a lie at that point, I was choosing to stay with them.

Neither of the officers looked convinced. It was below freezing, and all I had on was Jon's flannel pajamas patterned with mallards and rainbows and a bright orange puffer coat, both several sizes too large.

All I could think of was George, wherever she was. She hadn't been mentioned in the ransom letter. She wasn't part of this. Collateral. Collateral damage. If I got to her, she might be safe. If I got to her, maybe I could bargain for her safety.

"Really. I'm fine." I smiled as big as I could. "I'm glad folks are looking out for the unusual. I'd just hoped to sleep through the drive." I feigned a yawn and covered it with the back of my hand.

"Where are you all headed?" the dark-haired officer asked. "And what happened to your face?"

My kidnapper and I tried to answer at the same time, but he finished his reply first. "Into the city, and I fell into a bush trying to push our car out of a ditch."

The officer pulled a card out of one of his many pockets and pouches. "If you change your mind." He looked me hard in the eyes, one last unspoken invitation to leave this situation.

I took the card and shoved it into my coat pocket without looking at it closely. Tactical Jack asked if we were free to go, and the officers dismissed us. I walked back to the SUV, my new friend cupping my elbow in a way that might have felt protective, not possessive, if Matjaž had done it. I'd been presented twice with a window to escape and hadn't taken either of them. My stomach turned over at the thought, and I added to my petition to Minerva. Please, I need one more out, for all of us, when I get to George and Adrien.

CHAPTER 9

The freak early snow didn't let up, and the highway patrol closed the interstate, trapping us all at the gas station for the night. I tried to curl up against the door with my bag as a pillow. Between the coffee drink that sat souring in my stomach and Driverman Dan turning on the engine every so often for warmth, sleep didn't happen. I kept my eyes closed and feigned it anyway, mostly to keep any conversation at bay. If Tactical Jack did have a little fear of me, best not to dissipate it by running my mouth.

I spent most of the uncomfortable night with a head full of even less comfortable thoughts. I'm sure Adrien Senior had not been pleased to find that Matjaž and I—the coveted prize—had escaped into the previous night. I let a little spark of hope flicker up that he might be looking for us. With Matjaž—I'd probably ruined things for good there—it didn't take much to imagine the fear and guilt he must be feeling, he and Hilma pacing the cabin after extricating themselves from the closet. Garvey and Jon would have encountered the same storm, and it was doubtful they had gotten to them yet. And then there was George, the reason I had agreed to come with these two against any rational thought. It's what we do for family. George had done the same for me. Together we would figure out escape. It was hard to imagine someone as powerful as I assumed Adrien Junior to be being held for long, but maybe I was wrong about him having any magic. It happened sometimes in families.

Families. Mine and George's—equally fucked up but for different reasons. We'd found each other and made our own family as sworn sisters. It wasn't my family who had come for me that night. Everything had been planned. Theo was leaving town to go to an opening of his work at a gallery in Paris, and I had exams. He left, and I started packing—only the essentials, only what I had to have to move forward from there. Walk to the Tube station and meet George at Paddington, where we would take the train out to her family's house near Moreton.

Theo forgot his train tickets and came back while I was packing. His rage filled the house before it laser-focused on me. There was no placating, no bargaining. And there was no sparing my face or head or ribs. He kicked me when I fell near the stairs that led down to the front door and kept kicking until I tumbled down them to the bristle mat at the bottom. The door opened and George was there, incandescent in her own rage and her magic. If she hadn't come for me when I was late to meet her, I would have died from internal bleeding.

Driverman headed south with the many other cars finally leaving the safety of the gas station awning when the storm lightened with the dawn. I cracked an eye open as we crossed the George Washington Bridge and felt some relief in the familiar. We drove on, almost to the end of Long Island out to the Hamptons. I'd only been out this far twice in all the time I had partially resided in the city, and both of those trips had been on George's coattails for weekend house parties I hadn't enjoyed. I didn't have high expectations my third trip would be an improvement.

There was only a dusting of snow here, but the sky still hung low and dark even at midday. Driverman turned off the main waterfront artery into the drive of a house surrounded by a shimmering ward that flickered in my mind's eye as we drove through it. Whoever my host was, they weren't much interested in drawing attention. Once parked on the half circle drive at what looked to be the back of the house—the fronts tended to face the ocean in these neighborhoods—I couldn't see where we had come from. Fully mature evergreens and deep underplanting hid everything from the street. The house itself was a box of glass and steel that reflected the flat gray of the sky, negating any shine it might have had in fairer weather.

Driverman turned off the ignition and got out, immediately piercing the warm envelope of the car. I pulled the borrowed coat around me and waited. He opened my door and motioned for me to get out. He'd only said a few words to Tactical Jack back at the gas station, but I had seen both their injured faces and heard their voices at some point. That they hadn't bothered to hide their identities better made me doubt their boss had any intent of letting me leave alive after he'd gotten whatever he wanted. All the more reason to get to George—if she was still alive—and get us out of there as quickly as possible.

The main entrance door opened, and a man dressed in dark trousers and a heavy fisherman-style sweater stepped out to meet us, his face hidden in the shadow of the entryway overhang. Four steps away from the car, the wall of his magical presence hit me. I looked up to see Adrien Travere Junior smiling in satisfaction, not greeting. I'd seen that look before, on Theo's face when he told me he'd gotten me into a group show at the Whitechapel Gallery the night after he'd broken two of my ribs when I'd tried to leave the first time. My knees would have met the driveway if Tactical Jack hadn't decided to look like he was doing his job and manhandled me to the door.

Adrien glanced from Thing 1 to Thing 2 with their now fully

visible shiners and clawed-up faces. "It looks like you gave Joe and Marcus a bit of a fight."

The one I decided was Marcus, the driver, grunted in true henchman fashion, but Joe, previously Tactical Jack, answered. "She came willingly once we got through the wards."

"You two should see to those cuts. I can take her from here."

Joe and Marcus did as they were told and disappeared around the corner of the house. Adrien extended his hand, which I refused.

"I want to see George." Joe had deposited me on the bottom step, and I stayed there, clutching the strap of my messenger bag with both hands. The sourness in my stomach climbed up into the back of my throat. I would have preferred to find George in the hands of an unknown assailant. Instead it was Adrien, billionaire charmer, powerful magician, and—if my trauma-honed senses were correct—malignant narcissist.

"You will." He turned his back to me to walk inside, knowing full well I would follow.

Adrien Senior's fake chateau in Westchester had been permeated with a gentle hum. Walking through Adrien Junior's pad in the Hamptons was like walking through a forest of glass shards. The air was thick with magic and scattered intent, some of it protective, some of it generative, but with an underlying hint of desperation and paranoia. And jealousy, so much jealousy. Adrien Travere Junior had some serious unresolved daddy issues.

Adrien led me to a breakfast room off a sparkling glass and steel kitchen and gestured for me to sit down. "I'm assuming you haven't eaten much."

I looked at him but didn't answer.

"I made breakfast for George earlier, but she wasn't interested." He collected a plate of cold cuts and cheese from the French-doored fridge and added a couple of slices of bread to it from a basket on the counter before placing it on the table in front of me. "Would you like coffee or tea? Juice? There's cranberry and orange."

"I want to see George." A glass of water would have been nice, but I wasn't going to ask his sorry ass for anything.

He returned with two cups of coffee and took the seat next to me at the breakfast table.

I had no interest in the ham and whatever the pink thing was, but the cheese and bread looked good and I hadn't eaten since… hell, I couldn't even remember. No, Matjaž had made dinner. I ate then. Still, fainting from hunger would make me of zero use to George, so I arranged some cheese on a piece of bread. He waited until I had taken a bite to begin his sales pitch.

"I know my father scooped you up after he got the demands. I can easily best whatever he offered you." He leaned in too closely.

"Bold, considering you have no idea what he offered me." I choked down another bite of my open-faced breakfast and considered the coffee before Adrien Junior found a response.

"Well. What did he offer you?"

"I'm sure that's not how negotiations work. What are you offering?" I sat back in my chair to get away from the heaviness of his aura. It clung to him like a fog of cobwebs.

"Besides George?" He smiled that same satisfied smile I'd seen on arrival. The smile of an asshole who could never believe he doesn't have you exactly where he wants you.

"Why did you involve her in this?" I wrapped both my hands around the warmth of the mug I'd been given and slowly let my senses push out to explore the house. It was harder to do with my personal wards all the way up, but still possible. It would have been easier with Hilma to help. Thinking of her led to thinking of Matjaž and the look he'd had on his face when I'd closed the closet door on him. It had taken a lot for him to do as I asked and not try to fight our way out of the cabin.

"Joe and Marcus had a bit of trouble getting through your wards on their own at your house. I moved to Plan B. She means more to you than I do, obviously."

"Obviously." I nodded. "And what do you want me for?" I didn't know what he knew, and I wasn't going to give anything away.

"To repaint the Raphael portrait. I would have thought that was also obvious." He looked at me like he was reassessing my intelligence.

How half of the New York art world had learned of my "gift" was still a mystery to me. Knowing the rumor had spread from the Art Squad in Venice made it more baffling. It was understandable that Adrien Senior believed George had to be the ultimate source, but I knew that was impossible in my bones. She would never betray me like that, not even to save herself.

"And what makes you think I can do that?"

"My father believes you can."

Daddy issues for real.

"And why not let him enjoy his fun and convince me to paint it for him? Why all of the tactical, commando, drag me from a lovely retreat in the Catskills garbage?" A fiery warmth was creeping back into my chest, pushing out the chill that came with the recognition of what Adrien Junior was. Anger would make me careless. I took a deep breath.

"Because he would just sell it or trade it to one of his cronies."

"And isn't that exactly what you're going to do?" It was always about money—money and power—with these assholes.

"Not to some art history fetishist, no. To a museum."

I laughed, which might have been a mistake, given the ugly twist in Adrien's features. "Based on what provenance? No museum with any integrity is going to touch a painting like that with a ten-foot gilded pole."

"That isn't your concern."

"You made it my concern, and I don't understand your motive here. Why start a pissing contest with your own father?" That struck a nerve. Adrien's whole aura shifted from the foggy cobwebs to spikes.

"My father only understands two things: money and power." I'd already figured that out about Adrien Senior for myself.

"Are you just trying to get daddy's attention?" I may have said that a little too sarcastically.

Adrien stood and grabbed me by the arm. "No. I am beating him at his own game." His grip tightened, and he pulled me to standing.

I shrugged my way out of his grasp. Whatever his issues were with Adrien Senior, I was here on a totally different mission. "I want to see George. I'm not coming to any agreement with you about anything until I see her." I looked him straight in the eye. The emptiness there was shocking, only because I had completely missed it that first night in the pub.

"Fine." He strode away toward the central corridor of the house.

I followed, still wrapped in Jonathan's puffer coat with my messenger bag slung across my torso. He led me down a flight of stairs, made of yet more glass and steel, that took us to beach level. Watery daylight gave way to warm electric lighting at the end of the central hallway, where Adrien rapped lightly against a matte gray door before punching in a code hidden from me with his hand.

"There's someone here to see you."

"Go. The fuck. Away."

"George." Her name came out in a croak, my throat having tightened with the relief of hearing her voice. George, with the poshest possible swearing, angry and scared, but alive.

Adrien unlocked the door, and George stood in the gap. Her makeup was a mess, and her eyes were puffy. She'd at least been escorted there in street clothes. Adrien planted his hand in the small of my back and pushed me into the room. Even through the layers of nylon and faux down, his touch was repulsive. The door locked behind me, and the sound of his shoes on the cold tile of the hallway echoed away from the door.

George hugged me until my ribs squeaked before stepping back and placing her hands on both sides of my face, as if she were going to kiss me. "Verity, I am so sorry. I am so so sorry I got you tangled up in this."

My heart sank. Had she told Adrien Junior what I could do? I stared at her, not knowing how I could forgive her if she had.

She let go of my face and turned away. "I don't know how he

found out about what you can do. And I feel like an idiot for falling for his bad boy bullshit. I know better." Turning back to face me, she said, "How could I be so stupid?"

Because as much as she thought she wanted to find me a partner, she wanted someone for herself more, and Adrien played right into that.

"You didn't tell him?"

Her face fell. "No. Oh my god, you can't believe I would do that?"

She sank to the edge of the unmade bed.

The room was far nicer than the average jail cell. Two double beds, one slept in—or at least mussed—and one undisturbed. A plain but expensive-looking dresser and a desk with a pad of paper and those fat pencils children learn to write with arranged like a bouquet in a chrome organizer. The carpet looked like wool, which had to feel nicer on the feet than the large white tiles in what I'd seen of the rest of the house. There wasn't a window, though, and that told me all I needed to know about Adrien Travere Junior.

I sat on the bed opposite her and pulled my messenger bag strap over my head before shimmying out of Jon's coat. It was much warmer in this room than it had been upstairs. "I didn't think that you would, but Adrien's dad asked me if you could and said he'd heard a rumor from someone in the Venice Art Squad."

George's head shot back up from where she'd been staring at the floor. "That doesn't make any sense. You haven't been to Italy in years."

I shrugged. "I don't know. Maybe Theo had some idea, and

that's why he was so keen on keeping me under his thumb."

Theo had been the heartbreaker in the London art scene when we were at Central St. Martin's—a serious painter, pushing the envelope and partying his way through the city like he was hell bent for leather to end up like Basquiat. We met at a gallery opening, and he latched on to me like a lamprey, his infatuation inexplicable to everyone in the crowd we ran with. I didn't have money. I didn't sell a painting for more than street art prices until I came back to New York, and I didn't look like George or any of the other art students who could have stepped out of one of her reputed great-great grandfather's pre-Raphaelite paintings. I'd been as baffled as anyone as to why he'd shone the spotlight of his enormous personality on me. And then I'd been horrified and too embarrassed to admit what was happening as his adoration turned to drunken accusations and fists to the ribs.

"Don't go there. Theo is dead. No one would have taken anything he said about something like that seriously." George knew how easy it was for my thoughts to go trailing down that particular dark corridor.

Theo was dead. It hadn't been a Basquiat-like, 27 Club blazeout, but a train on the Circle Line. Whether he was pushed or jumped was still the gossip of the London art scene, and I was happy to have already put an ocean between us when it happened. Our connection had made it into several tabloid stories at the time of his death, and I still got the occasional fishing call from a journalist or two around the anniversary.

"Maybe not then. But people remember things. The Storm." It hadn't just been the tabloids outing witches and magicians and other oddities after The Storm; The New York Times had run an article on the "Witches of Wall Street." No one had taken up pitchforks and torches, yet, but any magic user with a brain in their head laid as low as possible. Which is probably why Adrien Travere Junior could hide what he was from George, Matjaž, and me. I didn't want to think too long on what he'd had to do to keep up that kind of personal ward. Witchcraft for the most part is a gray area when it comes to all that "are you a good witch or a bad witch?" nonsense, but there are people capable of real evil in every walk of life. Magic users had the added layer of being able to stray all the way over into maleficia if they chose. There was real power there, but it cost more than most people could bear.

"Maybe. I'm sorry. Please know I would never tell anyone about you. Not that stuff." George shook her head and looked back down at the ground. "I would die first."

She meant it and I felt it, in my bones. I reached out and took her hand.

"Why didn't you tell me it was Adrien when you came to the cabin?"

"I didn't know. I was blindfolded and gagged. And too scared to get anything to work until I was left alone, and I went looking for you. Adrien came in then and took off my restraints. At least he doesn't know what I can do." I'd never used or thought much about the word crestfallen, but it captured the look on George's face and the set of her shoulders perfectly. She had really liked him, believed the glamor he hid behind.

"What are we going to do about getting out of here?"

"I've had a look around. This place is a fortress. I could tell you ten ways to break into his flat in the city, but this place? The wards are strong, stronger than anything I've seen." George looked at the wall where Adrien, or his cell decorator, had hung a painting done in the style of The Storm on the Sea of Galilee, Rembrandt's painting that had been stolen from the Gardner Museum in Boston. "I've tried taking that thing down. It's hideous."

"Is it bolted to the wall?" I walked over to it and inspected it more closely. It wasn't just done in the style of Rembrandt's work, it was meant to be a copy but the glazes were all wrong. I'd never seen the work in person, but I'd seen enough Rembrandts up close to know this person had never seen it before it was stolen either.

I ran my fingertips over the prow of the boat, where the central light of the original painting had glowed even in photographs taken before it was stolen. Percy. I drew my hand back but reached out again, tentatively placing the pads of my fingers on the dark lower corner. Unmistakably Percy.

My memory, not the magic, took me to him standing at the door of the studio at the farm when it had been my mother's receiving area for clients. He looked so much like our father, blond and fair. It would have been easier to believe he was George's brother than mine. We'd fought because he said the drawing I made was stupid copying, like a baby. Mother had stepped in, pointing out that I was still learning, that copying was a way to learn. He'd yelled at her about always taking my side and stormed off. It wasn't true, she almost always sided with him—her golden boy, but in that argument she had defended me, and that was the only fight between us my mother remembered. He was gone the next day. And though she'd never said it out loud, I knew she blamed me.

I hadn't sensed George come up behind me and jumped when

she spoke. "It's not actually a Rembrandt, is it?"

"It's Percy." I didn't know how it could be or why, but the thought was enough to smother me.

She peered into the painting, seeing all the flaws I had seen. "I thought you said Percy was good?"

My hackles went all the way up. "I was eleven the last time I saw him."

She apologized and maneuvered me back to sit on the bed.

"When did he paint it? Can you tell where?" George looked down at me, her eyes raccooned with smudged mascara and eyeliner.

Adrien was a shitty host if he wouldn't even give her a washcloth for her face. I wondered if I had any makeup wipes in my bag. I had underwear and a toothbrush, surely I had put something—

"Verity! Look at me."

I did, look at her, but her questions didn't register because I didn't have any answers. All I'd gotten was Percy. All these memories, Percy, Theo, and now trapped in this room with them, with George, and Adrien was upstairs plotting who knew what. Things had truly gone off the rails.

"Why is that here?" I looked up at George again, expecting her to know, to have an answer. She didn't. I didn't. And I didn't want to look at it anymore. "Can you cover it or something?"

George took one of the pillowcases from the bed and tucked it over the top of the frame. The room was less close with it out of sight.

Neither George nor I mentioned that the painting meant

Percy had been alive at some point after he'd disappeared, but it was old. It didn't have that new paint smell that fades from oil paintings with time. Adrien Junior had acquired one of my brother's paintings completed after he'd run away. Someone who had priceless art in his collection bought a horrible, amateurish copy of a well-known missing painting and hung it in their windowless room with a door that only locked from the outside. A room that now held George, and me—one of the few people in the world who would know who painted it. Adrien knew Percy. There was no doubt in my mind, but how?

I looked up at George as she walked back to sit on the bed next to me. "We have got to get out of here."

CHAPTER 10

A polite knock on the door interrupted my next thought.

George's face screwed up in disgust. "I said, go away." She didn't yell, but she put her heart into it.

The lock turned in its mechanical way, and the door opened. Joe stood in the doorway holding a stack of towels and a shopping bag with a boutique logo splashed across the side. His eye was still swollen, but his face was clean and patched up with some butterfly tapes. "Mr. Travere thought you might want to shower and change clothes before you talked again."

Now that I was here, Adrien was being nice. George had been here more than a day and hadn't even been offered a washcloth. He wasn't nice or kind though. This was another way to manipulate.

"Are you going to watch?" George stood up and catwalked toward the door with her sarcastic come-on.

Joe's face reddened, but his expression didn't change. "No, I'm to stand outside. Who . . . who wants to go first?"

"I can wait." I'd at least had a wipe down at the cabin, whenever that was.

Joe handed George a stack of clothing out of the bag then held the bag out toward me. "The rest of this is for you."

I got up and took it from him and peeked inside at what looked to be a completely black outfit with black underwear to match. "Thanks." He tucked the towels under his arm, motioned George outside, and locked the door behind them.

I set the bag on the bed and walked back over to the covered painting. After untucking the pillowcase and looking more closely at the brush strokes and glazing, I ran my fingertips over the prow of the boat, trying to read the ridges and dips in the paint. Turpentine and the nutty, vegetal scent of linseed oil, morning light from an open window, and the sound of traffic outside and below. But that was as far as I could go. I couldn't see the canvas or the brush in my hand, Percy's hand. There was an opaque film between me and the painting's past. Was I too close to him, or had he gone somewhere beyond death? My tiny kingdom for a primer on the mechanics of this gift.

There wasn't much else to do in the room. I sat back on the edge of one of the double beds and stared at the door, waiting for George to return. She didn't seem afraid, only angry and disappointed in herself for not seeing through Adrien's narcissism. On the drive down, I was sure I was putting myself in danger, but I feared for her more and needed to get to her, see her. I hadn't anticipated this being some elaborate plan on Adrien's part. How could I have anticipated that? Narcissists couldn't be trusted not to turn on you for the smallest deviation from their plan or for no reason at all. If Adrien had me—one of the things from his fake ransom wish list—he no longer needed George. Except to motivate me, if he meant what he said earlier.

That tiny voice poked me in the ribs again for leaving Adrien Senior's lair. Maybe I would have been safer. I wouldn't have endangered Matjaž or put him in a position where he had to watch me walk into the custody of criminals. He had every right to be furious with me. If Garvey and Jon had gotten to him, Garvey would be consoling him for being bullied, and Jon would be appalled that he'd just let me go. I doubted either approach would sit well with Matjaž. He would probably go back to Travere Senior, but neither Matjaž nor the elder Travere knew it was the son who had set things in motion. I threw myself back on the bed, my head spinning with all the horrible possibilities my future could hold.

Joe returned with a scrub-faced George in a beltless, white spa robe she held closed with one hand. She laid the clothes she'd been given on the untouched bed. "It was too steamy in there to get dressed."

"Your turn." Joe looked at me warily. The cabin wards had definitely made him afraid of me.

"Adrien is still a complete twat, but that is a great shower." She pulled down the towel she had wrapped around her head and started rubbing chunks of her hair to dry it.

Leaving my own change of clothes, I followed Joe—it was hard not to think of him as Tactical Jack—back down the hall to turn into another short hallway that ended in a wall of glass. The ocean lay beyond, flannel gray and roughed with white wave tops under gunmetal skies. The bathroom shared the same glass wall, but it had been tinted for privacy.

Joe pointed to the remaining towels. "Don't take too long." He shut the door before I could make a snippy remark.

The bathroom was as big as the room George and I were being kept in, but the glass and the view made it seem bigger. I had my choice of a soaking tub or a walk-in shower with a rain head. Since Joe was worried about me dallying, the shower would do. I shucked off my borrowed PJs and tossed them on the marble vanity.

As the water ran over me, I imagined it taking the funk of fear sweat and the acrid paranoia of the house with it down the drain, there was also a flash of Matjaž's hand under the small of my back when he lifted me up to him when he was inside me. I couldn't think about that now. I washed my hair with the over-perfumed shampoo and stood under the water a little longer. My only bargaining chip with Adrien Junior was my ability to paint the Raphael. If I agreed to do it if he let George go, there was no way for me to verify she was safe. Unless she could come back using her bi-location and let me know. Adrien didn't know she could do that, or he would have taken different measures to lock her up or set up wards to prevent her astral body from leaving. He'd underestimated her because he only saw her as a means to an end.

Joe knocked on the door. I turned off the water and toweled off. Some lotion would have been nice for my sandpaper winter skin. Another spa robe hung on a peg next to the shower surround. The tiny voice and I agreed that shitty people had nicer things than they deserved. Dry and swathed in another beltless robe—did Adrien really think George and me capable of subduing Joe with a strip of terrycloth?—I opened the door. Joe took a quick appreciative look then avoided making eye contact. That was a surprise. Joe liked scary women. Another scrap of information to tuck away should I need it.

When I got back to the bedroom, it was empty.

"Where's George?" I wheeled around on Joe, forgetting my robe didn't tie.

He motioned for me to cover back up, pointedly looking away. "Boss said she had done her part and could go. She's upstairs talking to him now."

"She was going to leave, just like that?" I doubted she went quietly, but I hadn't heard a thing from down the hall. I tried to push past Joe to run upstairs.

He stopped me with a sidestep and a hand to the shoulder. "No. She pitched a fit and said she wouldn't leave until she could see you, but Mr. Travere didn't give her a choice." Joe hemmed. "Get dressed if you want to catch her."

"How would George get back to the city?" I grabbed the bag of clothes on the bed and pulled on the underwear with my back to Joe.

"Marcus is going to drive her, why?"

"Is Marcus really going to drive her back to the city?" I hoped I was giving off more anger than fear.

"Yes. Marcus isn't like that." Joe seemed offended that I thought he might be like that. "He wouldn't hurt her. Get dressed, and I'll take you upstairs." He stepped back and closed the door. His empathy was a strange development to juggle, but it could prove to be useful.

Adrien, or Joe, or whoever, had done a decent job of getting the sizes right, though I struggled to get into the slim-fit jeans with damp skin. I quickly finger-combed my hair out of my face and opened the door. Joe turned and started to smile before he caught himself.

"Marcus wouldn't hurt George, even if Adrien told him to?" I put my hand on Joe's forearm.

His face softened the tiniest bit. "No, he wouldn't."

No mixed signals. He believed that of Marcus. I couldn't, and I sure as hell couldn't believe Adrien wouldn't hurt her.

"Thank you. And thank you for telling me about George." I patted his arm and followed him down the hall again.

Upstairs, George and Adrien were at a standoff. George stood face to face with Adrien next to a wide low couch that almost disappeared in the white on white room overlooking the beach. Her hair was still damp, but with her aura having puffed up like a hedgehog, she radiated power. Adrien couldn't be dull enough not to sense it.

"I'm not leaving her here alone with you." George gave me a tiny nod when I walked in. I joined her next to the couch.

Adrien's whole presence was a self-satisfied smirk. "You don't really have a choice, princess."

My guts clenched at "princess." Theo had preferred "your highness" in public—and "cunt" in private.

Adrien glared at Joe but didn't say anything to him for bringing me upstairs.

I ignored him the best I could and focused on George. He'd hurt her if she stayed, but I was more afraid of what he'd do to her if he "let" her leave. She knew way too much about what was going on. Joe might not think Marcus was a murderer, but I had my misgivings.

George stared at me. I would have traded every single supernatural and natural talent I had in that moment to be able to read minds. Maybe she should go and go to Dr. Mar. I no longer trusted our boss wasn't involved in some shady shit, but maybe she was a better option than Travere Senior. I had no clue who to trust aside from George. It had to be better if we stuck together.

I shook my head just enough for George to see my no.

I turned back to face Adrien as Marcus, always the driver, joined our tableau.

"I'll paint your picture, but only if you promise George can stay with me until I'm finished, and you let us both go together. And you tell me about the painting in the room downstairs."

Adrien's mouth was half open before I got my sentence out. He closed it and looked at us both in surprise. "Sure."

I took George's hand. "I'll need supplies."

"Give a list to Joe."

"I can't paint in that hole you put us in."

"I'm aware of that. I've set up a studio."

Cocky shit. It would still be a challenge to paint a Raphael in the encroaching winter light of the Hamptons.

Adrien dismissed us with a wave, and Joe escorted us back downstairs.

"I'll go into the city tomorrow and get what you need." Joe failed to hide his eagerness to either leave the house again or help me in some small way.

"It isn't a grocery list. It may take a some running around."

He suppressed a smile that showed up at the corners of his eyes anyway and nodded before shooing us inside again and locking the door. Maybe I was making too much of his seeming to be on our side. It could all be a ploy designed by Adrien for me, for us, to again let our guard down.

George plopped on the edge of the unmade bed and fanned her skirt out around her.

"I suppose that's his idea of a joke?" I asked. Where Adrien had picked standard artist black for me, he'd dressed George like an extra in *The Sound of Music*.

She rolled her eyes. "I'm tempted to put my stinky dress back on."

I'd left my pajamas in the bathroom, so I didn't even have the option of refusing. "My heart sank when you were gone. There's no way he would really just let you go. Everything unravels as soon as daddy knows the kidnapping was bullshit."

"We may have played right into his hands. I don't think he was really going to let me go. He fancies I will somehow come around to liking him again."

"You can't be serious?" But I knew better. Egos like Adrien's—and Theo's—knew no bounds.

"He definitely isn't going to let you go. He thinks you're his goose that lays golden eggs." George didn't do pity, but her expression veered into that territory. We both knew how things ended for the goose. "You can't paint for him. It won't stop with the Raphael."

"I have to at least agree to do it. Does he have the rest of the list of demands?" I could agree to do it all day, but I wouldn't get anywhere without the study for *Portrait*. As far as I knew, I couldn't randomly offer myself up to dead artists without the gateway of an artwork.

"I don't think so. Joe might tell you." George smirked.

"You caught that too?"

"That boy has it bad for you. What did you do to him?" She sat next to me on the bed.

"I might have neglected to tell him that I didn't set those wards on Jon and Garvey's cabin." We shouldn't have been laughing, given our situation, but it felt good anyway.

"He must like it rough." She picked up my bag. "Do you have a brush in here?" She pulled out the two papers I'd printed off about fugitive pigments and spectrometer tests on paint samples and put them on the bed.

"There should be. I dumped it out at the cabin. There was a bug like you said." I picked up the articles and stared at the title. We needed to bust out of here, but if I was going to have to paint this damn thing without selling out absolutely everything I believed in, I could make sure the painting itself was worthless.

CHAPTER 11

"I'll need a panel—Raphael used poplar—from the 1500s, Italian. Boiled walnut oil, no just get walnut oil. I can boil it myself; modern alkyd oil has additives that would show up." Hell, anything modern would have chemical traces. "No get the boiled walnut oil. It'll save time." This whole endeavor was a farce, but I handed Joe my list. "These pigments. I'd usually order those from Germany, but Blemen's may be able to get most of what I need, except the lead white. You'll need to go here." I pointed at the address at the bottom.

"I'll also need some white glass powder, chalk, and rabbit glue." I handed him another list with my best guesses as to where he could find those things. "Oh, and a heat gun."

He gave me a quizzical look.

"To dry the paint faster."

He nodded and started to head out.

"Wait, does dipshit have brushes and a muller at the studio?"

Joe gave me a half smile before reverting to his stone face. "The studio should have all the equipment you need, if not, I can get it."

"Does he already have the sketch?" Joe might not know about all the things on the ransom list, but I wasn't about to ask Junior.

"He doesn't, but he will tomorrow." He turned and left.

Either that meant Adrien Senior had given in or Adrien

Junior was planning on stealing it, or—more likely—having it stolen.

I knew how to sabotage the painting so no one would ever think, even for a moment, it was the real deal. More importantly, I had to keep George and me safe, which most likely meant catering to Junior's ego enough to keep him mollified. How fast could I paint this thing? Would it even work the way both Adriens thought it would? It was going to obviously be a new painting. Van Meegeren's trick of adding celluloid to the varnish and baking the painting wouldn't get past electron microscopes and mass spectrometers. I could use as close to period ingredients as possible, but I couldn't add in a few centuries of time and grime with the pigments. As far as I knew, material time travel wasn't possible, so there was no taking the painting back to Renaissance Italy and hiding it a cupboard for 500 years.

After Joe's footsteps had stopped echoing in the hallway, I sat on the bed, exhausted. I hadn't had a decent night's sleep since the night we met Adrien and Matjaž at the pub, and I didn't much think I was going to sleep well under Junior's roof. George had been quiet while I was giving Joe his marching orders.

"What now?" She sat next to me and leaned her head on my shoulder. It was a funny reversal of our relationship. She'd always been the ringleader. She'd encouraged me to apply at NAMA even though I already had an offer to stay in London. We shared her apartment. She was the person who scheduled our social lives—I wouldn't have had one at all otherwise. Now it was down to me to make sure Junior didn't crack and take us both out, his plans for lucrative forgeries be damned.

"I'm exhausted." I said it as punctuation to my thoughts, but George took it as a problem she could actually solve and ran with it.

"You should take a nap." She got up and started fluffing pillows and turning off lights.

"This mothering turn of yours is weird."

George started to smile, but her eyes narrowed with concern. "Have you thought about how much energy this is going to take? This is serious magic over the course of days if not weeks. How are you going to sustain that?"

She had a point. I'd never done any kind of magic that took weeks, or at least not weeks of sustained concentration. Magic requires power, something to draw upon. For small things, I tended to draw on my own power, or hit up Minerva or my ancestors. For big things . . . well, I hadn't done big things in a long, long time. And though I'd gotten away from Theo, the runup to leaving had almost killed me, and in the end my magic hadn't worked. I didn't even know how long the connection to Raphael could last. What if I got halfway through, and he decided he'd had enough? Where was Raphael, his mind or soul, even going to be during all of this? Where would I be?

"I don't know. I'm going to have to figure out the equivalent of magical batteries, and fast." I wasn't sure I could call on Minerva to do something as nefarious as out and out forgery. Magic always has a cost. It isn't necessarily a dangerous one—witches make offerings to deity or ancestors or the spirits of the land, the house, whatever. But big magic, the kind that Adrien Junior apparently indulged in, tended to require a sacrifice. Sometimes it was just the energy or the sleep of the magic user. Sometimes it was ritual sacrifice, the blood of the magician, or—somewhere I was never willing to go—the blood of other living things spilled in part or wholly. I had nothing much to offer this magic except myself.

George motioned for me to lay down and scooch over. She laid down next to me and put her head on my shoulder again. From above we probably looked like a beatnik and a lederhosen fetishist having a sleepover.

"We can worry about it later. You need to sleep. And then we'll figure out how to get out of here."

***

I woke up in an unfamiliar dark room with George snoring softly on my shoulder. My thoughts eventually organized themselves enough to reorient me to our situation. Without a window or a clock I couldn't even guess at the time, but I'd slept long enough to be rested and didn't feel the need to go back to sleep. I got up, trying not to wake her, and found my way to the desk to click on the dimmest light in the room, which still blinded me when it came on.

I read through the papers on preserving Rothko's work that I'd shoved into my bag in what felt like a different year and thought about marking the painting I was about to do. I had sensed Raphael's spirit in that drawing at Adrien Senior's, and a small part of me wanted to feel that again. That made ruining his work feel wrong, despite how wrong it was to even be doing this thing. Maybe my brain was just getting all muddled with everything that had happened. I put the paper on the desk and tried not to think of Matjaž and Hilma staring at me out of the closet or the flood of emotion that washed over me when he'd kissed me goodbye.

That little voice chirped up to tell me to focus on the painting.

There was a lot of time between Rothko's use of novel pigments and house emulsion and Raphael's studio with its swirl of apprentices grinding rocks into colors and prepping boards, but some things hadn't changed. Artists, the great ones anyway, did tend to lead interesting, if not tortured, lives. When we were together, Theo liked to say artists were washed up by thirty. Whenever I found myself thinking of him, I wondered if he still felt that way at thirty-five or thirty-six. Was he thinking that at thirty-seven, standing on the platform at Blackfriars station—the same age as Raphael had been when he died, maybe not so mysteriously. After centuries of rumor and speculation that Raphael had died of syphilis from his overly amorous lifestyle, it turned out that he probably died from the prescribed treatment for pneumonia—bloodletting. Maybe leeches killed Theo too. He'd squeezed everything he wanted out of the art world: famous friends, more money than he knew what to do with, his paintings hanging in galleries, museums, and private collections all over the world. The only thing he hadn't gotten was his membership in the 27 Club. He'd had to settle for mysterious death at thirty-seven. Just like Raphael.

The fact that I hoped someone pushed him always makes me feel like a bad person, but part of me still roots for all the others out there he'd hurt and the possibility one of them had their revenge. It's not as satisfying to think gravity was the only one who got a lick in before all those dark paintings shot up in value. I ran into his sister at a holiday party at George's parents' house when I was back in London the year after he died. All that money hadn't erased the haunted look in her eyes, because Theo's death had chained her to him forever as the executor of his estate.

No one wants to be a starving artist, but at some point—in the

1990s, maybe—people stopped talking about the art world and started talking about the art market. The art market was always there, but a sheen of culture and cliquishness kept the baser instincts of capitalism at bay or at least under the expensive Turkish rugs. Now it is just about money, the investment, the peevishness of owning something "priceless" and locking it up in a vault where no one else will ever see it, or worse—using artwork as currency or leverage. Thumb through the catalogue raisonné of any artist that your average person may know the name of and count how many works are in "private collection." Adrien Junior's museum scheme wasn't about the art, however noble it sounded to sell a "restored" painting to a museum. It's still about the money, the power, and probably, for him at least, the giant fuck you to his father.

George rolled over and mumbled. "Where'd you go?" The hamster wheel in my head came to a crashing halt, having rolled far away from my original task of figuring out how to paint a sabotaged painting without burning myself out—and then getting the hell out of here.

"I was going to go for a windy, moonlit walk on the beach to clear my head, but there's this whole being imprisoned against our will thing going on."

She snorted. "What time is it?"

"No clue. I'm hungry, but that could mean dinner, midnight snack, or breakfast."

"Think we can request a clock?"

"Do you think Adrien thinks either of us capable of MacGyvering a bomb out of a tampon and some clock innards?" The thought had occurred to me that nothing in my art education prepared me for escaping evil clutches, and my teacher hadn't included it in my magical training either.

"Shame neither one of us has lock magic." George turned on the light between the beds and stood up to stretch. "Jesus, I need to take a piss."

"I don't have lock magic, but I do have some temperamental telekinesis with some firestarter tendencies." The little voice in my head laughed at my sheepishness for not remembering this sooner. I countered with enumerating the traumas I'd experienced over the last few days.

"Since when?" I could practically hear George's head swivel on her shoulders.

"The Storm."

"Hmm. Well, I neglected to share my new party trick with you, so I guess we're even. Want to try it on that lock on the door?"

"Aside from attempting to blow the doorknob off, I have no clue how to use it to open a digital lock. I kind of need to be able to see the thing in my mind for it to work, and even then it's hit or miss. I set fire to the bushes on the front lawn at Adrien Senior's trying to break a twig to make some noise."

"So about that. I only got whatever Adrien, Junior I guess, felt like monologuing about after I warned you. Which was basically some whiny spiel about his father not appreciating the potential of magic. What's dad like?" George plopped back on the edge of the bed, her full skirt fluttering around her with comic Julie Andrews effect. What would someone do with a problem like George?

I inspected the locking mechanism, or at least what I could see from our side. "Massive woo. More asshole than narcissist. Well-kept, exceedingly wealthy, silver fox territory—like if Gabriel Byrne had Cher's plastic surgeon on speed dial. He doesn't reveal much aside from what he wants or needs from you in the moment. If he were my dad, I would probably have a chip on my shoulder too." I mean, I do have a chip on my shoulder about my dad, but it's different. "And his magic? Serious old woo. Not the kind you get at Stonehenge—more the kind you randomly walk through in cities that makes your bones cold for a moment."

George laughed. "So what you're saying is I should have held out for the original model."

"He is more your type. Did you ever get anything off Dr. Mar?" When I touched the lock mechanism, I got a strong jolt of magic.

George's energy focused. "Dr. Mar. Yes, but I chalked it up to her just being badass. Magic, huh?"

"Definitely, and the old kind like Travere Senior. Nothing so spiky and spiteful as Adrien Junior."

"Do you think Senior knows Junior kidnapped himself?"

Adrien Senior's clipped delivery of the news hadn't revealed much, but it had been easy to tell he knew more than he shared. "He knows something, but I don't know if he figured that part out." The sense of the magic in the lock didn't match Adrien. It was more deliberate and organized, professional. Someone else had warded the lock, which meant Adrien wasn't the only player here.

I looked up at George. "Do you think you could get to Adrien Senior with your new party trick?"

She cocked her head at me. "I don't think so. Like you said about yours, it's new. And I've only ever been able to get to places I've been before."

"What if I went with you? Is that possible?"

Her eyes widened, and she sat back on the bed. "I have no idea."

Astral projection—aside from that one disastrous time I'd tried MDMA at uni—had never been in my bag of tricks, but my mother had always insisted it was something anyone could do if they wanted to. She also on occasion said she was channeling aliens, so take that with a fifty-pound bag of road salt.

"At this point it can't hurt to try, right?" I rummaged around in my bag and then remembered I'd stuck my emergency magic kit in the pocket of Jon's coat. I had one stub of candle, a vial of salt, and two matches left. I'd learned from my teacher how to set myself into a trance watching a candle, and I could protect our space with the salt.

George took the salt when I handed it to her. "What am I supposed to do with this?"

Aside from her innate gifts and the new Storm-enhanced one, George wasn't much interested in ritual magic or witchcraft. Her parents would have been thrilled for her to follow in their version of a Hermetic Order of the Golden Dawn revival. Instead, George embraced a kind of aesthetic chaos—not chaos magic—just chaos where magic was concerned. If it happened, it happened.

"Make a line in front of the door, since it's the only way they can get in, but save a little bit in the vial."

While she warded the door, I set my kit on the table between the beds and lit the candle stub. A couple drops of wax on the lid of the tin was enough to stick the bottom of the candle in to hold it up. George handed me the vial. I wrapped my fingers around it and closed my eyes. Up from the line of salt on the floor I imagined a grid of blue light spreading over the door and how the light would turn red if the door moved, activating the salt on the floor and the salt in the vial to shake or heat up to warn me in time to slam back into my body.

I tucked the vial into the tiny front pocket of my pants. George sat on one of the beds and I on the other, both facing the candle. I watched it dance through half-closed lids, and I remembered walking through the grand foyer of Adrien Senior's house and into that dining room where he'd originally sprung this whole thing about the kidnapping on me. George took my hand, laced her fingers through mine, and I added her to the memory. The two of us walking toward the door, her warm hand in my cold one. Adrien Senior's butler, Fontaine, holding out his arm to let us into the room ahead of him.

The hum of Adrien Senior's house buzzed in my ears as I floated in the doorway, waiting for someone else before I could go in. I looked behind me to see who it might be, but there was only darkness and the thin silvery thread that held me to my body in Adrien Junior's cell room. George squeezed my fingers and reached for the lintel of the door with her free hand.

She ran her fingertips over the wood like I had touched Percy's badly forged painting, then gripped the lintel. "You can go now. I can find my way back. You need to rest." She let go of my hand, and I was alone in the darkness. George and Adrien Senior's house disappeared, if it had ever existed. The space around me expanded out farther than I could imagine. Someone else was out there, untethered in the ethers, looking for me, calling my name so softly. I drifted toward the sense of the sound, focusing every cell in my body to hear them say my name again.

Heat. Like a fire raging up my pant leg. No. I needed to find whoever that was. Hotter now, and sharper—like a brand to the hip. I turned and touched the silvery thread and went flying back toward the other end, toward my physical body. This was not going to be a gentle reentry.

It was like flopping into a cold lake face-first.

I blinked my eyes open, flat on my back on something hard enough to not be the bed. George looked down at me and nudged my shoulder with her bare foot.

"Are you in there?"

I nodded. Which was a mistake. The floor tilted under me, and George's face blurred as my stomach tried to find something to throw up.

"Are they here? Did someone come in the room?" I tried to get up but immediately thought better of it.

"You should stay down there for a minute. I kicked the salt line. You were still gone when I got back." She bent over and put her hand on my forehead like she was checking for a fever. "Where the hell did you go?"

"Nowhere. It was just dark."

"You know that's not good, right?" George offered me her hand to pull me up off the floor. "You can't just go wandering around in the ethers like it's Central Park."

"Thanks for the advice." I didn't have any plans to venture back anytime soon, and I didn't tell her someone had been looking for me. That was probably against the "rules" too. "Were you able to see if anyone was there?"

"That place is like a rabbit warren. I did eventually find

someone, the butler, I think. I startled him when he came around the corner, but he scared me, too, so I lost the connection."

"Then you need to go back." More awake, but that voice calling for me in the darkness… it lingered and made me want to go back too.

"I couldn't get back, I tried. I did have a look around here again. Adrien had a visitor."

My stomach was roiling, and I was doing my best to push down the need to be sick. "I think I'm surprised that he'd be entertaining guests while he's supposed to be kidnapped."

"I'm fairly certain this person is aware of the goings-on. They were looking in a box at what looked like a pewter plate with engravings I couldn't read. The man told Adrien that he had better not be late on his side on the bargain."

"The painting probably."

"My guess as well. The visitor saw me, though, or sensed me. I didn't think that was possible in the astral." George's face darkened. "I left quickly and came back here expecting you to be awake."

I didn't know what it meant that she'd been seen or sensed, but it could only be bad. "Do you want to try to go back to Adrien Senior's?"

"Not now. I don't have anything left in me. That was way more than I usually try in one go." George flopped back on the bed. "I need some food and a piss."

Food would probably be a good idea, except eating didn't sound good. Apparently astral travel messed with my stomach, but putting calories in to keep all the bits working was a necessity. "We definitely need to ask for a clock or something. I don't even know which meal we should be waiting on."

A light knock at the door before it opened revealing Joe—our jailer—with a tray of something that smelled of food.

"I didn't wake you up?" He stepped into the room, leaving the door open behind him. I couldn't tell if the light in the hall was daylight or can light.

"Is that dinner or breakfast?" George got up and walked closer to him.

"Breakfast. It's about eight." He set the tray on the bed closest to the door before George got any closer to him. "Eggs and bacon."

"Did you bring something for Verity too?" George looked up at Joe and smirked.

"Um, there should be enough for both of you."

"Verity is vegetarian. But of course Adrien wouldn't have noticed that—or remembered if he had." George poured coffee from the small carafe for both of us and handed it back to Joe. "Some fruit, toast, or veggie sausages would be nice, and we'll need a lot more coffee than that."

Joe stepped toward her. "Boss told me to give you this and to put it on you."

A gift from Adrien couldn't be anything good.

"What is it?" George held out her hand to take it, but instead of laying the gift on her open palm, Joe clamped it around her wrist. It made a tiny whirl and tap.

George tried to pull it off, but the bracelet wouldn't open or budge down her arm.

"What did you do?" She looked up at Joe, anger and panic

dancing in her eyes.

"Boss said you would know, and I should take you both to the studio by nine." He turned to leave, closing the door behind him.

Before it shut completely, George called out, "Could you at least bring us a fucking clock and maybe another change of clothes?" After the door had closed, "That don't make me look like I'm tanked up for Oktoberfest." She swore again under her breath and dished out some eggs and bacon for herself. "Would you like some eggs? The protein wouldn't hurt."

I nodded. I wasn't averse to eggs in general, but the slight sulfurous smell and pale yellow wobbliness of the scramble weren't helping on the not-hungry front.

The bracelet gave off old-magic vibes, with a menace in the glints of silver chasing.

"What do you think it does?" I had a horrible vision of it bending George's will to whatever Adrien wanted from her.

"I've never seen one, but my father wrote about them in one of his papers. I think it's an astral lock."

"Is that really a thing?"

"Only one way to find out." George sat still on the edge of the bed, her open hands palms up in the folds of the skirt on her lap. Her eyes closed, and her breathing deepened. Then it quickened enough to scare me.

George's eyes flew open. "I can't find the thread."

"What does that mean?"

"When I move into the astral, I can see a silver thread connecting my astral body to the part of my spirit that remains in my body body." So the silver thread I saw in my own experience wasn't just a me thing. "But the thread isn't there. I stepped out of my body, and it wasn't connected. I was dying—or I knew my body would die if I left."

An astral jail wasn't made of bars.

"How do you get it off?"

"With the key." She pointed to an oddly shaped void in the silver next to the latch. "Or magic bigger than anything I've got."

Bigger than anything I had either.

"There are other ways to get out of here. I should eat. You should eat. We won't get far if we are fainting of hunger." George attacked her breakfast again. "I guess his guest really did see me and ratted me out."

"I'm sorry. I'm guessing he's gotten the Raphael study, too, if he wants us in the studio." I scraped up a forkful of egg. They were criminally under-salted.

"So what happens if he does have it?"

"I paint the thing, knowing full well it's a forgery that will look like Raphael painted it himself. Except in the twenty-first century. No one is going to buy this. I don't really understand what either of the Adriens is up to."

"To go through all this trouble? Junior already has a buyer, and they are either too greedy to care, or he's told them exactly what he's doing and they're on board." George put her empty plate back on the tray. "The guy who brought him that artifact said not to be late with his end of the bargain. Maybe it's the painting. He didn't seem like he was fucking around either."

There were so many bad actors in the art market. Forgers were one thing, but organized crime was something else completely.

The possibility of magical organized crime hadn't occurred to me before. I mean, I knew it existed, but that I would ever have a brush with it? This whole thing was exactly why anyone with real magic was smart to lay low and stay off the radar of anyone looking to use magic for nefarious purposes. If Adrien Junior had already begun telling his "clients" what—who—he had at his disposal, I really was the goose that laid golden eggs, and I wouldn't bet on a happy ending to my story.

CHAPTER 12

Adrien's studio had everything an artist could need, except the ability to walk out of it whenever I wanted. The watery, late autumn Hamptons light filtered in through the floor-to-ceiling plate glass window in a pale imitation of the warm Mediterranean light Raphael would have enjoyed in Rome. Joe had set up the easel with a wooden panel that had probably held some unknown sixteenth-century artist's finest work before it was washed away with modern chemicals.

A manila-colored, acid-free portfolio propped up on a smaller easel sat next to the one with the panel. I ran my fingers over the cover, knowing what was inside. It had the power to take me away and let Raphael take my place here, and I could almost hear it whispering.

Joe's voice startled me. "Do you need anything else right now?"

"Is Adrien not going to stand over my shoulder while I work?"

"Mr. Travere has other things to do." And probably other ways to keep an eye on us, but maybe not. "I'll be at the door, though, if you need anything." He didn't need to add "or if you have any ideas about getting out of here."

George asked for more coffee and some water and settled herself onto the hard-looking sofa in the corner. Adrien read, apparently, or he'd had one of his henchmen acquire a stack of books to keep George occupied while I worked. I doubted Adrien's reading extended beyond questionable, tattered grimoires purchased from edge lord-infested, dark web auctions. I snorted to myself and waited for Joe to leave.

Before I opened the portfolio, I wanted to prep the panel and make my paints. There was no point in ripping Raphael out of whatever he was doing to do the work he would have had an apprentice for. Maybe I needed to figure out how to channel an apprentice? Joe had fulfilled my shopping list and gotten some other random things, like a large, pointy palette knife. I laid it on the table and focused on the tasks at hand.

Since only the paint layer and a couple layers of gesso had been wiped from the panel, I didn't need the rabbit glue. I did need to even out the gesso layer, and it would have to dry overnight. I had forgotten to ask for sandpaper, but there was some in the low cabinet next to the easel with a respirator mask and some other supplies. Adrien, or more likely Joe, had done his homework.

"You might want to step out for this." There was only one mask in the drawer. "No telling what's in this old ground. Definitely put our drinks outside too."

"Here we go." I pulled the respirator straps over my head. George gave me a sarcastic thumbs up and went to the door with our drinks. It didn't take long to sand down gesso. I tried to avoid going down to the layer of linen size. I could build the gesso back up, but no modern linen would look like fabric handwoven on a loom. I applied a layer of fresh white mixed with the ground glass and leveled it out as smoothly as possible with my very modern sponge on a stick and hit it with the heat gun. I could get three or four layers on and let it cure overnight. One of my secret weapons in making sure this would never be mistaken by anyone for the real deal needed to be deployed now though. Adrien and Joe being out of the room made it easier, but it would have been hard to pick out white on white at a distance anyway.

I picked through the drawer of pigments and paints Joe had acquired for a tube of Old Holland Cremnitz white, better known as lead white. I can only imagine what it cost. Last time I checked, if you could find it at all, it was pushing $300 a tube. I put on some gloves, as I wasn't about to sacrifice brain cells for Adrien Junior's lark. Real lead white has real lead in it, which is—as I'm sure you know—real bad for you. And that is why it's expensive and generally going the way of dodo. I squirted a small amount of paint onto the corner of a paper palette pad. I chose a fat sable brush and worked the paint into the brush before, very deliberately and with little flourish, painting "fuck you, Adrien Travere XX Verity" in stacked white letters on the white gesso. One simple X-ray and the jig would be up.

I hit the lead white with the heat gun, respirator on again—just in case—and finished the gesso layers for the day. I tidied up my work area and made a hazard pile of anything that had the white lead paint on it, including the solvent-wetted rag I used to clean the brush. I hoped whoever scraped this panel had taken as much care with the lead dust and contaminated solvent that would have been produced. I'd have to be especially careful with my sanding tomorrow to not go down to the leaded layer.

George returned and handed me back my coffee, which had been poured into a travel mug with a lid. I set about mixing pigments into oil mediums to have them ready for tomorrow. The pot of Verona green, or terre verte as Raphael most likely knew it, reminded me of my inpainting misadventure with the de Graaf. Odd now, to think I had been so worried about that. I used the palette knife to tip out a pile of the pale greenish-gray powder onto the sheet of glass. This particular green earth, celadonite or glauconite, had come from England and probably varied from the deposits in Italy and Cyprus, which were more likely to have found their way to Raphael's palette. I dropped in a small amount of walnut oil and started working it in with the knife. It would have been easier to work with a smaller knife, but I had what I had. Once all the pigment had mixed into the oil, I ground it with the muller on the glass to refine it. Then I did the same with the other pigments I would need for the large blocks of underpainting, decanting them into screw-top tins as I went.

With my studio prepped for the next day, I opened the portfolio—careful not to touch the work. I wanted a peek at the sketch, not a peek of the past. Even without touching it, it was hard not to imagine a youthful Raphael putting reed pen to paper while he studied his reflection in a looking glass. What had he seen in his own eyes? What had he believed about the young man staring back at him? I closed the portfolio.

"He didn't think he was a fraud." I said it softly, as much to the imagined Raphael as to myself, but George perked up from her book.

"Are you done? I'm starving." She stretched when she stood and walked to the door to give a couple loud knocks.

Adrien Junior opened the door and strode past her to make a beeline to the easel.

"That's all?" He looked from the white coated panel to me back to the panel.

"Rome wasn't forged in a day."

"How long is this going to take?" He glared at the board and then at me.

George had nailed his character with her pronouncement of twat. I would add peevish.

"Do you know anything about art?" George yawned from the couch.

That landed hard. His face flushed.

"Raphael didn't prepare his own ground or paint. He had apprentices for that. And even if he had prepared his own ground for this piece, it's too much of my energy to get him here to do grunt work. I'll finish the ground and charcoal sketching tomorrow and then summon our painter." I sounded like I knew what I was talking about. It was entirely possible it wouldn't work. Not that I believed it wouldn't, because the study had been practically begging me to touch it all day, but the less Adrien understood about what I was doing, the better.

"You've got two days."

I laughed. "You've got to be kidding."

He didn't say anything else but spun on his fancy leather-soled shoes and strode out. *Must resist calling him a twat out loud.*

Joe came in after Adrien had left and asked if we wanted lunch in the studio.

"It's best not to eat in here. A lot of those pigments are not something you'd want to accidentally ingest." Who knew if I would live long enough for doses of lead or cobalt to have any lasting effect? On the off chance, though, I'd play it safe.

He nodded and herded us back to the kitchen, where Adrien had first tried to ply me with coffee and charcuterie, of all things. A serviceable lunch of cheese sandwiches—because apparently that is all vegetarians eat—then back to our room where at least there was now a clock on the desk and another boutique bag with a change of clothes for George and me. There was also a pair of lightweight coveralls on the bed I'd been sleeping in. Pretty sure that was Joe's doing. Adrien couldn't possibly be that thoughtful.

Our keeper took his leave and left us to stare at the walls until dinner or tomorrow morning, depending on Adrien's whim. A magazine or a television would have been nice. Were we on the news? Surely Adrien Junior's disappearance was notable, if not that of two restorationists from NAMA. Had we been reported as missing? By whom? Dr. Mar or someone at work? By Garvey or Jon—or even Matjaž? Or maybe Adrien Senior could keep everything out of the news with Dr. Mar's help. It would be pretty easy to say George and I were on vacation. But if we were known to be missing, I wondered how my parents were coping. They didn't exactly shower me with their love and affection, but having another child disappear would have to suck.

George poked around in the bag and pulled out another all-black ensemble and a frilly summer dress that looked like something from a 1970s douche commercial. Two guesses who the hippie drag was for.

"Are you kidding me?" She handed me the bag. "There's also pajamas in there."

"Adrien apparently has a thing for costuming you."

"I think 'twat' might be too good for him." She flung the dress over the desk chair and paced back and forth. "How long do you really think it will take you to paint this thing?"

"I mean, I can finish one of my own paintings in a week." Though I usually lingered over them longer than that. "But I'm not painting this one, and I don't even know if it will work to get Raphael to stick around to finish, or even paint Portrait. I mean he could just go off on a tangent." I could too easily imagine Peevish Twat Adrien's reaction if something other than *Portrait* showed up on that canvas. I wanted to be done with this, not just to get it over with but to see if Adrien would keep his word about telling me about the painting in our room.

"George, do you think you could remote view the other side of the door? The ward on the lock didn't stop us, so it's only to prevent us using magic on it. If we knew the code and one of us was outside the room—maybe?" I didn't like the idea of being separated, but it would be one way to try to get out of here.

"If I can't get into the astral, I can't remote view either. Also no bi-location. I need the thread for all of them."

"Do you think he knows you can bi-locate?"

"Doubtful. Like your thing, it's rare. Anyone can learn to astral project with some work." Or enough Ecstasy in their system. "You should take a nap. You need all the rest you can get."

A knock on the door later woke me and announced dinner: a tray for me and an invitation for George to have dinner with Adrien. It was as George suspected, the invitation came with a request to be sure to wear the Prom Queen 1978 dress, which George obliged. A quickly whispered conversation set her off with a plan to turn the small talk around to what would happen after the painting was complete. If we couldn't immediately use magic to get out of here, we'd have to rely on smarts and planning.

Surprising no one, I had a cheese sandwich and an undressed salad for dinner. I chewed my way through it and conked back out. Sleep comes too easily in a windowless room.

In the darkness, a voice was calling my name. Softly at first.

Then a disembodied murmur in my ear. The light thrum of all three syllables was comforting and tantalizing, coaxing me more deeply into the void of unconsciousness.

CHAPTER 13

Matjaž's lips smoldered a path up my neck before gently pulling my earlobe into his mouth. His breath was quick in my ear, and the slow heat building low in my belly radiated out to every nerve ending he brushed with his lips or his hands. We lay facing each other on the bed, my leg thrown over his hip, pinning us together.

He moved his hand down my arm to my elbow then skipped to my waist before pushing up my shirt to get to the clasp of my bra. I pulled my mouth away from his long enough to awkwardly push the shirt over my head.

"I can smell the forest on you. It's in your hair, leaves and damp earth." His voice trailed off before he covered my mouth with his again.

Everything was too slow. I wanted him inside me, over me, below me. And it was too fast. We hadn't talked about anything that had happened. How was he not angry with me for leaving him? Neither of us stopped. My hands pushed his shirt up, and he did the same twisting maneuver to free himself of it. The tattoo in better light was a caduceus, Mercury's with the double snakes and wings. Every place our skin touched warmed as if sitting too close to the fire. His hand in my hair, cupping my breast, tracing the line of my clavicle to the tendon of my neck. Maddening.

"You didn't have to leave me. We could have run together." He cradled the back of my head in his hand and pulled it with a handful of hair pushing my chin up and toward him and left a silent trail of kisses in the hollow under my jaw.

"Verity." Those breathy syllables in the dark. "Do you trust me?" He rolled us over so he was on top of me, pushing his body between my open legs. Every nerve ached for him. I'd never wanted anything more than I wanted him, but something in my brain was pinging with fear.

"Do you trust anybody?"

Why ask me that now? I opened my eyes to look at him but there was only darkness. A lightless room. A small form jumped onto the bed at my shoulder, hissing. Hilma. Her rough tongue licked at my temple, and the weight of Matjaž was gone. The room was cold as well as dark, and my skin was crawling with the sensation of someone else's magic in my head. I wouldn't put it past Adrien to try to keep us unbalanced, but based on what I'd learned about his magic, I didn't think he could pull that off.

***

The studio was bright with early winter light. George curled up on the sofa with a book about Catherine the Great, and I laid down a few more gesso layers to even the ground on the panel. I'd been asleep when she'd come back from her dinner with Adrien, and we had been woken up and ushered into the studio before we had a chance to catch up. George was ace at keeping her emotions under the surface when she wanted to. I'd have to wait until we were locked back up to get anything out of her.

I couldn't see yesterday's message in white lead, but I smiled to myself when I thought of it. It was a shame there was a real possibility I wouldn't live to see Adrien's face when it was

X-rayed. After some light heat gun work and stepping out into the hallway to eat a granola bar and down a cup of coffee, it was time to see if Raphael would trade places with me.

George set her book down when I opened the portfolio. "Do you need me to do anything?"

"Maybe give me a shake if I don't come back this afternoon?"

"How long is a reasonable amount of time to be 'gone'?"

"No clue. I'm guessing if I faint with exhaustion or something, the connection would be broken."

George nodded but didn't return to her book.

I made sure there were charcoals at hand. Deep breath.

The acid-free paper of the portfolio was smooth under my fingertips. The vellum was more textured, calf or goatskin. The irregular edge was the only place I felt comfortable touching it. Even there, where Raphael hadn't made any marks, it was alive. Whispers and scents. Bright morning sunlight and quiet laughter.

Charcoal in hand, I made the first long marks, blocking out the lines of the head and cap, the drape of the clothing. One elbow on the table, the hand loose and open. The other hand close to the heart, holding the edge of a sable thrown over my shoulder. An open window in the wall.

I added finer details from the study I had done observing my own face in a glass. The soft lines of nose and mouth and the eyes looking back at me brought the figure to life. It is me and not. A me from days ago captured on vellum as Margherita teased, but now I am alone, or as alone as one can be in the city, especially this workshop.

Pietro joined me briefly to observe. I asked him to bring me my palette and brushes. He had already prepared the terre verte, lead white, and yellow for underpainting the skin tones and the wall.

For most works, I would have Pietro do these first layers, but Margherita was out for the day to see a friend with a new child. If she returns early, I will leave this board to him and pursue other pleasures. With the underpainting for the wall and table completed, I focused on the green earth for the skin tones of the face and hands. These painted features would be paler than my skin. The warm sun of Rome had bronzed my face and hands on many walks through the quarter. Margherita had commented about the strong line on my chest where my shirt covered the skin. She was more careful to stay in the shade, but even so, her skin was a variety of tones and mixtures of white, yellow, and the palest vermilion.

Pietro came for my brushes to clean them when I had finished. I tucked the study behind the panel so it would not be caught in a breeze and went back to my rooms in search of food. I also hoped Margherita had returned. Thinking of all the colors of her flesh had made me hungry for more than bread. I was not disappointed.

Margherita's scent—a floral water she made herself mixed with her own musk—greeted me at the door. I called to her, but she did not reply. It didn't take me long to find her in the bed chamber, clad in the thinnest of shifts and reclining against the many pillows and bolsters. She, too, was interested in sustenance other than bread. The corner of her pale red mouth turned up, adding to the mischievous cast in her dark eyes.

"I heard you coming up the via, chatting to the neighbor." She tilted her head, indicating I should join her on the bed.

I stripped down to my shirt and crawled to her from the foot of the mattress, locking my eyes on her like a great hunting animal.

Her face and chest flushed the most delicate crimson, not of shame—we were long past the first awkwardness of new lovers—but in anticipation. When I was even with her, eye to eye, ready to cover her inviting mouth with mine, her expression changed.

"Your eyes. They are different." The blush lingered, but the lilt of flirtation left her voice.

I narrowed my gaze at her. "I am not Raffaello, but a beast come to devour you." I growled low and made to pounce on her, but she yelped and moved away.

"You mean it." I sat back on my haunches, keenly aware of my cock standing at attention.

She tucked her legs underneath her to kneel and looked me in the eyes, her soft hand cupping my face. "You are different."

"I am not, but I have been staring at my own eyes all day. Perhaps they have turned inward."

That sufficed, and the flush and flirtation returned with a warm kiss as her hand moved lower. How she made me ache for her.

"Verity!"

I slammed backwards, landing on a floor, hard and cold under my head. A white ceiling in a room lit by bright electric lights was the only thing in my field of vision until George bent over me, her hair hanging in two golden braids.

"You okay down there?" I couldn't see her expression. A can light above her head cast her features in darkness with a coronal halo like an angel in a medieval painting.

I pushed myself up to a sitting position and nodded my head. I was fine, if you ignored the fact that I was aroused to the point of distraction. For Raphael's hot mistress. Who'd probably been dead for a solid 500 years. I looked up at the panel on the easel. All the blocking and underpainting had been completed. That was good. I remembered doing that but in Raphael's studio.

"You scared the piss out of me." George offered a hand to help me up.

"What time is it?" It was fully dark outside the window, turning it into a giant black mirror where our interaction played out in reflection.

"About six."

I'd been gone for almost eight hours.

"What happened while I was there?" I touched the edge of the panel but didn't feel anything besides the edge of the board.

"You painted and occasionally mumbled to yourself in what sounded like Italian. Then you just stopped and stood there. I didn't want to do anything at first because I wasn't sure what was going on, but after about half an hour, I got freaked out and yelled at you."

"And I fell over?" I rubbed the back of my head, expecting it to be tender or for there to be a bump. Nothing.

"No. I mean yes. But, like, in slow motion?" Describing it seemed to bother her all over again.

I nodded. I didn't really remember leaving, and I definitely didn't remember coming back.

"Don't do that again, okay?"

"I can't promise you that." Thankfully things in the general crotch and nipple areas had calmed down despite reminding me of the dream I'd had about Matjaž and how unsettling it had been. Him but not him, me but not me. Magic as interference and amplifier. The ebb of sexy time endorphins came with a massive crash. I would have sat down hard again on the tile if George hadn't caught me.

"Couch." She walked me to the low sofa where she'd taken up residency for the day. "I'll get Joe to take us to the kitchen."

Three taps and Joe's face appeared in the open door.

"We're . . . she's done for the day. Can we get her some food?"

Adrien followed Joe into the room and went immediately to the easel. Joe took one look at me and decided I needed food, and some tea. Joe as the clucking type was unexpected. Adrien stopped us before we made it to the door.

"That's all you got done today?" If yesterday had been Adrien pouting, today was Adrien pissed.

I started to defend myself, but George stepped in. "She worked for a solid eight hours on that. If you think you can do a better job, then we'll happily be on our way."

Adrien's expression changed mechanically, like a puppet's when the strings are pulled. "Yes. I'm sure the layers need to dry." He stayed behind to stare at the canvas.

I happily followed Joe down the hallway to the kitchen. He put down two plates on the counter and started pulling things out of the fridge before putting on a kettle and playing sandwich artist.

Joe had just put two remarkably good-looking baked tofu sandwiches down in front of George and me when Adrien joined us in the kitchen. "George will be having dinner with me. Put Verity's dinner on a tray and take her downstairs."

George stiffened and looked at me pointedly. Scared. Angry. Resigned. There was so much in that one hard glance, but I was still a little too scrambled between today and five hundred years ago to see it all. Adrien Junior's "charm" offense with her worried me though. Eventually "no" isn't flirtation to someone like him, like Theo, and the monster shows his face.

Joe busied himself putting the sandwiches, the tea, and some cookies he'd pulled from the cabinet onto a tray before motioning to me to head downstairs. I looked back at George, who imperceptibly nodded. I headed back to our room with Joe and my dinner behind me.

Neither of us spoke until he'd set the tray on the desk.

I touched his wrist. "Is George okay alone with him?"

Joe was surprised I'd asked him, or surprised I'd touched him again.

"Honestly, I don't know. I don't think he would . . . you know, force himself on her." His face reddened with an emotion I expected wasn't embarrassment. "But he's been more unpredictable lately."

No lies there. Or at least he didn't think he was lying. It didn't make me feel any better.

"You gonna be okay?" He moved away from me, back toward the door.

"I think I'll feel better after I eat." I sat in the desk chair and picked up half of a sandwich.

"Maybe you shouldn't do that thing for so long." His concern felt genuine, even without touching him, but the source of it stumped me. He could simply be less of an asshole than his boss.

"I don't think that's an option. He wants this painting yesterday." I took a bite of the sandwich and gestured toward him with it. "This is good. Thanks."

He did come closer to blushing. "It won't be the last one."

I looked up from my mug of tea. "Last sandwich?"

"No. It isn't just this one painting he wants from you."

That wasn't news. George and I had already discussed the goose with the shiny eggs problem.

I nodded. "Well, he'll have to get more source material." Maybe that would slow him down enough for us to figure out how to get out of here.

Joe looked like he had more to say but thought better of it. "Enjoy the sandwich. I found some vegetarian recipes online. I figured you couldn't just eat cheese all the time."

"Thanks."

He left, locking the keypad behind him. I listened to its beeps and whirs, as if that would tell me anything about how it functioned or how its magic worked.

I polished off the sandwiches and the tea and cookies, but I was still hungry and restless, despite the exhaustion. I didn't want to conk out again before George came back. I needed to know what was going on. What if Adrien was trying to assault her or, I don't know, hypnotize her like some Rasputin? I really should have asked for the whole pot of tea. I tried reading through the papers on pigments and spectrometers again. They hadn't been riveting the first time, and I kept nodding off and nap jerking myself into a headache that started at the base of my skull.

Walking around the room kept the blood flowing better, but I was a dog in a run. I didn't even own a TV but would have been happy to have something to distract my brain now. Humans are terrible at estimating the passage of time under the best conditions. I was especially bad at it, more so in a windowless room. It could have been two hours or four before the lock sang its song of beeps and whirs again.

George slid through the barely opened door with her back to me. She pushed it closed and put her head against the door frame.

You okay?"

She jumped and spun around. "I thought you'd be asleep."

"Your face." Her cheek was red, and her lower eyelid was swollen with a thin purpling line curving from the tear duct to her cheek bone. "What the hell?"

"I told him no." She was angry. Not cowed. "I also called him an idiot. Apparently that's his trigger word? Slapped the shit out of me." She prodded at the puffiness with her fingertips.

Theo had rarely hit me in the face. The first time he'd let go, he'd managed to black both my eyes and had been so drunk that he didn't remember anything had happened until the next morning—when I'd looked up at him from where I was cleaning up the vase of flowers he'd shattered, spraying wet glass under every surface in the kitchen. I lost track of the number of times he apologized that day. We were supposed to go to an opening together that night, but I'd called George and told her I had the flu. No amount of makeup would have softened the coloring, and even then, we all knew what it meant when girlfriends showed up with sunglasses on at night indoors.

"I hit him back."

"What?" I stared at her, convinced the bruise had spread in the moment we'd been standing there.

"I hit him back. I think I may have broken his nose. Bloodied it at least." George laughed. "Enough that he couldn't stop it."

"He's going to kill us both." I laughed, too, but mostly out of fear.

"Not if I kill him first."

CHAPTER 14

George and I followed Joe to the studio the next morning. He kept glancing at George's face, seemingly as upset by the state of it as I was, but he didn't say anything to either of us about it. I didn't want to leave George alone, and going back to sixteenth-century Rome felt like doing exactly that. I'd slept fitfully. Between dreams about Theo coming at me in the house we'd shared and dreams of Adrien doing worse to George, it was surprising I'd slept at all. I certainly wasn't rested enough for eight hours of magic.

George curled up on the couch again, book in hand, waiting while I prepped my palette and calculated how much we could get done today. How quickly had Raphael painted? What if he'd had one of his assistants take on part of it—would I be able to complete those portions? Had he worked on the background of the painting before working on the portrait itself? I'd know more tonight, if I managed to make this work again. I wanted it to work again, not for Adrien, but for me. As much as I didn't want to be there, I wanted to go back to renaissance Italy. Raphael himself called to me, as did his vixen of a lover.

I opened the portfolio with the study, and I was standing in the studio, morning light beaming through the windows and highlighting dust motes in the air. Pietro had set up my palette and brushes and a glass for me should I need to peer at my face in more detail. I worked quickly and silently, filling in the large areas of color and the beginnings of shadow and light, larger details. Pietro brought me a plate for lunch, but I left the fruit and cheese to slump in the afternoon warmth of the studio.

Margherita's absence was keen. My thoughts kept straying from the forms appearing under my brush strokes to her form. An idea for another portrait of her had been taking shape in my thoughts. She paid no mind to the perceived impropriety of posing nude for me, as I had seen and touched every measure of her soft flesh. Capturing her intelligence and spirit would be the challenge. The nakedness of her gaze would be far more scandalous than an exposed breast—that was neither here nor there. The self-portrait would need to be completed first, and then there were many commissions requiring my attention.

The sun sank lower and darkened the studio beyond working light. I could have called for candles, but this piece required daylight. Pietro instead came to collect my palette and brushes.

"You have made much progress today. Will you complete it before the sabbath?" Pietro was ever the planner, keeping me on task.

"Perhaps. There is another painting I would like to begin—"

"There is always another painting." He smiled and left with my brushes.

I picked up a piece of browned fruit from the plate he had brought earlier and evaluated the day's work as I chewed. Something of this work felt so familiar, as if I had already painted this same portrait in a dream, a dream of a younger me painting my future face. The thought put a shuddering chill down my spine. Perhaps we were never far from the spirit realm, but I preferred not to consider such things. I placed my smock on the low bench behind the easel and bid good evening to Pietro and the dust boy sweeping the studio. Margherita's embrace awaited.

It was fully dark by the time I reached my rooms. Candles had been lit, and the table had been laid for supper. Margherita sat in her usual place, the cook at her elbow waiting for word to serve. A deep line had etched itself between the older woman's brows, no doubt evidence of her consternation of preparing meals for me at unknown hours. Margherita nodded, and the cook disappeared through the serving door.

"You are later tonight." Her tone was cool but not unwelcoming.

"I made progress on the portrait and discussed commissions and such with Pietro." I moved my plate from opposite her to the seat beside.

"Cook will be more cross with you." Margherita tempered her scold with a smile.

"We follow so few rules and mores in this house, running my hand up your well-turned leg during supper would hardly be the worst of infractions she has witnessed."

Her chest and neck flushed, heating my own blood in turn.

"You are a monster." She laughed and placed my hand on her thigh. "I adore it."

"And I you." I turned to cover her mouth with mine, but she pulled away.

"Your eyes. I wish you would finish this cursed portrait. You are changed." She smoothed her skirts under the table, brushing my hand away again.

"Nonsense." The thought I'd had earlier, though, of having painted this version of my face before pricked at me. Could there be some folly or some danger in studying my own features for so long?

Cook arrived with a cold soup—one that was to be served as such—and crusty rolls still warm from where she kept them close to the fire.

"A light supper, I asked." The devilish glint in Margherita's eye, and the cup of her rosy lip promised the sweet course would be far more filling.

I brought the first spoon to my mouth and paused as a wave of nausea overtook me. The candlelight flared to brightness hotter than day and faded back. I dropped the spoon into the bowl, splashing the pale green liquid onto the table. Margherita startled.

"What, Raffaello?" Concern in her eyes, the same as all the times she prodded rest when I had worked too much.

"I don't know." The smell of walnut oil and the strong resinous odor of trementina, as strong as the vapors of the studio, watered my eyes. The light flared again, and a woman—an Amazon, an angel with darkly ringed eyes—peered at me through the brightness, her hand reaching out to touch me.

"Fuck!"

I blinked into the brightness and tried to focus on George's face, but Margherita's terrified expression still floated in my vision until the two were superimposed in their disbelief and concern.

"Let her go!"

My face stung with a slap from a soft hand. The Amazon. I could see her and a bright white ceiling with halos dotted along it.

She sat back on her heels and pulled my head and shoulders onto her thighs. She looked down into my face, her visage disorientingly upside down.

"You have to stop this. Fuck Adrien. You have to stop."

Adrien. The painting. George.

I scrambled to sit up and face her. "What just happened?"

"That's what I'd like to know."

"I was sitting at a table, eating dinner with Margherita and—"

"Who the fuck is Margherita?"

"My lover, Raphael's lover. We were eating soup, and I saw the studio and the dining room at the same time, your face and hers. Both places both times at the same time. Did you slap me?" My face still stung.

"No." George looked incredulous.

Margherita must have slapped me. Slapped Raphael.

Pain pierced my temples. "I need to lie down. Not on the floor."

George stood and pulled me up with her, steadying me as I wobbled. "This has to stop. It's going to break you." She walked me to the door and opened it without knocking. "Some help please."

I started to slide out of the vertical again. Everything would be easier if I was flat.

"Whoa."

Strong hands caught me and scooped me up like a child.

***

I woke up or came to, or whatever you call it when someone who has fainted opens their eyes, surprised to find myself in a new location. The bed was not the one in our basement cell. There were windows, black planes in the darkness. George, Joe, and Adrien stood at the foot of the bed, arguing.

"She will finish it."

"Look at her. It's killing her." George pointed at me but didn't look. "Do you want her dead?"

Adrien's silence said a lot there.

"Give her a day to rest." Joe had taken George's side. Adrien probably loved that.

"One day. Let her get some air and a walk or something. Do you want your fucking painting or not?" George didn't call him a fuckwit, but I'm sure she thought it.

"Fine. One day. Then she is back at it." If you had asked me to prove it, I wouldn't have been able to, but there was sheen of desperation in his voice. Maybe he was worried Adrien Senior would figure out what was going on. I didn't know how many days had passed since he and George had "gone missing."

I closed my eyes again. The thought of the elder Adrien Travere connected by dream logic to Matjaž and Hilma crammed into a closet full of winter coats and snowshoes, both sets of eyes pupils wide with fear. Fear for me. And a disappointment that hollowed out my chest.

I followed a silver thread back to the cabin, but it was empty of Matjaž, Hilma, and the few possessions we had brought. I stood in the kitchen where Matjaž had made that lovely meal of what he'd found in Jon and Garvey's cabinets, clad in my Adrien-acquired artist black, barefoot. Something of Matjaž lingered. His scent or his thoughts. I ached at the spot where the silver thread pierced my sternum. I touched it, and it pulled me through an indigo-dark sea of bone-white stars and snowflakes to the foot of the stairs at Adrien Senior's faux chateau. The house was dark and quiet except for the sounds houses make in the winter, rapping pipes and shrinking joints. Outside, snow was falling, but the flakes looked like they were illuminated from within like stars.

I walked up the stairs, trailing my hand on the banister, confused as to why I had pushed Matjaž away when he had come to me in the darkness. After a turn or two, I found myself at the door of the bedroom Fontaine had led me to, where I had only stayed long enough to nap. A week ago? How long had it been since Matjaž and I had run into the night?

The door didn't open, but I was inside. Matjaž slept in a T-shirt with the neck stretched out, the duvet pushed down to his waist. One hand was on his flat belly, and the other arm flung toward me, reaching out across the empty half of the bed. I was lying next to him, head on his chest, body curled to him before the thought to move fully formed in my mind. The arm underneath me pulled me into him as he turned to face me and whispered my own name into my hair.

"Verity." I slammed into open eyes and Joe's concerned face entirely too close to mine. "You okay? You were breathing funny."

I nodded and rolled over, unable to even think about going back to sleep. Though I was pretty sure that wasn't a dream. It had been the real Matjaž in that bed, not the fevered one that had come to me on a wave of malicious magic. Joe settled back into the chair next to the bed. Enough moonlight filtered in for me to see I was still in the bedroom they'd brought me to earlier. It must not have a lock on it, since Joe was here to keep me in my place.

Matjaž was safe, or at least as safe as he could be with Adrien Senior. He'd felt my presence. Would he remember or think anything much of it if he did? The little voice in my head, who'd been rather quiet these past few days, chided me to go back and wake him, that I wanted him to remember I'd been there. Tell him where we were. Great idea, except I don't know how I got there exactly. And even if I could go back, an astral body wasn't much use—not like George when she could bi-locate. Maybe Matjaž would remember. If that had been real, if he really had gone back to Travere Senior, he and Dr. Mar would be looking for us.

Joe's breathing deepened into sleep. I rolled over to stare at the ceiling. Escape would have been an option if I had any idea where my shoes were or if it hadn't been so cold so early in winter this year. And I couldn't leave without George, who was most likely locked up downstairs. At least I hoped that's where she was. And Raphael. Margherita. I couldn't leave without them, without the study, without the painting. It was mine now.

CHAPTER 15

Joe woke me gently with an honest to the gods breakfast tray.

"It's veggie sausage, though it looks pretty real." He waited for me to position myself before setting the tray down. "Eat. George thinks you need some air, so I thought we could go walk on the beach."

I laughed at the thought of Joe's online dating profile saying something like "makes a killer breakfast and likes long walks on the beach with captive artists." None of this was what I imagined kidnapping to be, but my ideas about kidnapping came from British mysteries and never involved people who had magic at their beck and call.

"What's so funny?"

"Nothing. My thoughts banging into each other before I've had any coffee." I shrugged.

"There's more coffee if you want."

I nodded my thanks and tucked in—or tried to. Everything smelled and tasted great, but all I wanted to do was go back to the studio, to Raphael. To Margherita. The need to be with the painting, and with her, was stronger than hunger. My thoughts were ripped into two streams—here and getting to safety, and there and finishing the painting, proving to Margherita I wasn't possessed by demons.

Adrien opened the door and came in, pulling George behind him. "See." He flung his hand at me and continued with a nasty bite of sarcasm in his tone. "Breakfast in bed. She's fine."

George's face looked worse than yesterday now that the bruises had fully developed. Adrien had a bandage across his nose, so George had clearly gotten hers in good. She crossed the room to sit on the bed next to me. Poking at the sausages and looking up at Joe still standing sentinel on the other side of the bed, "Those are vegetarian?"

I got dressed, and Joe brought up my coat and boots from our cell downstairs to head out to the beach. The sun was out, but there was a stiff enough breeze coming off the water that I didn't want to be out long. He walked behind us, and George and I chatted low, letting the wind take our words with it. She reached inside her coat and pulled out the pointed palette knife Joe had purchased with the supplies for the painting.

"Can you pretend to trip or something and get him close to us and distracted?" George looked out over the water and not directly at me.

"I guess. But what are you going to do? He's not going to let us run off."

"No but he might take us to a vehicle if there's a pointy bit at his neck." She slid the knife up her coat sleeve, and I took the next grouping of rocks as a good excuse to go down, in an awkward controlled manner.

Joe ran up to us as George bent over to check on me. When Joe's head was even with hers, she stood catching his arm, pulling it behind him, and put the pointy but not sharpened tip of the palette knife under his chin. There was no way I could have pulled that move off. She was a tall as Joe, but I was sure he had her on weight and strength.

He laughed. "What do you think is going to happen here?"

George motioned for me to get up with her chin. I stood up shakily, and I did my best to get control of Joe's other arm.

"You're going to take us to one of the cars so we can leave."

He sighed and wrested his hand free from me and had George in the same position she'd been holding him with almost no effort and without the palette knife at her throat. It clattered harmlessly onto the rocky beach.

"Look. If it was up to me, I'd set you both free of this crazy bastard, but that's not going to happen. Marcus and I are both as good as dead if you two escape." He let go of George and pushed her away enough to pick up the palette knife. "I can't promise you I can intervene if he gets more violent, but I'll try."

"Why do you care what happens to us?" In the brief time I'd held his arm, I hadn't gotten fear off him—of us or of anything—but his aura hummed with it now.

Joe looked up to the house and the large panes of glass that reflected the pale blue sky and the gray expanse of the Atlantic. "Because he's spiraling. He's made promises to people he should have known better than to get involved with. You aren't part of that." He shook his head and looked like he might say more but didn't. The little voice in my head chimed in about Joe's loyalties lying elsewhere, but it didn't make sense. They clearly didn't lie with whoever Adrien Junior was tangled up with.

"These other people he's made promises to, do they have magic?" It might explain the magic on the door lock and the artifacts Adrien had.

Joe hemmed. "Yes. But not like him. He's powerful but erratic. They, well, they're different. Professional." He wouldn't say more.

He walked behind us back to the house. We'd tried at least.

George and I returned to our cell for the remainder of the day. We were gifted a small television that struggled to pick up the local stations on the digital antenna attached. The midday news said nothing about a missing billionaire son or two unknown art and object conservators. Disappointing but not surprising. We were still well within the long windows of time that I went without speaking to my parents. They wouldn't suspect anything unless there had been a news item or someone had reported us as missing. Matjaž or Garvey and Jon might have called the police, but that would depend on what happened to get Matjaž back to Travere Senior's place. I doubted Travere Senior wanted the media and police crawling all over his business, and including George and me in the kidnapping would just bring more questions about his shady art dealings with the Restorationists. Travere had the money and influence to keep things quiet.

I napped most of the day, and George and I watched the late news after she got back from dinner with Adrien. There were no new bruises on her face, but he was getting pushier about her reciprocating his interest—at least physically. I shuddered at the thought of that man touching George's body at all, let alone in a sexual way. I had found him charming that first night on our double date, despite the sheen of his wealth, but his objective hotness had been forever obliterated by his personality. All I could see when I looked at him now was the lifelessness behind his eyes.

George still blamed herself for getting us into this mess.

"It's really the other way around. Though I think Adrien thinks he's got it bad for you now, he started this, approached you, to get to me." I didn't want George to feel used, either, but she definitely didn't need to feel guilty.

"I just feel stupid. I believed those first few days that things were like a fairy tale—I definitely know better than that. He love-bombed me, but he was charming and seemed surprisingly down to earth. I should have known it was too good to be true." She took my hand and apologized for the thirtieth time. "I also wish I could help you finish this painting. I mean if it's done, he'd have to leave to go deal with it, right? A window of escape opens wider, maybe."

George was great at her job of gluing fragments of ancient vases together or cleaning tapestries, but easel paintings weren't her area of expertise, and her traveling abilities were clipped.

"Please don't. No more apologies. We need to focus on surviving this—especially him trying his charm offensive that is mostly just offensive." It hurt me to look at her face—for her, and for the times I'd looked in the mirror at my own face and Theo's handiwork.

The perky blond woman on the eleven o'clock news segued from an upbeat story about New York City schools into the mysterious disappearance of art collector Adrien Travere Junior over clips of Adrien Junior ducking into black SUVs or holding up his hand to block the cameras in his face. There were no images of Adrien Senior when the newsreader mentioned he could not be reached for comment. George and I weren't even alluded to. At least my parents wouldn't be worried. I didn't think George's would be much bothered, either, as she tended to speak with her family even less than I did with mine.

The morning couldn't come soon enough. Partly because I believed George was right about finishing the painting giving us a better chance at escape. But I also wanted back to the studio, back to Raphael and Margherita.

***

I prepped my palette and brushes and stepped into the hall with Joe to down a glass of water and a protein bar. He was watching me as worriedly as George.

"Sure you're up to this?"

"Do I really have a choice?"

Raphael was whispering as soon as I approached the portfolio with the study. I opened the manila folder and brushed my fingers down the rough edge of the lambskin.

Pietro coughed softly and approached with a beaker of weak tisane. "Margherita said you were unwell yesterday. I thought this might help."

The liquid inside was the color of straw, or urine, and smelled of bitter herbs. He wouldn't be put off—I'd tried, to no avail, in the past. It was best to take the medicine so I could get to work in peace. He faded into the background, and there was only the painting and my face in the glass. Watching. The texture of the wall came to life with ochres, followed by the shadows and drape of the shirt with umber. I was avoiding the face but did fill in the skin tones and small shadows before I was taken away in a daydream of a room filled with such different light and moving paintings of the sea behind enormous pieces of glass. The Amazon angel I had seen in the dream at dinner sat reading quietly on a low bed of sorts and peered up infrequently from her book with a look of concern. Her strange clothes accentuated her pleasing curves, but her face was masked with lurid reds and purples I didn't realize were bruises until she looked up the second time and I stepped closer.

She didn't hear me when I called to her. The strange logic of dreams separated us that way. I continued to paint until the light had gone and approached her again. She looked up startled and spoke in strange Latin, asking for truth. The dream dissolved back to the studio and the canvas and the day turning to evening. A worried Pietro stood to the side of the easel.

"I'm fine." My head swirled, and my body felt as if I was moving through water, but I wouldn't worry Pietro more. "I think I will head home soon. You can go. I'll clean my own brushes today. It will clear my head."

The line of concern between his brows deepened, but he nodded and turned to leave. When he had gone, it was only the dust boy with me in the studio. I looked into the glass.

"Boy, bring some candles."

He hurried to do as asked and set up a large candelabrum on a small worktable he dragged to my side. "More. Whatever we have." Enough light to drive away devils. I nodded my approval when the studio was lit like day with every candlestick he could find, and I dismissed him.

My eyes had changed in the candlelight reflected in the glass, and another face seemed to flicker into focus with the dancing flames. I couldn't look too closely or it disappeared. Its lines were softer, more feminine—the eyes larger and darker, the lips fuller. I looked away, intent on working until the candles burned to the sockets.

Ignoring hunger and thirst, I worked feverishly with the urgent sense that I needed to exorcise this demon that had attached itself to me, tempting me with lusty specters, pushing me. I would not cause Margherita more fear. I would finish this before I returned to her.

The nose, the eyes and lashes, the light that played on the skin of the face and the hands. Quickly. The face was mine but still softer, that succubus in the mirror. The blond goddess resting on her couch approached, more demons to be pushed away. The candles burnt lower, and I worked on into the night.

The blond woman called to me once again, but I pushed her away. I would not be tempted.

***

I woke up on the hard sofa in the studio, squinting against the late morning light. No George. And no painting. The study was gone as well. My muscles ached and my head swam when I stood, but I made it to the door. Unlocked. And no Joe standing guard.

The little voice in my head suggested I was dreaming, but I don't remember ever having felt that shitty in a dream. I caught a glimpse of myself in a mirror hung near the end of the hall. If I had been a person unfamiliar with mirrors, I would have screamed at the "vision." My hair was a nest of tangles, coiled together and stabbed through with paintbrushes encrusted with what looked like a mix of umber and lapis. My coveralls were smeared with those same pigments and more. My eyes were sunken in a face the color of an old gym shirt. My eyes, and not.

I followed the sound of voices to the white on white living room where I'd agreed to paint this damned portrait. The image of Raphael's face in the glass reflected back at me with my eyes.

Focus. Where's George?

She was sitting on the white couch. The neckline of her *Sound of Music* costume was torn, and a bruise on her shoulder was doing its best to out-technicolor the fading bruises around her eyes. I caught her gaze before Adrien heard or saw me. She shook her head at the question that had to be naked on my face. He hadn't forced himself on her. But it looked like she'd paid a price anyway. The *Portrait of the Artist as a Young Man* by Raphael by Verity Green was propped against the wall. The face glowed in the sunlight. Pride swelled in me, but it wasn't mine. Relief did, too, and that was mine. It was done.

Adrien finally saw me. He crossed the space between us with two strides and grabbed my wrist, pushing the bones together painfully. He flung me on the couch next to George, who immediately put her arm around me and pulled me into her. She smelled like the overly perfumed shampoo from downstairs and roses. A different voice in my head wanted to touch her face, run my fingertips over the golden curves of her braids to see if this angel was real. I pushed it down and looked up at Adrien.

He was angry. He had his painting. What did he possibly have to be angry about? I mean, other than the fact that George clearly was not going to fuck him. Not even as a grudge.

Joe walked in and glanced at George and me before addressing Adrien.

"The car's ready."

Adrien nodded. "Figure out how to transport that without damaging it."

Joe picked up the canvas by the edges and walked out, holding it in front of him like it was haunted. Was he repulsed by the fakery? Or by what had happened to bring it into existence?

"Are we going somewhere?" Maybe he would leave us here and we could try to run. I didn't remember anything from my self-defense classes about a third location, but I doubted anything good could come of it.

Adrien gave me a withering look. "We can't stay here." He walked off after Joe and left George and I alone.

"What's going on?"

George put her hands on either side of my face. Her eyes were puffy and red beyond the bruising. "I thought you weren't coming back."

"Why?"

"It's been two days. You were speaking Italian. You came onto me in the studio, and when I tried to call you back from wherever it is you went, you stomped off and started painting again. I couldn't reach you, and when I asked Joe to help, Adrien stopped us and locked me out of the studio."

No wonder everything hurt. But two days? There had only been the night. And a demon in the glass. I was the demon in glass.

"Verity." She shook me gently. "No, you don't. You aren't disappearing again."

"I didn't go anywhere."

"You did. Your eyes changed."

"What?" That had never happened before. Or I didn't think it had. It was channeling. Sort of like my mother, but different. This wasn't possession, it wasn't like we traded places. "Or we were in the same space together."

"What space? What are talking about?" George was still patting my hair.

"Changed places. I think Raphael was here. He saw you. I was there. I was in Italy, in Rome with Pietro and Margherita." My chest flushed. Margherita. How scared her eyes were when she saw me painting like a man possessed at the studio. A man possessed.

"No no no. Don't do that. Who the hell are Pietro and Margherita?"

"It doesn't matter." It did matter. What had I done to Raphael's life? My heart raced, and two days of time travel channeling caught up with me.

"Why are we leaving?"

"I don't know. Adrien has been on edge. Something about the deadline and not being able to return the money. I tried to get something out of Joe, but he's been on edge, too, and would only say Adrien was mixed up with some dangerous people."

Adrien came back with Marcus and Joe. "Let's go."

"Where?" George stood up, and I wobbled on the couch before she pulled me into her hip. "She's in no condition to go anywhere."

Adrien didn't speak but motioned at us again. Marcus and Joe had George and me marching through the house before either of us could put up a fight. Let's be real, before George could put up a fight. I had nothing. Being upright without Joe holding onto me would have been more than enough of challenge.

We were being hauled toward the waiting SUV, no coats, no anything. I didn't even have shoes. Before Joe and Marcus could shove us into the back, another hulking black SUV pulled in behind. Great. Adrien had a posse.

Joe stiffened next to me.

Or maybe not.

The ward around the house pulsed and collapsed like tinkling shards of glass on the cold ground.

Adrien blanched. "Get them in the car." He spit the words out between clenched teeth.

The front passenger door of the newly arrived vehicle opened. A tall dark-haired man stepped out, looking like a cover model for a tech bro business magazine or one of the guys George would hook up with on a dating app. Adrien stood up straighter and leveled his gaze at the newcomer.

"She's done then." The man nodded toward me.

"Does it matter? You said the deal was off." Adrien Junior stepped forward half a step. The air between them crackled. I looked at George, but she was staring at the man who had emerged from the SUV. Adrien clearly knew him, but from George's expression, I would have sworn she did too.

The man smiled without any mirth.

The back passenger door of the SUV opened, and another man got out. His feet crunched on the white quartz gravel as he took a step toward Adrien Junior.

"I thought you were going to wait in the car." The man's expression didn't change, and he didn't look back when he spoke.

"She can come with me. That will cover the interest." The second man motioned to the SUV as the driver got out, another younger man with close-cropped sandy blond hair. "And the painting."

Adrien Junior protested with a string of garbled words and profanity. Again, I can only feel auras, and Adrien Junior's pulsed with anger, but he stank of fear too.

The man, still unbothered, motioned again to the driver, who popped open the back of Junior's SUV. "We can do this quietly or—"

Adrien Junior slammed the men with a pulse of magic that knocked them back for a moment, and then Junior came for me.

He twisted me out of Joe's grasp. I stumbled backwards toward him, and he pulled me against his body with a headlock. The asshole was using me as a human shield against this new—to me at least—threat. George yelled. The first man rushed forward but didn't get past the hood of the SUV.

"Let her go." The second man was the picture of calm in the chaos centering on Junior. "This is between you and me. She's too valuable." He locked eyes with me and smiled, almost apologetically.

Adrien Junior grunted out orders for Joe and Marcus to get George in the car and started pushing me forward with his body. I tripped and clotheslined myself on the crook of his elbow. My heartbeat pounded in my eardrums, and I gulped for air, sure my windpipe was crushed.

The little voice told me to calm down and take deep breaths.

Really? Now? Shut up.

George was still yelling and, given the grunts coming from Marcus, she had gone full wildcat on him.

The younger man from the SUV kept moving toward us. I was too busy clawing against Adrien Junior's arm and trying to breathe to pay much attention to anything that wasn't coming at my face. My little copilot voice was screaming to get my attention.

Break him. Break something. Like the twig.

What? I wanted a breath. My lungs were burning.

Break him.

Maybe? I tried to think about all those anatomy books for figure drawing, but nothing would stick in my head. There was only breathing, trying to breathe, and an image of DaVinci's Vitruvian Man with his mane of hair and those tendons sticking out on his neck like ropes. Adrien stumbled and tightened his grip on my throat, fully cutting off my air. My vision darkened at the edges, and I focused my mind's eye on the Vitruvian Adrien's ropy neck and cutting off the supply of blood moving up that artery to his brain.

Adrien went down on his knees, taking me with him but releasing his lock on my throat as we hit the gravel. I kept from nose-diving into the quartz with both hands out and tried to crawl away. Adrien grabbed my ankle, holding me fast. I'd used up the little energy I had, and the world was blurry at the edges of my vision again. I couldn't get a purchase on anything but loose gravel to propel myself out of Adrien's grasp.

Two deep thuds, and Adrien let go. George was screaming now, but I couldn't tell where she was. I could barely lift my head. I pulled in every scrap of magic and energy I had and threw myself on Minerva's mercy. Unseen fire engulfed me, and a bubble of energy worked its way over me like a mythical beast before it ended in ringing silence.

Adrien, his henchmen, and the new arrivals were all on the ground as if everyone had gone to sleep where they'd stood. I went to George. She looked stunned but pleased with herself.

"What the hell was that?" She stood on her own, which was good, because my arms and legs were shaky and barely holding me up.

"We have to go quickly. I don't know what I did, but we don't have time to see how long it will take to wear off."

"Whose blood is that?" The apron and skirt of her beermaid costume were splattered.

"Joe got shot and, I think, Adrien."

"We can't just leave Joe." He had said he would help.

"Verity, are you insane? Get in the car." George pushed me into the seat and slammed the door.

When she got in the driver's side there weren't any keys. "Shit shit shit." She looked in the console and laughed with relief when she saw it was a push start. "Hopefully they are in the car and not out there." But nothing happened when she pushed start. She pushed it again. Nothing.

"Did you break the cars?" My throat was raw from Adrien nearly choking me to death.

"I have no idea."

"Where did that come from?" The only thing close to that I'd seen from her is when she'd gone after Theo that night, but I'd thought then she'd been running on pure adrenaline. I hadn't realized it was her magic.

"Doesn't matter. We have to go." She got out and came around to get me. "Your hands are bleeding."

"I fell on the gravel."

She nodded and half carried me with her to the end of the driveway. I was probably not in my right mind in that moment, but I couldn't figure out how George thought we were going to get anywhere. I was fading fast and didn't have a coat or shoes. But we started walking back toward what we thought was the main road, me praying under my breath that whatever Minerva had done—using George as her conduit—would hold until we could hide or get out of there.

A few minutes later, another hulking black SUV came up behind us and followed slowly for moment before going on ahead a few yards and stopping. Two men got out from the back seat and came toward us, both dark-haired and one older, with more swagger than the other. There was nowhere to run now, and I couldn't have gotten more than a few steps anyway. The adrenaline was wearing off, and my feet were not happy about what I was subjecting them to.

"If you're smart, you'll stay back." George still had fight in her. "I don't know what else we're capable of."

I was surprised they didn't laugh given the wreck I was at that point.

"This is a rescue. Not a kidnapping. We're friends of Adrien Travere, *senior*," the older man said, his words accented in that same soft way the elder Adrien's were.

George whispered loudly to me. "Do you believe that?"

"At this point, I don't know. I'm ready for the devil I know though." To the men, now ten feet from us. "How do I know that's true, and you aren't with those people back there?"

"Bellissima, nothing I can say will prove you can trust me, but I can tell you that your Slovenian friend and your very angry cat are safe in Westchester."

My resolve to question them further crumbled with the thoughts of Hilma and Matjaž.

I was directed into the back seat of the SUV, and George took shotgun next to the driver. We took off as soon as the two men got in on either side of me and closed their doors. I waited for a wave of relief to wash over me. Unsurprisingly, it didn't. It was hard to believe we were safe, as I had gotten really good at jumping from frying pans into fires.

CHAPTER 16

I wiped blood from my cut-up hands on the coveralls Adrien had "gifted" me, adding bright red to the mix of earth pigments. I wanted to ask our rescuers who they were and what they had planned from here. I formed whole questions in my mind, but I couldn't make the action of asking connect to my mouth. Was this shock?

The windows of the SUV were tinted diplomat black, and the driver didn't say a word until the older man leaned up to tap his shoulder and said, "Take the back route."

"Yes, sir."

The combined magical auras of the three men in the car was enough to push the air out of the vehicle and my lungs. Sir's magical presence reminded me, like his voice, of Adrien Travere Senior's. It resonated with centuries—not decades—of life, of practice, and there was a hum to it, like putting your hand to a hive of quieted bees. Dr. Mar's presence had held it, too, when she'd had her personal wards down at Adrien Senior's conference table. It was the kind of magic I'd felt in the Mithras temple in London and at the top of the ridge behind my house in West Kill. I imagined those sites as places where magic pooled, but they had different flavors. City magic was peopled somehow, and magic like on the ridge was older than people—wilder and, in some places, terrifying.

The younger man clapped his hand on my thigh. "I guess we'll see if Sandro was telling the truth."

"Did you get a look at it?" Sir re-entered the conversation.

"Not really. I was too busy dealing with the aftermath of Travere's dime-store magician routine."

I coughed. That hadn't been Adrien Junior's magic, it had been George's. She shifted in her seat. They had to have been right behind us.

Sir laughed, like someone rib-punching a cello. "At least we have it."

By "it," they had to mean the painting.

"You are a quiet one, bellissima." I wasn't the only quiet one; George hadn't said a word.

The tiny voice in my head screamed something about "effing mobsters," which seemed unduly prissy given the situation. "Mobsters?" The word was out without thought, but it hurt to speak, and I sounded like I'd been drinking paint thinner.

Sir chuckled this time. The younger man said, "The mob wishes."

I couldn't get my voice to work again until we entered the canyons of the city. "Where are you taking us?"

Not Sir answered: "I would have thought you would be happy to get away from that psycho Travere. Looks like he roughed up your friend too."

My friend that I had brought with me into this new unknown, the friend that I was supposed to be saving, who was still saving me. My throat tightened again, making it harder still to get any words out.

"It's okay, bellissima." Sir patted my thigh, making me squirm again. Strange men getting familiar with my lap was not comforting.

"Is Joe dead?" I felt bad about that. Aside from the kidnapping part, he'd been kind.

"Unknown. Young Travere most likely. If not, Marcus will finish him off. But this Joe person? We don't kill bystanders. Though I guess he did help with your kidnapping." Sir coughed and searched his inside pocket, pulling out a linen handkerchief and coughing into it. "My apologies. Your coveralls, they smell of turpentine. Allergies."

"Who are you people?" I didn't really care if Adrien was dead. I mean, I'd been trying to figure out how to telekinesis him into stroking out, so I could have just as easily killed him. Wait. Did I really not care if I killed someone? That was something I'd prefer to keep in the abstract.

"It's best you don't know, bell—"

"Verity. My name is Verity."

"Signorina Green, it is better if you don't know."

Miss Green was better than "bellissima." And bystander seemed to be better than knowing anything. But how could I be a bystander? They were hauling a forged copy of *Portrait* that I had painted all by myself. Well, maybe. And more people knew about me—enough to know my name.

The driver pointed the SUV into the darkened maw of a private garage and stopped at the floor-to-ceiling glass doors of an elevator lobby. Sir and the younger man got out, and Sir beckoned me to do the same. The back of the SUV opened, and I slid across the seat and tried to stand. I was still wobbly, and it hurt to put my weight on my feet. George and Sir took my elbows and walked me slowly toward the elevator.

"I think you could do with a rest, bellissima. And perhaps

some shoes."

The four of us rode to the penthouse, *Portrait* carried by the younger man, carefully, as if it really were of great value. The elevator dinged, and the doors opened onto a sea of serpentine marble. The floors and walls, all the way up to the coffered ceiling, were polished to a reflective olivine mirror. I stepped onto the cold stone, and the chill momentarily dulled the pain buzzing in my synapses from the bruises from the gravel at Adrien Junior's.

I must have telegraphed the change in pain to Sir, who looked down at my bloodied hands and my bare feet.

He called down the cavernous hallway, and a man with dark, neatly cropped hair in a well-fitted dark suit appeared.

"Church, our guest is injured. Would you send for Dr. Begam?"

The man nodded and melted back into the shadow at the end of the hallway. The younger man quickly followed him, *Portrait* in hand, and left George and Sir to navigate me into the living area. I've seen lots of photos of garishly decorated New York penthouses—and even had drinks in a few of them, courtesy of double dates with George. Money does not buy taste and is often thrown at designers willing to gild every lily in sight for commission, but the receiving area of this apartment could have been teleported from one of the Venetian palaces along the Grand Canal. The decor was luxurious but lived in. Sir led me to the nearest place to sit and continued to hold my elbow as I lowered myself onto the pale silk upholstery of a chair that could have come from the Doge's palace. He pulled a matching one close for George, who was still unusually quiet.

The man who had appeared at Sir's first beckoning

returned with a folding tea table and a tray with a porcelain pot and a plate of delicate tomato sandwiches on brown bread. My stomach growled audibly.

"You should eat. Dr. Begam will be here soon to attend to your hands and feet and that mark." He gestured at my throat and gingerly removed a paintbrush from my hair. He sat down opposite us in a matching chair. He laid the paintbrush on the side table and picked up a salmon-pink edition of the Financial Times.

So many questions, but also ravenous hunger. Calories. I had to fuel my brain, and the sandwiches were delicious, if swallowing was a little uncomfortable. George took tea and kept staring at our rescuer, as if trying to place him.

The elevator chimed in the distance, and the click of high-heeled shoes on marble tapped closer. A woman in her early thirties in a mulberry-colored suit and impossibly high heels, carrying a large black bag, joined our little party in the receiving area. Her dark hair was pulled into a low ponytail, emphasizing the high planes of a bronzed face.

"Rinaldo, you couldn't get her somewhere more comfortable?" The woman tsked at Sir.

"She is injured beyond her hands, and I didn't want to make it worse." He pointed to my feet.

"And why, in December, is this woman not wearing shoes?" She tsked again and looked up at me as she crouched down with her bag. "Why don't you have shoes? And your hands are a mess."

Bottles of medications and gauze and tape came out of the bag. "I'll need a basin to wash out these cuts."

George followed her wordlessly and came back carrying a large bowl of warm water with a towel slung over her arm. The cleaning part wasn't pleasant, but Dr. Begam worked gently and quickly.

Rinaldo peered over his paper at us, blanching slightly at the pinking water, then returning to the financial news. Medication and gauze were expertly applied to my hands.

"Can I look at your feet?" Dr. Begam had squatted down again so we were eye level.

She lifted up my foot before I could reply.

"No lacerations, but you do have some nasty contusions." She prodded my instep, and I flinched.

"I can give you something for the pain. But you should stay off your feet until we can get you some shoes with some padding." She stood up and gestured toward my throat. "What about your neck?"

"I fell." I sounded like an entire family of chain-smoking frogs.

"The pain meds will help with that, too, but try to rest your voice." She pressed gently around the front of my throat. "I don't think you have any damage, aside from the bruising. What did you fall on?"

"A man's arm, while he was choking me." And while the fucker was trying to use me as a human shield.

She pivoted toward Rinaldo on her spiky shoes. "What have you dragged this woman through?"

Rinaldo folded down his pink paper and the corners of this mouth. "More than was necessary, I think."

***

I was again in a strange bedroom in a strange place, but

there were windows that provided a glimpse of the city below and the gray-green expanse of the Atlantic Ocean beyond. I had a television in a cabinet with a remote for changing the channels as well as for opening and closing the panels that concealed it and for the blinds on the widow. I'd been left with a stack of art history books in leather library bindings, a carafe of water, and a small pot of the same tea we'd been served on arrival, Ceylon I think. George's favorite. Church, Rinaldo's valet, had also shown me where the button on the remote was that would summon him, should I need anything. And, perhaps most importantly, there was no lock on the door. George was in an adjoining suite taking a hot shower. We planned to debrief once she was done.

Dr. Begam had said I should avoid speaking or walking, but she didn't suggest anything about not thinking. Unfortunately, that's all I could do. My thoughts weren't particularly organized, but they were rather unpleasant. I had run from the home of Adrien Travere Senior only to be somewhat voluntarily kidnapped to the lair of Adrien Travere Junior, and now George and I had been officially rescued by Rinaldo, a very wealthy older Italian man— let's specify Venetian man here—who was happy to off Adrien Junior but wasn't a mobster. No, he was someone the mobsters aspired to be. And he and his comrade knew someone named Sandro, who had known about me. The Italian or Venetian connection again, perhaps?

On this journey that I had first undertaken to protect myself and then to rescue George, I had endangered Matjaž and lied to him by omission before abandoning him in a closet with Hilma. I had failed to rescue George. She had mostly rescued us after whatever happened in Adrien's driveway. That was more and more like a dream that I was losing pieces of rapidly. Rinaldo and his compatriot were now in the possession of one expertly "forged" but unaged painting of Raphael's *Portrait of the Artist as Young Man*. I had also left Margherita and Pietro in sixteenth-century Italy with no way to return and perhaps fix whatever damage my presence had caused in their lives, and I couldn't explain why my heart ached at that thought. And back to Matjaž—the thought that I had permanently damaged anything that had blossomed between us lay on me like a lead blanket. I really didn't know what to do with that.

There was a light knock at the door, and Church appeared with a pair of comfortable-looking shoes in hand.

"Dr. Begam recommended these and said you would be able to walk a short distance. Would you like to have dinner with . . ." he paused briefly. "Would you like to have dinner at the table, or would you prefer a tray in your room?"

I didn't even know what I would have preferred. Possibly a return-trip ticket to two weeks ago. The tiny voice in my head was quicker to decide. "At the table, I think." I might be able to get some questions answered, if nothing else.

Church nodded. "I took the liberty of picking up some clothes for you, and there are linens in the bath if you would like to shower. I'll collect you at seven." He set the shoes on the floor by the door and closed it soundlessly.

Collect. Collect me. That seemed to be all the rage in the dark underbelly of the art world these days. I imagined Andy Warhol laughing somewhere at the shitshow of my fifteen minutes of fame.

George knocked on the doorframe of our shared door.

"How was the shower?"

"Good. I feel like a new person." She tightened the belt on her robe and sat next to me on the settee I was resting on to work up enough energy to take my own shower. I wasn't exactly sure how I was supposed to do that with my palms bandaged, but I'd figure it out.

"You've been pretty quiet."

George nodded and pursed her lips while looking up at the ceiling and around the room. "It's a lot to take in. Knowing magic is real. Being able to do magic. Those are things. But what happened back there—what was that? How did those guys just undo Asshole's wards like they were nothing? And who the fuck is this Rinaldo guy, and are we sure we aren't putting ourselves in worse hands here?"

"Where to start?" I had a few answers, but there were definitely parts I couldn't explain and didn't understand either.

"How about we start with what I did at Adrien's?"

"Maybe you didn't do it, maybe Minerva did." Saying it out loud made it real, and that feeling of fire and magic erupting around me came back vividly.

"I thought you were iffy on the reality of gods?" It truly was a question and not a criticism.

"Yeah. I don't know." Maddalena, my teacher, had never mentioned tapping into godlike powers as even a possibility. "I mean there was that night when I left Theo, but I'd always chalked that up to your righteous anger."

"Well, thanks. I guess. We can figure that out later. It worked and got us here, whatever here is." She looked around again at the well-appointed room.

"Did you know the other man in the SUV at Adrien's?"

She had looked at him so intently.

"Maybe. I think I went out with him once on a solo. His phone went off the whole time, and when I got up to go to the toilets, the bartender caught me on the way back to the table and said something about him not being a good guy. Something about the Polish mafia. But Rinaldo also looks familiar, and I can't place why. I mean, talk about an out-of-context situation. But in the shower, yeah, I think I do know Rinaldo—or I think my parents do. I have to call them at some point to check in. Unknown as to whether I share any of this or not, but I do want to ask about him."

"So what now?"

"I'm going to take up yon butler's offer of a dinner tray. Are you going to dinner?"

"I thought it might be a good time to grill Rinaldo."

"Good, it'll give me time to snoop around." She stood and kissed me on top of my head. "I hope this really is the beginning of some answers."

CHAPTER 17

Dinner was served in a tastefully decorated dining room with a chandelier made of pale pink and primrose Venetian glass blown into delicate dolphins and merpeople frolicking along chains of sea anemones. I don't remember seeing anything as fine and intricate, even in museums in Italy. To be fair, my time in Venice had been mostly directed by Theo, and I didn't get to take a vaporetto out to Murano, an island in the lagoon, because he wasn't interested in glassblowing. We had spent hours looking at paintings first at the Gallerie dell'Accademia and then at the Peggy Guggenheim on the Grand Canal.

He teased me about getting emotional in the small room with four Jackson Pollocks almost close enough in the space to reach out and touch the paintings opposite each other. I could feel Pollock in that room, the violence and brokenness of his life. The museum had been Peggy Guggenheim's home and was still divided into small rooms. The paintings were close and the space intimate, unlike the Accademia. Between standing in the sense of the other visitors' auras as they experienced the works and the pull from the artists from all those paintings, I'd wanted to leave almost as soon as we'd arrived. But Theo wasn't having it, and he'd let me know how much he wasn't having it when we returned to the dingy room he had rented off San Marco. He had money to stay anywhere in Venice, but he wanted to see the city "like a tourist." Rolling over on the lumpy bed had been especially painful against bruised ribs.

Church coughed politely. He was waiting for an answer.

"I'm sorry."

"Would you like me to take your plate?"

I had not eaten much of the delicate fish in butter sauce, though it had been delicious. The first bite had sent me spiraling back to the canaled city where I had first eaten it. I nodded, and the sad remains of the fish course disappeared.

"Are you not hungry, Signorina Green?" Rinaldo asked. He and I were eating alone at one end of the large table. Church had set Rinaldo's place at the head and mine to Rinaldo's right. Despite the empty expanse of highly polished wood and the size of the room, the dinner felt very intimate—made more so by the dimmed lighting and a candelabrum burning slender beeswax tapers. Their honeyed scent reminded me of spellwork, and I could almost sense Hilma twining herself around my ankles. She was going to hate me so much when I finally got back to her.

"Distracted. Unsurprisingly." Rinaldo had not been unkind, but I had no idea what he was capable of. Though either he or Church had excellent taste in clothes, as I had been left a pair of light woolen palazzo pants and a cowl-necked sweater in a deep shade of brown that was probably called "loam" in the designer's catalogue—though I would call it burnt umber.

He nodded sagely, picked up his glass of wine, and leaned back in his chair, as if to get a better look at me.

"I am sure you have questions, and I will answer them. But I have one for you first."

I was hardly in a position to say no.

"Who painted *Portrait*?" He nodded his chin, pointing to wherever the painting was beyond this room.

"It was painted by my hands, but I believe the thought and talent behind them was Raphael." The tiny voice in my head suggested that was enough information for now.

"Sandro was speaking truth for once, not just lying again to . . ." He was speaking to himself.

"I don't know who Sandro is, or how he knew about me."

Church returned with two small plates of insalata, bitter winter radicchios and frisee, lightly dressed.

Rinaldo took a bite of the salad course and nodded at Church, who disappeared again.

"Sandro is, as it turns out, of little importance. And he is dead, so he matters even less. He did offer information about you as a bargaining chip and, as I had expected then, it was one he had played before."

Well, that didn't answer any questions.

"Signorina Green—"

"Please, Verity is fine. And less jarring."

"As you wish. Verity, as I am sure you know, you are a rare thing, even in this realm of magic that we share." He set his fork on his plate and looked at me.

I nodded, pinned by his gaze. This wasn't going anywhere good. Conversations about magic, specifically my magic and what I could do, never seemed to.

"Good people would be tempted to use your talents for gain. Bad ones would happily try to exploit you. Like your lover, Theo."

It took a lot not to drop my fork. I had never told Theo what I could do.

"Since I learned of you through Sandro's attempts at salvation, there has been—shall we say—an uneasy truce between Adrien Travere the senior and his Restorationists and my interests. We don't have such a catchy name, but you could say we are more conservative in our aims. As long as you didn't attempt to use your ability to create forgeries or do anything else untoward, we'd both leave you alone. Neither the senior Travere nor I had any reason initially to think his son would be the one to break that truce." He polished off the rest of the blood-colored leaves.

"Adrien senior knew the kidnapping was faked?" My insalata was left to wilt. Adrien Senior had propositioned me to paint *Portrait* before Adrien Junior and George had been "kidnapped."

"Not at first. But Junior, while somewhat adept at magic, is quite pedestrian at everything else, including plotting a kidnapping scheme. You might have been better off staying in Westchester, though I did find Claus's story of your escape amusing. I didn't know you were a firestarter as well."

"Neither did I. Claus works for you too?"

"I suspect Church works for Adrien Senior. It's the way of the long-lived, I'm afraid."

Church appeared to clear the course as if summoned and before I could ask what Rinaldo meant by long-lived. Small pieces of a puzzle were coming together. Like clues in a Christie novel, when everyone is brought into the parlor for the reveal, the little voice in my head chimed in to say.

"Sir, would you like dessert served here or in the lounge?"

Rinaldo glanced a question at me. "The lounge, I think. And perhaps our guest would care for amaro?"

"Dr. Begam suggested I not drink with the pain medication."

My wine glass had been quietly removed by Church when I'd declined the pour with the antipasti.

"Of course. Perhaps just the pevarini." Church nodded and took away our salad plates.

Rinaldo stood and offered me his arm, reminding me of Matjaž on our first meeting. His old-fashioned manners were perhaps why I had trusted Matjaž so quickly. Rinaldo and I walked together to the lounge, and he made a fuss of making me comfortable on the most stuffed piece of furniture next to the softly crackling fire. In a high-rise penthouse. In Manhattan. Welcome to my life as a surrealist painting.

"As I was saying. By the time you'd fled Westchester, Adrien Senior knew for certain the kidnapping was faked. The only thing he didn't know was where Adrien Junior was. Or if he had… disposed of Signorina Burne-Jones." I appreciated his hesitation there. Thinking of Adrien murdering George as collateral to getting to me? I didn't need to go there.

"And you did know, because of Marcus."

"Yes—"

"I'm sorry, if you and your compatriots knew what kind of person Adrien Junior was, why would you leave George and me with him? Why not immediately come get us, or tell Adrien Senior? That asshole beat the shit out of George. And tried—" I'd overtaxed my bruised voice box and started coughing.

"When Marcus alerted me to Junior's abuse of your friend, we made our plans. I hadn't expected you to finish the painting so quickly."

Neither had I. "What happens now?"

"Adrien, the senior of course, is coming tomorrow, and we can discuss that."

"Is Adrien Junior dead?" A shadow slipped across Rinaldo's face.

"You had asked about Joe, Junior's other staff."

Staff? I guess at his level you don't have "henchmen" or "muscle," just various staff assigned to kidnap people or clear the table.

"Joe is alive. He's recovering from a gunshot wound that appeared to be a ricochet from one of the shots fired at Adrien Junior."

"Bystander."

"Yes. But what is your interest in his well-being? He was not a bystander to your kidnapping." Rinaldo took one of the lumpy cookies from the plate Church had delivered, along with a digestif glass of what had to be strega—by the glowing saffron color—for Rinaldo and a cup of chamomile tea for me.

"He was unusually kind and seemed protective of George and me."

Rinaldo seemed surprised for the slightest moment. "Perhaps he is not as good at being undercover as his employer would like to think."

"Did Joe work for someone else?"

"Perhaps."

Whatever Rinaldo knew about Joe, he wasn't going to share. "And Adrien Junior, is he dead?"

"Marcus believed him to be dead, but his body is currently unaccounted for."

***

What would happen next was a question that couldn't be answered over tea and strega and black pepper cookies. Apparently Rinaldo was going to insist on this meeting with Adrien Senior first, before anything was decided. He was kind about it, but I tried not to feel like he had patted me on the head and sent me off to bed like a toddler. I was too tired to seethe much about it and conked out quickly with the help of pain meds and the soporific tea.

The morning came with a light knock and a breakfast tray carried in by Church. A girl could get used to this luxurious life if it didn't seem to include kidnapping, murder, art crime, and gods knew what else.

"I disposed of the coveralls, but your clothes have been washed." He gestured to a stack of folded black clothing on the dressing chair with additional cream and silky-looking items on top. "And I brought you some more underthings."

"Thank you, but I prefer the clothes from last night." The underthings, swishy silk French knickers and a camisole, were amusingly old-fashioned but incredibly comfortable.

"Signor . . . Rinaldo would like you to meet him in the morning room when you're ready. He is expecting Mr. Travere this morning and would like you and Ms. Burne-Jones to join them." Church took the carafe and teapot from the bedside table. "Do you need anything, Ms. Green?"

"No, thank you. This has all been incredibly strange, but you have been very kind. Thank you." I still sounded like I'd been gargling drain cleaner, but there was improvement.

Church nodded his acknowledgment of my gratitude but left

without saying more.

I nibbled at breakfast, my stomach unsettled by this meeting that surely meant some sort of arrangement would be reached. I did my best to look presentable with help from the basket of toiletries and makeup that had appeared in the ensuite bathroom and headed downstairs to see what might happen next in this grand adventure I hadn't signed up for but would very much like to bring to conclusion. If there was to be bargaining, what did master-forger, dead-artist-channelers go for on the open market?

George was dressed and looking refreshed. She'd struck out in the snooping category other than to discover that the entire two floors of the penthouse seemed to have been furnished in Venetian doge palace. If there were secrets, they weren't being kept in the drawers of ornate writing desks. Church's taste was much better than Adrien Junior's. He'd outfitted George in a woolen combo similar to mine, but it had a scoop neck and was a deep royal blue that made George's eyes practically glow.

When we got to the morning room—another space transported whole cloth from some canal-side palace—Adrien Travere Senior had already arrived and been served coffee. He and Rinaldo stood when we entered the room, and I got a fleeting glimpse of them having completed that same old-fashioned courtesy hundreds and thousands of times.

"Please sit." Rinaldo gestured for me to take a seat next to him, opposite Adrien Senior. "You know our guest of course." George sat opposite Rinaldo. Neither of the men had their full guard up, and the room brimmed with their magic. It was intoxicating and made it difficult to focus on the reason we were here. George seemed especially distracted by the presence of Adrien

Travere Senior.

"Good morning, Mr. Travere." I nodded and took my seat.

"Adrien, please."

George introduced herself and shook Adrien's hand. She had that look on her face. Georgina, the never truly daunted.

The two men sat back down, and Adrien poured a cup of coffee for me. "Just milk, if I remember." He offered the same to George, who took hers black.

I took the cup and looked between the two faces. "I appreciate the politeness and niceties, but can we get on with it?"

"I do enjoy your directness." Adrien chuckled softly. "I'm here to take you home. More accurately, to my home."

"Don't we get a say in this? I thought this was to be a discussion about what came next?" The little voice in my head said something about minding my temper.

"Of course. But I can assure you it is the best option, and Matjaž is there waiting for you. And Hilma is there of course. She has finally stopped walking into every room and yowling, but I believe she is still looking for you."

I smiled despite myself at the thought of them together, in some semblance of safety. And Hilma pacing about, unhappy to be in a magician's space. There was going to be so much peeing in shoes.

"Can I ask how this decision was reached?"

Rinaldo started to answer, "Perhaps it is best—"

"Nope. Sorry. We are past that point. There is no more negotiating about me. You are now negotiating with me, and I'd like to know what was said before I arrived."

"As Rinaldo explained, there has been a truce between our interested parties regarding you that was, as you know, disrupted by the actions of my son. We have agreed to recommence the truce until such time as this current situation is resolved. As I have a more robust security detail than Rinaldo, we agreed that it would be best if you two stayed in Westchester until my son's whereabouts are known." That last bit seemed to strain his voice the tiniest amount. I couldn't know what it was like to be betrayed so fully by my own child.

"I thought Marcus had been instructed to kill him?"

Adrien didn't react to the mention of his son's possible execution by his rival.

"Be that as it may, Marcus did not succeed." He managed to keep his voice flat, but he did give Rinaldo the archest of eyebrows.

Adrien Senior's handsomeness caught me again and made me think how he was exactly George's type if it hadn't been for the ridiculous situation we were all sitting in together. "And you both think he'll come back for me?" I took a quick look at George, who had gone pale.

"He no longer has you or the painting to bargain with, and the people he has made himself beholden to are unlikely to accept a simple refund—if he is even capable of repaying their money." Adrien Senior set his cup down and turned the full force of his gaze on me. "So as you can see, your safety is of concern on multiple fronts."

"And the painting? You should both know that it is worthless. In addition to being newly painted, I left a message for Junior in the ground layer with some lead white. The first X-ray will ruin any chance of authentication, even if you do manage to age it somehow."

Rinaldo laughed. "I presumed as much, with your knowledge of authentication and restoration techniques. The painting may be worthless for its intended purpose, but it is priceless nonetheless. It will be preserved, off market." He glanced at Adrien, but neither of them was eager to say anything more about the painting or where it would end up.

"Do you have any things with you?" Travere stood and smoothed his fitted slacks.

"No." George and I said it in unison.

"Then we should go." He gave Rinaldo a slight bow and started walking toward the serpentine-clad elevator entrance.

"I don't know what to say. Thank you for getting me away from Adrien Junior, and for your hospitality." I took one of Rinaldo's hands in mine, getting the full force of his magical presence. There was a warmth there, not unlike what I'd felt with Matjaž, but it felt safer, steadier.

Rinaldo smiled, though there was an air of sadness in his expression. "The situation of our finally meeting is unfortunate, but I am glad to have made your acquaintance. When this business has passed, I would like to meet with you again. We have some further things to discuss." Rinaldo kissed my cheek and walked with Adrien Senior and George and me to the elevator.

Adrien Senior pressed the call button.

I turned to Rinaldo to ask him what he'd meant by "long-lived" at dinner. That hint of an explanation for the penthouse and manners and the magical presences that left me feeling like I'd walked through a temple where the sculptures and murals held the rituals of several lifetimes had started to form in my mind, and I was tantalizingly close to a solution.

The elevator chimed, and the doors opened.

Before I could register fully that the elevator was occupied, a blast of magic knocked me flat. I fell hard on the marble, and my ears rang with the pressure wave. Marble dust hung suspended in the air, now filled with muffled shouts and yelling. An alarm started going off. I tried to scramble to my hands and knees in an attempt to get up to run—where, I wasn't sure. The voice in my head kept repeating not to move, not to move, which made zero sense until I tried to stand. A wall of pain descended when I put my weight on my right arm, and my hand slipped against the marble. There was blood on the floor, blood running down my arm, too much of it.

I couldn't see Rinaldo, Adrien Senior, or George, but I tried to reach out.

Someone picked me up from behind, their arms under mine, and pulled me onto my feet. I yelled in pain and was twirled around and thrown over their shoulder, which pressed into my stomach, winding me and leaving my injured arm to dangle. The bane of being a relatively small person is being easily portable.

I'd had quite enough of that. I flailed at my new captor with my legs and fists. I was sick of this shit, and I was not going quietly this time.

Another person approached, their feet sure on the uneven, broken floor. The ringing in my ears hadn't stopped, but I could hear a little better, enough to understand first the words of an old blood-stopping charm Maddelena had taught me, then somnus and *Morpheus*, a spell of sleep being pronounced over my head followed by its darkness.

CHAPTER 18

Everything hurt. I was in the dark. A bumpy, rough ride, with the darkness close. The back seat of a car, the upholstery in my face. My mouth was taped, and my hands were bound in front of me, my ankles bound together. My head was resting on a slick and plasticky lump that held my neck up. Someone else read mystery novels or thrillers and knew enough to not let me asphyxiate from a weirdly cocked head. Panic bubbled up and ebbed, talked down by the tiny voice in my head, who I had to admit was right as often as annoying. Breathe. The smell of new car and sweaty bodies.

Wherever we were going was near a railhead or on bad roads. I bounced around enough that the pain shooting down my arm was almost enough to black out again. It was impossible to gauge time. Minutes? Hours? The panic and pain made it harder still. But the car stopped eventually, and the door opened into darkness. Night. It had been late morning when I'd been at Rinaldo's with Adrien Senior. We were nearing the solstice and 4 p.m. sunsets, so I had been out at least five or six hours. We could be anywhere.

"Okay, princess, time to go."

My removal from the car left much to be desired, but at least I was not slung like a sack of potatoes this time. Small mercies. I was carried into a low farmhouse building that even in the dim orange glow of a security light looked like it had seen better days. Perhaps sometime in the 1970s. After being deposited on a threadbare couch in a horror film set living room, I was left alone to panic some more.

I had just gotten my breathing under control, and calmed my heart to "running too hard" instead of "abject terror," when Adrien Junior stumbled in to undo my good work. He looked as bad as I felt. His skin had taken on the gray pallor of the very ill, and blood had seeped from a bulkily bandaged wound on his shoulder. He looked at me with a mixture of satisfaction and disgust, not an expression I'd ever experienced and not one I would recommend.

A cowed-looking woman in rumpled fuchsia scrubs came around him and tried unsuccessfully to remove what turned out to be medical tape from my mouth without hurting me.

She started asking questions about my injuries, glancing up at me with terror in her eyes as she awaited each slow answer. Between the earlier injury and the dryness of my throat, I could barely get words out. The tape around my ankles and hands was cut loose.

She inspected my exposed arm, pushing gingerly against the red, swollen flesh around a deep cut on the outside of my upper arm.

"It looks like it's infected. It should've been cleaned and stitched up." She spoke to Adrien without looking at him.

What had that monster done to her to make her so afraid of him?

"You need antibiotics." She looked at me with a pleading in her expression that I was currently incapable of addressing. "I can bandage it up to keep it clean for now."

"Be quick with it. They can get her medical attention." Speaking seemed to hurt him. Good.

The woman dug around in a box of random medical supplies and came up with a roll of tape. After sufficiently futzing with my arm and an industrial length of gauze, I was as bandaged up as I was going to get under Junior's care. He shouted for her to go back to the bedroom, and she went without a word or nod, an air of relief to be out of Adrien's presence following her.

"You are entirely too much trouble for what people seem to think you are worth." He might as well have spit on me after he said it, his words were so infused with disgust.

I didn't have anything to say, so I didn't. The tension and the sharpness of his fear was like sitting in a bag of broken glass, unable to breathe or move. Like living with Theo those last days before I finally got away from him. The smallest thing could set him off.

The flower of blood on Adrien Junior's shoulder began to unfurl. Whatever that poor woman had done to put him back together was being undone by his insistence on standing. I watched it creep, crimson purpling the blue material of his shirt, mesmerized by his life force if not his will leaking out of him. Did he in all his "high" magic not know how to stop blood? Maddalena had often said that was the problem with some magicians, they were too busy learning how to summon treasure-hunting demons to learn the simpler magic of healing.

"What are you staring at, bitch?" He looked down at his shoulder and quickly covered his own grimace of pain. "You should be glad I'm not dead, or my father and Rinaldo would be trading you back and forth like a prized whore."

Whatever had been attractive or charming about Adrien Junior when George and I had met up with him at the pub had evaporated, revealing a scared bully propped up by his magic and his money—neither of which seemed to be serving him in this moment. I didn't fully appreciate Adrien Senior's or Rinaldo's methods, but at least they weren't in this league of abusive bullshit. It distracted my anxious brain to try to imagine Adrien Junior with either of the old men's sense of decorum.

My continued silence seemed to irritate him more than if I'd snapped back. He moved surprisingly quickly across the stained living room rug to slap me, hard, across the face.

"I've wanted to do that for a while. Now that Georgina isn't here to protect you..." his voice trailed off as headlights filled the living room, spraying the looping floral pattern of the torn, machined lace sheers against the paneling. "Sooner than expected. Good. I'll be happy to be rid of you. Though I don't much think you'll care for their company. Funny to think you'll be wishing yourself back with me."

Car doors opened and closed, followed by shouting, a single gunshot, and the pop and reverberation of magic.

Adrien's smugness slid off his face, and he jerked me up from the couch to play human shield again. This time he wasn't strong enough to hold me upright, so he dragged me to the armchair in the corner and sat down hard with me halfway on his lap. I couldn't get a purchase on anything to push away from him. I gritted my teeth, but the pain throbbing down my arm made the edges of the world dark for a second, and I had the mother of all headaches building behind my eye where he'd slapped me.

The tip of something sharp touched the soft spot under my jaw. The blood on his shirt soaked through to the skin on my back, spreading sticky and warm between us. There was more shouting outside and another flash of magic that I could feel rather than see. It was controlled and precise, clean even, despite its violent purpose.

I never learned "combat" magic. That was something my teacher never felt was necessary, especially before The Storm. There was no way I was going to blast myself out of this situation, and I couldn't bet on Minerva, or whatever that had been in the driveway, showing up now. I knew enough of Adrien and his ilk through dealing with Theo that I needed to distract him before he hurt me reflexively. Or before whoever was out there got through the door. Whether they were worse, as Adrien threatened, or not didn't matter much. Everything in me told me I needed to get out of here before I had the unfortunate chance to find out.

"You said you'd tell me about the Sea of Galilee painting when I finished the Raphael."

"Shut up." He poked the knife hard enough that it broke the skin but backed off before he really cut me, though I couldn't tell if it was blood or sweat running down my neck.

"It was part of our deal. I haven't done anything to dishonor that. I painted the Raphael for you."

"Why do you care so much about that stupid painting?" He knew why, I could tell. He was afraid of what was outside, but there was something else about that painting that made his aura pulse with fear.

"Because I know who painted it."

"Some bum on the street in Venice, painting gondolas and copies of Old Masters to sell to tourists who wouldn't know a Rembrandt from a Titian." His heart was beating harder, and my back was getting wetter.

"No. My brother painted it. How did you get it?"

He laughed. "Your brother is dead because he made promises to the wrong people." He said it with conviction, but he was lying. I'd never gotten an indication that clear from anyone before.

"You seem to have that in common."

"I am delivering though." Uncertainty. Fear acrid enough to make me gag.

"Are you? You seem pretty afraid of whoever's out there."

The little voice in my head screamed something about neck ropes. You have to get out of here. Now.

I didn't think I could make the neck ropes, the cutting off of the supply of blood to the brain thing, work. It hadn't really when I'd tried before, but I could paint this whole living room with his blood. My teacher had insisted on my learning blood stopping charms. She was a big believer in magical first aid as a responsibility of those who could do magic. And if you can stop blood, you can make it flow. I stilled my breath as much as possible against my own panic and the pain threatening to take me into the darkness again, and I imagined the poppy of blood on his shoulder spreading out into hundreds and thousands of poppies until they filled the living room like the art installation at the Tower of London. George and I had visited her parents during the centenary and stood silent, looking out over the moat of almost 900,000 red ceramic poppies for the dead of the Great War. In my mind, poppies covered the rug and the horrible couch and drifted out of the windows in a cascade of spilled blood onto the porch and down the front step to seep into the cold December ground. I repeated the words of the ancient prayer Maddalena had taught me in my thoughts. It might have worked faster to say them out loud, but Adrien could've stopped me with the blade at my throat.

His will did struggle against mine, like crystalline shards pushing back at me. I was going to live through this, take that poor nurse out of there. See Matjaž and Hilma. I walked on in my mind, through the wall of glass, felt it crash around me in sparkling fragments.

The knife fell, and Adrien's head lolled. I pushed myself off him, trying and failing not to bang my arm around, slipping in his blood. I called for the woman.

"He's dead." Louder. "He's dead. Come on, we have to get out of here."

She came out shaking and looked in horror around her. I could see the monstrousness of my handiwork through her eyes: the floor and rug were slick with blood, and it had started to wick up the front of the legless chair, dip-dyeing the orange and brown plaid with black in the dim light.

"Is there a back door?"

She nodded. Together we walked out into the darkness, holding each other up in our pain and fear. She was almost as frightened by me as by what we'd left behind. A battle continued on the other side of the farmhouse, the percussive waves of magic and the occasional gunshot egging me on despite the throbbing in my arm. Farther into the woods, into the cold. Away from whatever devils Adrien had made a pact with and whoever they were fighting.

***

Sarah. I'd finally gotten her to speak her name if nothing else.

Sarah and I pushed on until we found the remains of a shack. We could no longer see the light from the house, and no other lights had appeared on the horizon aside from the half moon as it rose over the trees. It had been enough to navigate by when our eyes adjusted to the darkness.

We hid in the corner with the most amount of wall left and huddled together for warmth. My shivering was both from the cold and what I thought was a fever. The crumbling structure wasn't enough cover to keep us from hypothermia, but it was enough that I thought I could hide us with my own "invisibility" spell. I murmured it repeatedly until the words blurred into sounds, asking Minerva to hide us from those who would do us harm. Her presence felt closer than it had any other time I had petitioned her, and I had to wonder if I'd drawn myself closer to the goddess of wisdom and art—who was also sometimes the goddess of war—by spilling Adrien's blood. There had been more of it than I thought a body could contain.

It wouldn't do to dwell on it while I was still trying to survive and keep Sarah alive with me. Her silence shamed me. I had done the unspeakable. I might not have shot Adrien, but I had drained him. In self-defense, yes, but I had taken a life, and that would require recompense.

That Adrien had lied about my brother being dead was the smallest comfort. If the people Percy had gotten tangled up with were anything like Adrien Junior's business partners, there probably wasn't much hope he was still alive, whether Adrien could confirm that or not.

Those thoughts, too, would have to wait. Whether we would freeze to death out here, and what we would do once the darkness could no longer conceal us, were more immediate problems. I would love to say I was one of those witches who knew exactly what time it was by moonrise, but even if I were, at that point I couldn't with certainty tell you what day it was. I didn't even know if we had hours of deep night to go or if we were approaching dawn.

My stomach rumbled, and Sarah laughed. A little nervously, but it was something.

She stopped laughing when we heard a shout, still far in the distance.

Her aura tensed, and she started shaking. I started murmuring the spell again, interwoven with Shelley's "Homer's Hymn to Minerva"—one of the few poems I know by heart because it's good to have some praise in your back pocket, even if I think he was wrong about the "Cerulean-eyed" thing. Surely Minerva was a dark-eyed beauty of the Mediterranean.

The shouts got closer: multiple people and what sounded like a woman in the mix. Torches—excuse my British affectation— flashlights began to flicker through the trees and the cracks of the rotting shed.

"Verity! Where the hell did you go?"

George. That put-on East London over the poshest possible accent was a dead giveaway.

I tried to stand, but Sarah had a death grip on me.

"It's okay. It's my friends. They're looking for us."

She let go, but just enough for me to push up over the rock foundation on my good arm and peer through the broken walls to see three flashlights sweeping our way.

"George!" There wasn't much left of my voice.

One of the flashlights stopped swishing back and forth. The other two stilled, then trained our direction.

"George!" It felt like her name took the flesh of my windpipe with it, but it was as loud as I could get with all the magic I had left in me behind it.

The three beams converged on the shack and moved quickly toward us. I thanked Minerva under my breath, knowing that I owed her, again.

CHAPTER 19

"There was so much blood. I thought you had to be dead." George insisted on riding with me and Sarah in the ambulance to the nearest hospital.

We were somewhere in the woods of New Hampshire north of Manchester. Adrien Senior and Matjaž followed in a car behind. Apparently there had been others at Adrien Junior's makeshift compound, but that had gotten cleaned up before George and Matjaž and Adrien Senior had found us.

I hadn't asked about Adrien Junior, and no one had offered anything. Sarah was curled up on the stretcher next to me under a matching silvery blanket and hadn't spoken aword. I can only imagine what seeing that kind of magical violence up close had done to her mind. And gods only knew what Asshole did to her before I was deposited there. I wasn't sorry he was dead, but I still hadn't fully wrapped my thoughts around the fact that I had killed him—and what that would mean for me. I had only accepted that it had happened and that there would be fallout. And that he had put us in the position where I'd had to make the choice about which of us was going to live.

I soon realized I had not anticipated how much Adrien Travere—no need to call him senior now that his son was dead—could sweep under a rug woven of privilege and power. Once I was deemed stable enough to be released from the ER in Manchester, the four of us were in one of Adrien's cars being driven back to Westchester with the sun rising behind us. One of Adrien's "staff" stayed with Sarah to make sure she was cared for and that when she started talking she didn't tell everything she knew. I wondered if Adrien's people would send her into their version of the witness protection program. I hoped she'd be safe whatever happened.

Matjaž hardly spoke to me at the hospital beyond saying he was glad I was safe. His warmth with me had become a wariness that told me that whatever connection we had begun to forge was broken. I hoped it wasn't a permanent situation.

The ride to Westchester was quiet, and I slept because I'd been given something at the hospital. There was probably conversation around and over me and most definitely about me, but dreamless, drug-induced slumber had been a gift.

I must have woken up enough to move from the car to a bed to sleep the rest of it off, because it was afternoon when I awoke to Hilma happily licking my face. I snuggled her up, relieved by the purrs and the warmth of her tiny body. I would have happily stayed there, building my emotional fortitude for all that was coming, but I seriously needed to pee.

I managed to get to the bathroom, but I was going to need help finding clothes and food. I wandered through the bedroom and into the hall. I wasn't sure how I'd gotten upstairs and undressed, but I remembered a glimmer of being carried yet again. It had to have been Matjaž. That he had been kind enough to carry me earned a check in the Pro column, but I guessed I'd earned several checks in Matjaž's Con column. It now likely totaled "more trouble than she's worth." That's what Adrien Junior had said too.

Adrien Senior's butler, Fontaine, rounded the corner carrying a stack of neatly folded clothing and immediately came to my assistance.

"Ms. Green, you should have called for me." He led me back into the bedroom, where he set the clothes on the bed.

"How?"

"There's a remote here for the curtains and lights with a call button." He picked up a slim black rectangle from the bedside table. I'd thought it was a phone charger or something.

"Sorry. It may have been explained, but I don't remember getting up here."

"Of course. I brought you some clothes. Mr. Travere sent me to your apartment to pack up some things for you and Ms. Burne-Jones. Would you prefer I get her to help you dress?" I was sore from my crown to my soles and probably looked like a bruise-colored Rothko. Fontaine didn't look the least bit embarrassed about helping me.

"If you aren't uncomfortable, I'm not uncomfortable. Thanks."

Fontaine couldn't have known every muscle in my body would hurt, but he'd chosen well for my current state. He deftly helped me into a long wool skirt and a cardigan sweater. I would have given anything for another pair of those French knickers from Rinaldo's penthouse, but Fontaine and I managed the underwear as best we could. I had a whole new respect for the man and told him as much.

"I made up a room for you downstairs this morning. I thought it might be safer until you've recovered your strength." He followed me to the staircase and walked next to me, his hand in the small of my back ready to grab me should I take a light-headed tumble down the carpeted stairs.

"Would you prefer to eat in the kitchen on your own, or are you ready to meet with Mr. Travere and the others?" Fontaine made sure I was steady before stepping back. Nothing in my psyche liked the idea of butlers and valets, but I was grateful for navigating this first bit with Fontaine. I dreaded what I could only assume was going to be an emotional firehose with Matjaž and George and Adrien Senior. Adrien.

"How many others?"

"Mr. Belak and Ms. Burne-Jones."

"I can handle that."

Fontaine led me back to the dining room, where I'd met the Restorationists before the truly awful part of this adventure had begun. The tiny, snarky voice in my head pointed out that I wouldn't be so banged up had I not taken it upon myself to run. I told it to shut up. I already had enough guilt to float a barge on.

"I'll let the others know, and I'll be back with a tray."

"Thank you. For everything."

Fontaine nodded and left.

George got there first and took the seat next to me. I hadn't really gotten a good look at her last night, but she was back in her own clothes and her bruises were healing. The astral jail bracelet was gone.

"I am so glad you are here, and safe." She put her hands on both sides of my face and kissed me on the forehead. "I want to hug you, but I don't want to hurt you." She gently patted my shoulder.

She didn't get a chance to say anything else before Adrien and Matjaž joined us. Adrien took his place at the end of the table, and Matjaž sat opposite me, his expression inscrutable. We sat in silence for moment, maybe to mark that we were all here again. Adrien was the first to speak.

And I cut him off. "I'm sorry about Adrien." I was sorry Adrien Senior had lost his son, but I had done what was necessary to save myself and Sarah. I'm sure she would have been killed when she was no longer useful or necessary.

"Then you know he is dead." I wasn't touching Adrien, but I didn't need to know he already knew that and knew I was responsible.

"He was badly wounded when those people came for the painting and me. I'm guessing he or someone else took Sarah to patch him up. When whoever that was showed up last night, and things started, he pulled me onto him as a shield . . ." George took my hand under the table and squeezed hard.

Matjaž's expression was easier to read now. It was one of pain and anger.

"I took advantage of the open wound on his shoulder and used magic . . . to . . ."

"To let him bleed out." Adrien finished my sentence.

I nodded. "Then Sarah and I went out the back and into the woods."

Matjaž was staring at me now.

"What happened at Rinaldo's?" I looked at Adrien. "No, wait. What happened after we left Adrien Junior's?" I squeezed George's hand back.

Adrien Senior answered. "Marcus thought Adrien was dead, and while he was trying to move Joe into the SUV, Adrien disappeared."

"Like literally?" Did anyone have that kind of magic?

"A blood trail. That led us to believe he was alive, but Joe was the priority." Adrien Senior looked between George and me.

"Is Joe okay?" I still wasn't sure what had been going on there, but something was up with him.

"He was when I checked yesterday, but he's gone missing as well."

"He wasn't working for you? I thought—" Adrien cut me off.

"No. Marcus does work for Rinaldo, which led us to figuring out where you were. But Joe seems to have been working for someone else."

"Okay." I accepted we were at the fill-in-all-the-blanks stage and could pick over the details later on some of this.

"Then Rinaldo picked us up." George looked at Adrien.

"Yes. I had, as I believe Rinaldo told you, already figured out that Adrien wasn't kidnapped. Rinaldo had informed me where Adrien was keeping you and George—"

"Then why didn't you come and get us?" It came out in a croak more pathetic-sounding and less angry than I was. I would be glad when my voice was healed.

"Because I didn't initially know who Adrien had made promises to and what he would be willing to do to keep them." He said it so matter-of-factly, as if what George and I had gone through hadn't factored in at all.

"He could have killed George, and he was willing to turn me over to gods know who."

"He was going to trade you for his life to an organized crime syndicate specializing in stolen and forged art and money laundering. He had initially offered them forged paintings that would withstand any and all scrutiny in exchange for certain magical artifacts they came across in their work. Then he missed the first payment because you took longer than he thought, and things started to unravel." So much for Junior's grand pronouncements about doing it for the art.

"Were you just going to let him?"

"No. We were planning to intercept Adrien with you two when he left the house, but the people he was dealing with got wind he was going to run. Rinaldo may have less security than I would advise, but he has a better network of informants. He got there first." Adrien paused. "However you feel about killing Adrien, you should know that he was already marked for death. Your actions were kinder than what he would have experienced had the syndicate gotten to him."

"I don't know that that makes me feel better, but I'm still processing all of that. What happened at Rinaldo's? You two look like nothing happened. Is he okay?"

"He is shaken but fine. He sends his greetings and is very glad you are safe. He hopes to follow through on your plans to meet soon." Adrien let a wry smile escape the corner of his mouth before he continued. "Adrien sent what was left of his crew to Rinaldo's with an artifact that would do maximum damage without loss of life. We have people looking at the remnants now. They took you, and Rinaldo and I continued looking for Adrien, tracking him to that farmhouse—one of handful of properties he'd bought over the years and done nothing with. We were lucky to arrive at the same time as the syndicate's 'courier' and his entourage."

The little voice in my head laughed about luck having nothing to do with it.

"I had not anticipated that you would rescue yourself. My apologies for underestimating you. Once things were under control, we went looking for you."

"The syndicate wasn't just going to trade with Adrien." They would have killed him and any witnesses, and taken me. That seemed clear, and Adrien nodded confirmation. I took Adrien Junior's life, but I saved Sarah's.

Fontaine returned with a tray for me.

Adrien stood. "I'll let you talk with your friends. I would like to meet with you before you speak with Rinaldo, if you are amenable."

"Of course."

George stood up too. "I think you and Matjaž have some things to talk about. We can chat later." She kissed me on the top of my head and followed Adrien out, taking his arm once they were in the hallway.

Matjaž hadn't said a word. I thought he might move to Adrien's chair, but he stayed where he was.

My lunch tray was tomato soup with a grilled cheese cut into neat triangles. George must have told Fontaine my secret comfort food, but my appetite was gone. I pushed the tray away.

"You should eat." Matjaž moved the tray back a half inch. Enough to suggest but not be pushy.

"I think we need to talk first. I'm sorry. I'm sorry I didn't give you a choice at the cabin. I just—"

"You don't need to apologize for that. You acted on instinct. And though I don't think they would have hurt me—or Hilma—who's to say what Adrien would have done when his men showed up with extras? It was awful to watch you leave and feel powerless to help you, but your reasoning was sound." It was good to hear, but his saying it didn't offer me any relief from the dread weighing in my gut.

"I thought we were moving toward something, before this began and at the cabin before you left." He sounded so hesitant, I needed to reassure him that I wanted to give this a chance.

"I did too."

He smiled briefly. "I'm glad of that. We talked about some things in my past, but not everything. I could love you, Verity. I thought that from the moment you walked into the pub with George. But not like this. Not in the middle of chaos and violence. It never works out, does it, when you get thrown together by circumstance and then the adrenaline subsides? I don't want to hurt you, and I don't want to be hurt like that."

"What are you saying?"

"I'm saying that I'm going to step back and let the dust settle. I've taken a commission in Venice. There's a lot of work there now with the inundation, and I need some space from this. I thought I'd left all this behind me in Ljubljana, and I don't know if I can do it again." The words were firm, but the emotion behind them wavered.

Maybe that was why he didn't sit next to me. He knew if I touched him, I'd know and maybe try to persuade him to stay.

And I wanted him to stay. He was the good thing in all of this, but he was right to be wary. This was shaky ground, and if he didn't want magic in his life, there was no way I could promise him that. My secret was out, and I had seen enough to know that things were never going to be the same for me. We'd both had so much heartbreak in our lives, maybe it was better not to risk it again—however much I wanted to.

"I want you to stay, but it would be unfair to ask that of you." Words did not want to come out. "Our timing sucked, didn't it?"

He moved to Adrien's chair and cupped my face in his hands before kissing me goodbye. That warmth that crept into me every time he touched me was still there, pooling in my chest where my heart was breaking. He left without another word, and I mechanically chewed my way through the last grilled cheese I'll ever eat.

CHAPTER 20

Despite Adrien's best efforts, the news of his son's death—if not all the details—were the main story for much of New York's and then the world's news. "Billionaire playboy, son of reclusive art collector, kidnapped and murdered" was in headlines and lead stories everywhere. The whole sordid tale had too many interesting facets and was like catnip for true crime fans and snooping journalists. George's name came up first, in that she had been taken with Adrien Travere Junior from his "heavily secured" penthouse.

My replacement phone started ringing. I had spoken with Garvey and Jon after Matjaž let them know we were all safe and accounted for. They drove down and visited with us the day after I got back to Westchester, and I promised to let them know when I would be back in West Kill. They both seemed reluctant to leave me there, but I assured them it was for the best for the time being.

I would have happily taken more of their calls, but the messages that were stacking up in my phone were from my mother, and I wasn't ready to go there. George's name had probably been enough to get her to call. My father imagined himself aligned with her family because of our friendship. I can't say George's family felt the same, though they were intrigued by my mother and her spiritualist work.

I had to cave and answer when my name hit the papers. truths that I had gone looking for George because the police weren't helping.

The tale of my intrepid and foolhardy derring-do made it to my mother and led to one of the least-bad conversations we'd had in a while. She didn't even open with her usual sarcastic jab about how good it was for me to take her call.

"Do you need anything? Are you hurt?" Her voice was almost motherly in her concern.

"I got banged up in the fray, but I'm fine." As far as she and most of the world knew, the police and I had made it to the farmhouse in New Hampshire at the same time, and I'd been caught in the struggle to free George and Adrien from their captors. My being kidnapped, our escape and rescue, and my second kidnapping with the "unrelated" explosion at Rinaldo's were all missing from public accounts. Along with anything about a recovered painting.

"Well, I'm glad the mysterious Adrien Travere has taken it upon himself to provide for your care." I had to wonder if she was calling to check on me or because my father was curious about Adrien and what he could get out of him.

"He is. But I'm planning on going back to West Kill in the next couple of days. I need to be in my own space for a bit." I did want to be back at the farm. I was less sure about being alone, but I had some magical work to do that I felt comfortable performing only there. Adrien Senior had assured me that I didn't need to worry about the syndicate coming after me now, and, given the expression he'd had on his face, I had to believe him.

"You may want to wait. Bunny called to tell me they'd been overrun at the cafe with reporters trying to find your house."

"Great." I guess I'd be staying in Westchester awhile longer. George's apartment wasn't an option. Reporters had already found it. And Matjaž, as far as any of us knew, was on his way to

Italy—not that I would have asked to stay with him. Maybe in a different timeline, he would have offered.

"You could always stay here for a bit. It's almost Christmas, and Lily Dale knows how to keep reporters out."

"Mother, I don't—"

"Verity, I get it. We aren't all happy families. But I've already lost one child, and I just found out I almost lost the other."

She was right. And I couldn't tell her that there was the slimmest possibility that Percy was alive because then I'd have to tell her the whole story. She didn't need any of that, and—though it pained me—I wasn't sure I could trust her with it. I knew I couldn't trust my father with what I could do, and telling her was telling him.

"Point taken. Give me a few days to make arrangements. I'll come after New Year's."

I could almost hear her self-satisfaction at beating me into agreement through the phone. "And bring George. I'm sure she could use a rest. It's quiet here in the off season."

"I'll ask, but I can't accept on her behalf."

"Verity, whatever you may think, your father and I do love you."

"Thank you." It was probably shitty of me not to say "I love you" back. I did love them because they were my parents, but I didn't like them much as people. And that made it complicated.

Placating my mother didn't stop the calls. Now they were from reporters who had linked my name to stories about Theo's death in London. Being able to block numbers is the best kind of technological magic, and it worked for about two days—

until the tabloid articles about Adrien Travere Junior being a black magician doing blood sacrifices for drug cartels hit the newsstand.

Most New Yorkers know that the tabloids trade in high-fantasy gossip, but since The Storm, their yarns were much easier for people to believe. Thankfully, the tide that turned against Adrien Junior—away from his tragic death to his comeuppance for getting involved in the magical crime world—didn't include any hint that his father could also be involved with "the dark inner workings of secret society magic cabals dedicated to increasing their wealth with shadowy rituals." It did, however, manifest with reporters camping in the street at the entrance to the Westchester property.

"Rinaldo would like to come to talk with you this afternoon." Adrien didn't usually eat breakfast with George and me. In the few days we'd been there since the events in New Hampshire, George and I had pretty much had run of the house despite Fontaine hovering "to see if we needed anything."

"I'm surprised he's willing to brave the horde outside." I took a sip of coffee and tried not to think too much about what Adrien wanted to discuss first.

"That would hardly be a deterrent. Meet me in the studio when you've finished." He set his napkin next to his plate and left.

"What do you think that's about?" George had been reading the arts section of the *Times*, charmed that Adrien still had the printed paper delivered every day. It was one of the many things that charmed her about Adrien.

"As you heard, he and Rinaldo and their separate 'interests' have had an ongoing discussion about me and what I can do. I suspect I'm about to get competing offers I can't refuse."

George folded the paper over and set it aside. "What does that mean?"

"I'm not sure, but it probably means I am not going back to work at the museum." Another thing lost along the way, along with my apparently false sense of anonymity and any chance I had with Matjaž.

"I was already thinking about not going back."

"Really? That's a surprise." George had practically dragged me to New York to work with her at NAMA. She loved her job.

"Adrien already made me an offer." She looked down at her plate and then up at me through her eyelashes.

"And you were going to tell me this when?"

"When I'd decided to take it or not. But if you aren't going back . . ."

"Because of the flat? I do actually have my own house."

"No, because I assumed he'd make you a similar offer." She looked a little guilty. I had to wonder what else Adrien had offered her.

"Are you going to tell me now what that was?"

"I said I wouldn't, until he'd spoken to you. I'll spill after. I promise."

***

The sky was low and gray outside the large studio windows. It looked very much like snow and matched my less than festive mood. All of the workstations were bare except for the one where Adrien stood waiting for me. He had several worn books and museum catalogues stacked neatly on the work surface.

"These may be of more interest to George," he gestured to the diaries, "but I think you will be interested as well."

I looked over the bound books. "Are these Edward Burne-Jones's notebooks?"

"Some of them."

"The last time you brought me in here was to show me a priceless Raphael study. That's been recovered, right?" I had kind of assumed he had it again. Someone on Adrien's staff had gone to his son's house to retrieve my bag with my wallet and, thankfully, had scooped up the puffer coat I had borrowed from Jon with my emergency magical kit and the other "prepper" supplies I'd squirreled into the pockets.

"Yes. And secured. At your suggestion, it will make its way to the public light in good time." He flipped open one of the notebooks. "But this is what I want you to see."

There was a small watercolor of a woman reclined on a divan, her pale arm hanging loosely, the blood from her slit wrist dripping into a bronze bowl.

"Is this a copy of a painting?" I'd never seen this composition, not exactly, but there were a lot of Burne-Joneses and other pre-Raphaelite paintings floating about unaccounted for.

"I believe so. Perhaps by Rosetti. Though I think it is Burne-Jones's work." He closed the book.

"You don't want me to do my thing on it?" I smirked at him. Why else would he have brought me back here?

"Of course I want you to. But, not just this. Not just today.

I'd like you—and George—to come work with me and Dr. Mar and the others. You'd be well paid and have the opportunity to lay low for a while to heal." He glanced at the bruises around my neck, which had faded into shades of green and yellow, but I got the impression he meant more than that. I don't think there's magic to fix what was broken between Matjaž and me. "Nothing would need to happen right away."

"Rinaldo is going to make me the same offer?"

"Possibly. But I think he'll ask you to accept my offer and feed him information."

"Are you asking me to accept his offer too?"

"Yes. It probably seems a bit James Bond to you, but Rinaldo and I have been at this for a long time."

"And this?" I pointed at the notebooks and catalogues.

"I understand your mother has invited you to Lily Dale. It would be a good opportunity to gather a piece of this puzzle." He was close but not uncomfortably so.

His aura had a magnetism to it, and I wasn't so heartbroken that I couldn't see why George was attracted to him. I was drawn, too, but mostly because I knew wading in deeper might let me find answers about Percy—and about this Sandro person who had sold me out to save his skin on multiple occasions.

"If I say yes, am I signing my name in the devil's book for eternity?"

"No. We, I, don't work like that." He pulled an envelope from a drawer in the work table.

"What's this?"

"Your advance."

"Do you always pay in cash?"

"No, this is a special case. You'll need to officially resign from the museum and take care of mundane matters. We can deal with the particulars on our end later. You should know, I made Matjaž the same offer I made George." Trust was building there, very slowly. But there was still something below the surface that made me wary.

"He turned you down though. He's gone to Venice to work."

"He didn't turn me down. He's working in Venice for me. He requested a first assignment away from here. I gather he left you on final terms, but that could change."

"Why are you being kind? You don't have to be. I'm not really in a position to refuse. I can hardly go back to my life of obscurity now."

"You are a remarkable talent, Verity. But it is more than that. You have abilities you actively chose not to exploit. You have to know that's a rarity, in my world at least. I won't ask you to step outside your ethical lines, but I may question why you've drawn particular ones." He handed me one of the Burne-Jones notebooks. "Take these and read through them. I think you'll find there is a small mystery to be solved."

"I'd like to want to say yes because it seems the better option, not because it's the only one." I took the book and had the slightest sensation of Edward, pen in hand and bent to his desk in contemplation.

"I hope in time you will come to see it is the better choice." Adrien turned to walk away but stopped. "And you aren't beholden. You can decide at any time this isn't for you."

I had to believe George had coached him in this approach, as it was so different than our first meeting.

***

Rinaldo and I met in the gallery surrounded by Adrien's collection of near priceless paintings. He was waiting by the large leaded windows, peering out through the clear panels at the lawn. With his dark hair and his expertly cut suit, you'd never know he was pushing seventy, if he and Travere were contemporaries. All that magic pays off, or something else was going on.

"Before we discuss anything else, I'd like to ask you about something you said at dinner."

"Of course." He smiled knowingly.

"What did you mean when you said 'long-lived?' You were talking about you and Adrien trading spies back and forth." I looked up into his darkly handsome face. Like Adrien, he had the presence of old, old magic about him.

"I did let that slip, didn't I." He walked toward one of the enormous battlefield paintings to the right of the windows. "Adrien, Hannalore—your Dr. Mar—and Dr. Askew—I believe you met her here at Adrien's. Jennifer?" I nodded. "We've all been at this for a very long time."

"How long is a long time?" My blood chilled at the thought that maybe vampires were real and I'd just agreed to help them out like a brainless thrall. Given the past month, I don't even think I'd be surprised.

"Hannalore under a different name was born here, a free woman of color in New Amsterdam. Adrien was a cardinal in the time of Charlemagne. Jennifer is younger; her family escaped famine in Sweden in the 1860s and settled in Chicago."

"And you?"

"Ludovico Manin, the last Doge of Venice."

"And I'm just supposed to believe that most of you have been alive for hundreds of years and Adrien is over a thousand years old?" It explained a lot but also made my head swim.

"It isn't something most people can adapt to instantly."

"No. I'm going to have to sit with that awhile. And Adrien Junior. Did I kill a practically immortal person?"

"No. We rarely pass this on to our children. It was always a point of contention between the elder Adrien and the younger. Adrien Junior resented he would never have his father's power or the time to amass his wealth, since he wouldn't be inheriting it."

"Were there other Adrien Juniors over the centuries?" Did those words just come out of my mouth?

"No. Adrien did not sire many children. He had been a celibate man of god, and when he did have children later, they were all daughters."

"Except Junior. Who I murdered."

Rinaldo turned to me, his eyes now flashing. "Whatever happened to Adrien Travere Junior was set in motion by his own hand. You saved your life and that of the poor woman he abducted. I doubt his father will ever speak to you of it, but I can assure you he understands this and does not blame you. Life is precious, Verity, and I can speak to that even more than those who have lived average lifetimes. You acted in defense, of yourself and of another. Never doubt that Adrien would have let those people take you. And they would have killed the nurse and happily tortured Adrien for his failure to meet his end of the bargain."

Rinaldo looked up at the bayonets and furling cannon smoke of the battle of Waterloo. "Adrien already offered for you to join his Restorationists?"

"Yes. I'd forgotten that's what they called themselves." In my mind, Rinaldo's group had become the Conservationists, based on our earlier conversation about his organization's more "conservative" methods, whatever that meant in reality.

"You said yes, but I'd like to make an additional offer." He walked to the next painting—a landscape by a minor Impressionist.

"He said you would."

Rinaldo laughed. "As I said, we've been at this a long time."

"Are there many others like you?"

"There are, though we tend to stay in our cliques. I can't say I know more than an additional handful personally, as we are a secretive and insular bunch. I don't want you to spy on Adrien and his colleagues; I know plenty about his business. I would like you to track someone down for me when you begin your new work. And I'd like you to promise you won't put yourself in danger again." He gave me a stern but genuinely concerned look on that last bit, then took an envelope out of his breast pocket. "The name of who I am looking for, some contacts, and a check for you."

"I don't need your money. Adrien has promised to pay me well."

"What is money to Adrien or me? We have taken advantage

of our long lives and compound interest." He laughed. "Consider it a Christmas gift."

"I can't promise not to put myself in danger. I didn't do it intentionally before."

"You need to talk to someone who can help you with the channeling. Someone like your mother." He stopped me before I could interrupt him. "I know enough. If not her, someone in Lily Dale should be able to assist you."

"Surely you must know most of the spiritualists are true believers but not truly mediums—" He started to interrupt me. "But I'll look into it." I took the envelope.

"I do know, but there are others there like your mother who hide in plain sight. She will know who they are."

"Why did you think Theo knew about what I could do?"

"He came to me with ideas about riches to be made off your abilities. I think he got the information from Sandro because neither of them really understood what you are capable of. Your Theo was involved in shady dealings. He had talent too. It's a shame his greed got him killed." Rinaldo's tone was flat, but his expression betrayed his disgust at what he thought Theo was. "I'll leave you to enjoy your holidays in peace." He turned toward the arched entrance to the gallery.

"Rinaldo, did you know my brother? Was he in Venice?"

Rinaldo stopped and turned. "Do you remember what I said about bystanders?"

I nodded.

"Your brother wasn't a bystander." He left me standing there with my envelope and a knot in my stomach.

Most likely Percy was dead, then, and he'd been mixed up in gods knew what.

CHAPTER 21

I spent New Year's Eve with George and Adrien in Westchester. Adrien suggested I invite friends, so Garvey and Jon joined us. They weren't impressed with the house and its trappings, but they'd warmed up to Adrien Travere. As had George. No one set out to make me feel like a fifth wheel for the evening, and Fontaine stepped in to do the New Year's kiss honors with a chaste peck on the cheek at midnight, but I still felt set apart in time and space from the three people I loved most in the world—and from this one new character in my life whom I seemed to be stuck with. For now. But if I was honest, Adrien Travere was growing on me too.

The next morning, Claus drove me to West Kill so I could take care of a few things and officially shutter the house. I'd be going back to Westchester after I'd had enough of my parents, found whatever information I could on Adrien's Burne-Jones painting mystery, and met with Rinaldo's contacts in Lily Dale. That would all take at least a couple months, even with George's help.

An enormous sense of relief washed over me when I opened my front door and freed Hilma from her carrier. I was home, inside the gentle hum of my own wards, set with my own magic. My parents were coming the next day to pick me up and I had a lot to do, but in that moment there was a release from all that had happened over the past month. I mentally tapped on each point of pain or sadness—like testing a tooth.

I had accepted the situation of Adrien's death to the best of my abilities. I had made choices that would drastically change my life in agreeing to work for the Restorationists and the Conservationists. George was safe, though currently smitten with a certain very much older magical billionaire. Garvey and Jon had forgiven me for abandoning Matjaž at their cabin. Hilma had stopped peeing in my shoes. The only thought that still ached when I let myself touch it was Matjaž. I'd let my guard down, let him in, let myself believe.

Adrien seemed to think reconciliation was possible. I wanted to believe it, too, but I didn't have Adrien's confidence in the matter—or his long life to wait for it to happen. Matjaž had not shared more than a sliver of his past with me. That glimpse revealed deep wounds—ones mostly related to injury caused by magic and, it sounded to me, by time with another witch who had dragged him into a situation where emotions and danger had run high, until they hadn't. I didn't want to be another source of pain in his life. But I did want to be in it, and I wanted him in mine. Now, though, we both worked for a man, for an organization, that could keep us from crossing paths indefinitely.

I wanted to let it go, at least for now. Matjaž had said his piece and made his feelings clear. I had other things I needed to attend to. But I was further gone than I had let myself believe, and his absence—his removing himself from my presence—left a hollow feeling in my chest and a chill everywhere I had felt his warmth.

Cue all the distractions. One being closing up the house and packing properly to be away for a bit. Adrien had suggested hiring a caretaker, but I wasn't ready to be a person who had staff. That was still far too weird.

More important things first. I needed to offer some thanks to my ancestors and deities for getting me back here. I dusted and cleaned my altar and refreshed the offerings that had evaporated and grown stale in my absence. Fresh water for the ancestors and dried yarrow petals for Minerva. I burned incense made from the junipers on the ridge and dried herbs from my garden. My working room smelled again of magic. I had survived an ordeal, and more was yet required.

I dressed in my working shift and swept the room of lingering stale energy before calling to my ancestors and Minerva. I offered my thanks to them and bid my ancestors stay if they wished but said my goodbyes if they had other places to be.

Minerva and I needed to talk.

I sat cross-legged on the floor in front of my altar and stared into the flame of the beeswax pillar candle I lit for her anytime I came to work or talk with the spirits. I still don't feel like I have much talent with astral travel. Those trips to Travere's house, first with George and then to Matjaž while we were at Adrien Junior's, had to be flukes born of duress. I was good at trance states, though, and that's why I continued to stare into the candle flame hoping for another fluke.

My breath and my heart rate slowed as I watched the light flicker, the candle guttering then regaining its strength, burning bright and straight. I watched as the flame grew brighter and became the light of a torch held tight to a temple wall in an iron sconce. I was no longer in my working room in West Kill, but this didn't feel like any trance state I'd achieved before, and it didn't feel like astral projection. I pinched the top of my thigh. Very much awake.

A sense of awe, in that true old meaning of the word, crept

up my spine. I was in the presence of Something. Something old and much, much bigger than me. I walked on, down the corridor of torches. Other figures retreated into side passages, their skirts or robes billowing behind them. A pull in my sternum kept me moving forward, though each step was a struggle against a mounting fear, and every nerve ending was telling me to run.

The corridor opened into a lavishly decorated room filled with Persian rugs, Greek vases, Etruscan statues, and chests of treasures and trinkets telling tales from across the known worlds of the ancients and of today. The smell of roses and honey hung in the air. A woman was seated on a divan on the far end of the room with a table laden with platters of food and jugs of wine to her left. As I got closer, I could see the flash of her eyes, amber and gold flecks that caught the torch light and dazzled like stars. She beckoned me to her without saying a word or moving her hand. I sat on the rug in front of her, like a child looking up at the teacher, and noticed the paintings behind her, work by the famous and the obscure. More women I recognized than men.

"Verity, I cannot give you the thing you ask for with your heart. I can tell you that all is not lost, but much patience will be required. Of the things you have come to ask with your mind, you will know the answers in time."

Minerva's voice sounded like I had always imagined, rich and honeyed and accented in a way that one would never be able to tell where she was from. Her worship had been carried to the corners of the trade routes and on into new continents with colonists and settlers and those who had rediscovered her.

How does one address the goddess? I had called her name in devotion and prayer and sometimes sensed her near, but I had never been in her presence. Of that I was now certain.

"Minerva, Goddess of Wisdom—"

"You do not need to struggle so. I have invited you here as a friend. Witches know better than most, I think, that we work together."

I nodded. "I have accepted my role in Adrien Travere Junior's death, but I feel as though I must try to make amends. I killed the only son of a nearly immortal man. And I'm still struggling with the reality of a nearly immortal man."

"Adrien Travere has not asked this of you, to make amends. Why do you seek to do so?"

"Because I don't wish to be someone who kills, even though I know his death was in self-defense and defense of another."

"You are not a soldier, Verity. I do not think that is a concern."

"Still is there nothing?"

Minerva reached into a small chest at her side, moved aside a fancy smartphone, and pulled a medallion on a gold chain from the tangle within. She smoothed the chain with her hand and held it out to me. "Wear this."

I took the necklace from her and looked at the medallion closely in the torch light. Two large topaz eyes stared back from the face of an owl, its feathers expertly carved and cast in gold.

"Those who know will know you have chosen to work with me. And you will know that you have the responsibility of the wise."

"Just wear this?"

"Of course, it is not so simple. It will allow me to call on you when it's time to make these amends you insist upon."

***

I woke up the next morning, cold and stiff on the floor of my working room. The candles had thankfully only burned to the sockets and not burned down my house. I had to believe Minerva had been watchful. A lot of strange things had happened in the past few weeks, but I couldn't say if they were stranger than meeting a goddess outside of time and space.

After I showered and got dressed, I went back to the working room and stood facing the altar. I needed to put things away and decide what should travel with me and what to pack away. It took longer than it should because I kept expecting to find that necklace tucked behind a candelabra or under a cloth.

Later, as I stood at the sink eating a pot of yogurt I'd brought with me, it was hard to unravel what had happened. Visiting Minerva in her shrine should have put paid to any agnosticism I had about whether the gods were real, but there was always the possibility that it had been a dream. I looked out over the raised beds, remembering that I needed to fill in that hole with compost, because I will almost always focus on the practical to avoid the complicated. In all that had happened, I had mostly forgotten the break-in and what they took. A doe, possibly the one I had seen before, made her way to the farthest box and ate what was left of the kale down to the dirt. Better that she eat it since it wouldn't get through the hard freezes to come. In that moment I didn't even know if I'd get to plant my vegetable beds for the spring. Maybe a caretaker wasn't such a bad idea, but how does one even go about hiring one?

I wasn't going to be able to garden, but I would be able to paint. I needed a way to think and set things in some kind of order in the fire sale of my mind. I would miss the studio, but

I had been gone so long already, and I practically ached to put brushes and fingers to canvas. To my own work. Not de Graaf's. Not Raphael's, though I did still wonder what happened after I left them. I know the history—that he never married the noblewoman he was engaged to and may have secretly married Margherita, his mistress, the baker's daughter. He would paint her near the end of his life, breasts exposed with a ring on her finger later covered by his apprentices, perhaps, to hide that secret marriage. I could only hope that they had been happy or something like it, and that my intrusion into their world had not haunted them long after.

The studio was chilly and carried the scents of nut and seed oil mediums and turpentine and the flat metallic tang of a room shut up for an extended period in the cold. I turned up the thermostat to something above meat locker and rummaged through the closet for my travel easel. Of course all my supplies don't fit into the storage compartment, so I also have an old metal tackle box I use for paint pots and brushes.

Once I had those packed and ready to take into the house, I wrapped up the painting I'd been working on in some craft paper and wrapped three other canvases in the spirit of ambition and hopefulness for how productive the next couple of months would be. I looked through some completed pieces, as my mother had asked me to bring her "something for the den." I would never have asked her to buy my work, but I did find it amusing that she insisted on hanging my paintings in her cottage at Lily Dale and bragging about her daughter the artist when she had never attended a single show. A small study of my angelica in bloom that I wasn't particularly attached to— and that didn't really mesh with the turn my subject matter had taken over the past year—seemed a good choice. She would prefer this "happier" image anyway.

Maybe my work taking on this darker, more ethereal dreamlike quality had been a harbinger of this dramatic shift in my life and abilities, but that could also be retrospective thinking. I didn't have the energy to dwell too much on that now. As I was rearranging the canvases, facing them back against the wall, I noticed one that seemed much older than the others.

The canvas was more yellowed, and the painted edges looked a little worse for wear, like it had been shoved into a frame or moved around a lot without one. I turned it over and almost dropped it. It was a copy of *The Storm on the Sea of Galilee*, much smaller than the original, but perfectly proportioned. I picked it up with a clean rag from the bin where I kept them and laid it on my work bench.

Unlike Percy's work I had seen at Adrien Junior's house, this was a true representation of Rembrandt's technique of layering glazes to achieve depth in the background. The light at the left center of the painting, focused on the cresting wave crashing over the edge of the small boat and the clustered disciples around the main mast holding on for their lives, glowed in the daylight of the studio. I braced myself, expecting to get Percy again, but when I touched the painted storm clouds, I got me. Child me, sitting on the floor of this studio before it was a studio, and Rembrandt, a young man in his thirties standing at his easel, looking in a glass at his own face to paint the one sailor who looks out of the painting at the viewer, a tiny self-portrait of Rembrandt himself. The face in the glass was mine.

I stepped back from the bench, from the painting. I had no memory of painting this as a child. No memory, as myself or as Rembrandt. This painting had not been in here after the break-in. Someone had brought it in since then. They had slipped my wards without signaling me. They left a painting in my studio that I had no memory of painting. One that my brother had also attempted.

What it could mean was more than I could deal with, but I couldn't leave it there either. I wrapped it up in craft paper, being careful not to touch the painting itself again, and put it with the easel and canvases. It would be a problem for tomorrow Verity. The tiny voice in my head had been very quiet since my conversation with Adrien Senior about working with him, but it chirped up now.

Percy is still alive.

AUTHOR NOTE

Some of the artists and artworks mentioned are figments of my imagination and, as far as I know, did not or do not exist in the real world. You most likely won't find de Graaf if you go looking for him. *Plum on Red* is a fictional Rothko, but the story of the Harvard paintings is true. I've taken a few liberties with Raphael's timeline but tried to stay true to his story, or at least what is currently believed.

If you'd like to keep up with new releases, events, and the occasional subscriber exclusive, please follow me on Substack. And if you'd like to help other folks find this book, please consider leaving a rating or review where you purchased it.

Other Books Available from 1000Volt Press at
1000voltpress.com/shop

The Voices of the Dead series and companion cookbook
Victoria Raschke

Changing Paths
Yvonne Aburrow

Conjuring the Commonplace
Laine Fuller and Cory Thomas Hutcheson

Victoria Raschke creates worlds where magic is real, but it isn't always pretty. She is the author of the *Voices of the Dead* contemporary fantasy series, which begins with *Who by Water*. She and her partner co-own 1000Volt Productions, which includes 1000Volt Press and the *WitchLit* podcast, hosted by Victoria. Because clearly she still needs hobbies, she does embroidery of medieval illuminated letters with modern slang, and she occasionally bakes. When she isn't traveling—or can't travel—you'll find her working at home with a cup of coffee and a cat curled up nearby.